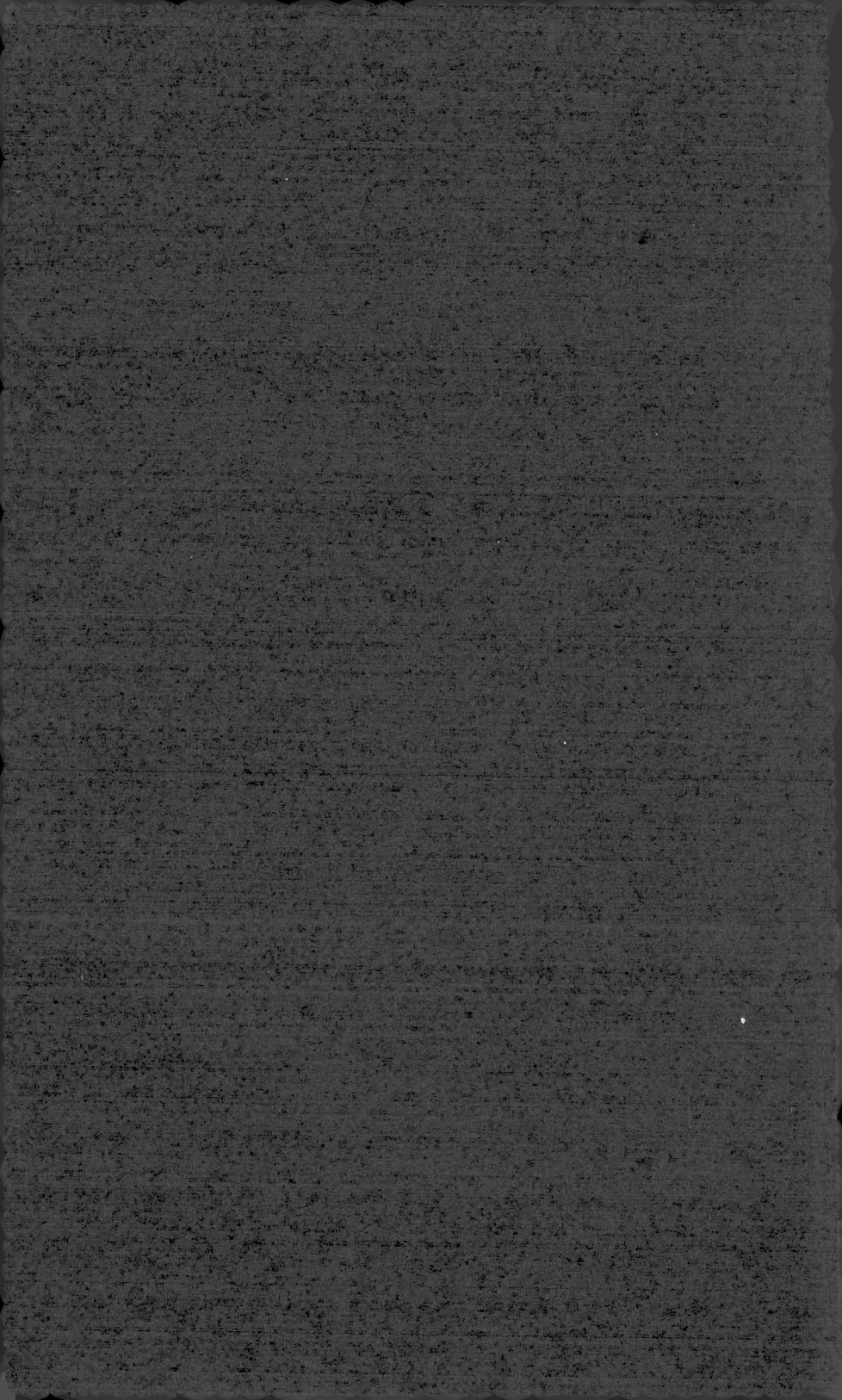

Cold Fire, Calm Rage

Published by bluechrome publishing

2 4 6 8 10 9 7 5 3 1

Copyright © Joe Stein 2004, 2007

Joe Stein has asserted his right under the Copyright, Designs and Patents
Act 1988 to be identified as the author of this work

First Edition: 2004
Second Edition: 2007

bluechrome publishing
PO Box 109,
Portishead, Bristol. BS20 7ZJ

www.bluechrome.co.uk
www.joestein.co.uk

A CIP catalogue record for this book is available from the British Library

ISBN   978-1-906061-01-2

Song: 'Times are Changing' by Joe Stein © 1993

Cover photography by Tim French © Tim French 2006

my thanks go to:

Gary, for use of his office and computer all that time ago

Richard, for reminding me of the truth

and to Kathy, of course, for everything else.

This 'story' is dedicated to the Lucky Club, those of us that are left. It is the only recognition we are ever likely to get.

Cold Fire, Calm Rage

Joe Stein

It was raining in Brussels and the two men who approached the apartment block on the Rue Royale were dressed for the weather, wearing overcoats and hats pulled down to shield their faces from the rain.

'4c,' said the older, heavier man.

His associate pressed the bell and on the answering buzz, pushed the building door open and held it for the other man. Not in a deferential way, but out of respect, because that was part of their working relationship.

'No lift,' the older man thought, 'at my age there ought to be a lift.'

They climbed the stairs in silence noting that although the building was old, it was in good condition, obviously well looked after. It would not be cheap to live here.

The door to 4c was open and they did not pause or knock, but walked straight in and turned into the main lounge. A woman of about thirty was standing at the other side of the room leaning against the wall, her arms folded across her chest. The older man stopped several feet short of her and took off his hat. He had met her briefly once before, but then she had been dressed up, out on the town. Now she seemed older, the dirty blonde hair was duller, the manner defensive. 'Maybe she's just scared,' he thought.

'Good morning, Sabine.' His voice was quiet, pleasant even and it was difficult to detect that he spoke French with a slight accent.

'Why did you bring him?' the woman said, gesturing with her head at the younger man. 'I know what he does. You needed him to come and talk to me?'

'Sabine, I don't need him to be here, but you might talk to me more *easily if he is. Michel, check the rest of the apartment, just in case we miss the obvious.' He looked at the woman. 'Do you mind if I sit down, I've reached the age where four flights of stairs has an effect.'*

'Do what you want. He is not here.'

She half turned away from him and moved a couple of ornaments on a bookshelf. It was a nervous reaction and the man noted it.

'Of course he isn't,' he said, sitting in a deep armchair. He almost added that he knew the apartment was empty. That the point of searching was not to find anything, but to show the woman that he could walk through her home, her life, as and when he chose to.

They stayed in silence until Michel returned. He didn't say a word, there was no need to, just shook his head once and took up a position by the door.

'Sabine, where is Jean?' The tone was still pleasant, an old friend asking a simple question.

'I don't know.'

Her voice was sullen, but he noticed an undertow of fear creeping in. Something to work on.

'Sabine, Jean has done something very stupid. I don't know how much he has told you about what he does, but in essence he is a book-keeper, an accountant, my accountant. Sometimes he makes appointments for me, hotel reservations, things like that. Now he has stolen from me. Not money, but an object and I want it back. So I will ask you again,' the tone hardened, 'where is he?'

'I'm telling you, Monsieur Julot, I do not know where he is.'

Michel shifted his position in the doorway and Julot smiled to himself. Perfect timing. A little threat. Letting the woman know that he was still there. Not that she had forgotten.

'You keep him away from me. I don't know where Jean is. He called me, but I don't know where he is.'

Julot paused for a moment and then hauled himself out of the chair.

'You know, I believe you, Sabine. I don't think you know where he is, so let's start with what you do know. When did he call you?'

The woman relaxed slightly. Here was a question she could answer and it wouldn't help them either.

'*Last night, about half past ten.*'

'*Where did he call from?*'

'*From the airport. He didn't say where he was going.*' *That would fix them, she thought. Now they would realise that Jean could be any-where and they would leave her alone.*

'*Now, Sabine, this is very important, what exactly did he say?*'

'*He didn't say anything. Just that he was about to get on a plane and he would call me later. Which he didn't,*' *she added quickly.*

'*And that is the last time you heard from him?*'

'*Yes.*'

'*And you have no idea where he would have gone, to family, to friends somewhere?*'

'*No, I'm sorry.*'

Julot smiled at her and put his hat back on. They are going, she thought, they are going. It's going to be all right.

'*Thank you, Sabine, you have been helpful, but I must ask a favour of you.*'

'*What favour?*'

'*If Jean calls, you must tell him to contact me. Tell him that it is okay if he comes back now. Everyone makes a mistake sometime.*'

'*Yes, I'll do that.*'

'*Oh, and I'll be sending someone round to stay with you, you know, just to make sure that you are all right and that you do this little favour for me. They won't be rough in any way, you'll hardly know they are here.*' *He moved towards the door, Michel in advance of him.* '*You won't go anywhere until they get here will you, Sabine, no of course you won't, you're a sensible girl.*' *Without looking back, he closed the door behind him.*

They stood on the landing and Michel realised that although no-one else would have known it, his boss was in a towering rage.

'*Get a couple of boys to stay with her, shift work. Someone with a brain, she is not a fool that one. Then get on to the airport. Find out which flights left soon after 10.30. He said he was about to get on a plane, that would be within say half an hour, maybe forty-five minutes. If you can get passenger lists so much the better, although he could be under a different name. That depends on whether he planned this properly or not.'* He stopped for a moment. *'It is probably somewhere near, or he would have said that he would call her tomorrow, not later. Where would he go to?'* Michel remained silent. *'He is not that clever to run far. He will go somewhere easy, somewhere that he knows the language, France or Britain.'* He started down the stairs, Michel following. *'Check on who he knows in France, who would be interested in what he is selling, and check up in London as well.'*

'Should we not wait for him to call her?' Michel asked, his voice quiet, almost a whisper.

'If you were selling that disc, would you come back for her?' Julot shrugged. *'Maybe he will, maybe he won't, but he must know that we will be with her. No, we cannot rely on that, we must force his hand. If there is a possibility of him going to France we will cover that, but I do not want to go to London. We would be too conspicuous there with the language and the accents, we might scare him off. Get hold of someone suitable in London to be on standby in case he surfaces there. If he wants someone to buy, then he has to let people know he has something to sell.'*

They emerged from the building into the grey rain of the city.

'This was supposed to be the easiest job that I had ever done.' Julot sighed out loud. *'The easiest and maybe financially the biggest. And I've been crossed by a book-keeper.'*

He looked up at the sky, at a plane flying overhead.

'I want this bastard found, Michel, if possible I want him alive when I meet him. So that I can look into his eyes and tell him what it means to cross me, before I put a bullet into his head.'

*

I opened my eyes and closed them again quickly, but it was

too late. I'd seen the time on the clock radio by the bed. 09:37. I didn't need to know the time, but once I'd seen it, there was a fix on the day that I couldn't ignore. If I stayed in bed now, I'd know exactly how long I'd stayed in bed for.

It was Thursday, wasn't it? I used to like Thursdays. When I stopped training I still used to go down to the gym on Thursday nights and work out on the bags. Now Thursdays held no special interest for me, just like the rest of the week. I stole another glance at the clock. 09:42. That was a mistake. Making a conscious decision like that meant that I was awake and that meant crunch time. Get up and get moving, or roll over, pull up the blankets and go back to sleep. A major effort and I was sitting up in bed looking out of the window. It was a bright day; winter was giving way to spring, although late as usual in London and not without a struggle. The High Street outside was busy. The fruit and veg shop across the road was crowded which was good. The busier he was, the less time he had and the more likely he was to give me his delivery work.

I stayed sitting up in bed – not enough reason to move yet – and looked around at my bedsit: a nine-foot by twelve-foot box with one badly stained plywood cupboard which, since it didn't shut properly, was open to show a mirror on the inside of one door and a rather poor selection of clothes hanging inside. There was the single bed I was in and a stack of drawers with a television on top; one straight-backed chair with my tape deck on it and two slightly-unpacked cardboard boxes that contained anything movable that I owned. Apart from that, there was just my clock radio and a bedside lamp which were standing on what the landlord laughingly called a 'bedside unit' – in other words, a square box with a space where a drawer had once been and another space underneath it for 'storage'. I was sure I could sue him somehow on some advertising or trade descriptions act, but what the hell. He probably had a better lawyer than I did.

At the bottom of the cupboard was a mess of dirty clothes lying on top of my working boots and my pair of good shoes. My trainers were obviously hiding somewhere else in the room. The clothes reminded me that I had to do the washing and suddenly the day had a purpose, a reason to exist. No longer was today just Thursday. It was, instead, the day I would do my washing. I could move at last and start the day. I had a reason. I had a mission. I had my washing to do.

I creaked up, shuffled the two steps to the stack of drawers for my soap, grabbed my towel down from the hook on the back of the door and wrapped it around me. I opened the door a fraction and peered out straight down the corridor. The two other bedroom doors were on the right side of the corridor. Both were shut. The kitchen door on the left was open and I could see the payphone. Not in use. The bathroom door was slightly open at the far end of the corridor, also on the left. Beyond that, directly opposite me, was the front door. No post on the floor. Linda, who lived in the far room, would be at work. Mex, who lived in the first room on the right, next to me, would not be and I didn't want to bump into him. If I did, I'd have to listen to how he'd pulled this wonderful woman last night and brought her back here and everything that they'd got up to. It would all be lies, but I'd have to listen to it. No point in hurting the poor guy. I knew it was all lies, because one night he *had* brought someone back. Some poor girl who worked in the supermarket, he said and I heard everything. And I mean everything! I tried not to, I even jammed my head under the pillows, but the walls are very thin here. It would have been funny if it hadn't have been tragic. She didn't stay till morning and she didn't come back. I think Mex shops at the local stores now.

Out of some cruel and perverse curiosity, Linda and I went to the supermarket to see if we could work out which girl it might have been. We didn't come to any real conclusion, but we did stock up the kitchen.

I listened hard, but I couldn't hear any sound from Mex's room. I started to pussy-foot down the hall. It wasn't that I disliked the man, which I did, but unlike most of the people that I dislike, I had to share a kitchen and bathroom with him.

The bathroom is by far the best room in the flat. It's bigger than my room and must have been refitted not long ago. A bath, separate shower unit, toilet and sink, as well as new tiling. The only drawback is the one that seems to afflict all bathrooms in the morning, natural light. Natural light, of course, always makes you look awful.

I looked in the mirror.

I looked awful.

A little voice somewhere started up.

– *Pale, very pale. Maybe you're anaemic.*

– Don't be stupid, I'm just naturally pale.

– *You look grubby.*

– I feel grubby.

– *And there's another grey hair.*

– Ah, shut up.

I decided to drown the little voice and have a quick shower. Talking to myself is okay, it's losing the argument that I can't handle. I got out of the shower and onto the scales. Force of habit from when I was training. Eleven stone, five pounds. That's all right. Only three pounds over my training weight. The structure might be shaky and the face might be a little worn, but outwardly at least the bod was still in good shape.

Damn. I'd forgotten my shaver. It was back in my room. I haven't wet shaved in years, ever since I seriously considered slitting my throat with one of the razor blades. I didn't really want to kill myself, at least not on that particular morning, I just sort of wondered what it would look like to see myself commit suicide in the mirror, like it was happening to someone else, seeing my life flow away and then suddenly... nothing. Or maybe something. Fascinating. I wondered how I would react. Would I see the blood and panic, would my natural instinct for self-preservation take over, or would I just watch it happen?

Anyhow, that was the last time I wet shaved. I reckoned that using an electric was taking temptation out of my way.

There was a knock at the door. Well, a hammering. Mex.

'Hey, Inglis, you in there?' He calls me Inglis. I think he read part of Hemingway once; *For whom the bell tolls*. Probably an extract from a magazine in a waiting room somewhere. I was tempted to shout 'no', but even idiotic sarcasm would have been wasted on him.

'Yeah, Mex, I'm on the way out.'

'Well hurry up, I gotta get moving.'

I opened the door.

'An' I tell you again, I'm no Mexican. I'm from Honduras.' He pronounced it *'mehican'*.

'It's close enough, mate. They're both south of Croydon.' God, I can be cruel sometimes, but when a couple of your eggs mysteriously disappear from the fridge, it soon becomes guerrilla warfare. Every comment counts.

Back in my room I pulled on my jeans (reasonably clean) and found my trainers hiding under the bed. I took my shaver out of the bottom drawer, pulled out the mains lead, the only socket was in the bathroom, and dug out the batteries from the mess that was my middle drawer. I fitted the batteries and the shaver dribbled into life. And then dribbled out again. I chucked it back into the bottom drawer and decided to grow a beard.

*

'You need a shave,' said the lady at the launderette. I usually do most of my washing by hand, but I had no soap powder left, so since I had to go out anyway I thought I'd do it properly for once.

'I'm growing a beard,' I replied.

'Oh no,' she said, 'you shouldn't do that. Women don't trust men with beards.'

'Women don't trust men anyway,' I said.

'Look at all those politicians,' she went on, ignoring my comment, 'they don't have beards do they – 'cos they want to earn our trust. Men with beards have something to hide.'

'Yes,' I said, 'their faces.' I sat down and the conversation ended.

I checked my watch and left the launderette to buy the evening paper, which actually hits the streets before lunchtime. Pat, the newspaper man, was at his usual pitch.

'Afternoon, Mr Garron, Standard for you.' He folded the newspaper and passed it to me. 'Report inside on the fight last night,' he said, 'Did you see it on the box? Bloody rubbish that Dagworth – you could've had the both of them, Mr Garron.' He looked at me almost apologetically. 'Probably still could, couldn't you?'

There's always one, somewhere, who recognises you and wants to talk. About you – your fights, the old fighters, the new ones, and they think you want to talk as well, to relive the 'good old days'. They never think that you might want to forget the good old days and leave them behind you. They only remember the good times – you remember the bad.

I smiled at Pat. 'Not anymore, Pat. Haven't got the legs

for it. Once you hit thirty, they just want to put you out to seed. I wouldn't mind being put out to stud, but seeding seems a bit boring.'

He laughed. 'Bye, Mr Garron.'

'See you, Pat, take care.'

I went back to the launderette, automatically turning to the sports pages first. The reporter agreed with Pat. Dagworth was apparently not worth the entrance fee, although he had lasted the ten rounds, only losing on points to the Frenchman. The reporter got stuck in with relish. Another British failure to report. His wasn't a name that I knew. I wondered if he'd ever been in the ring himself, with nowhere to hide when it started to hurt. I felt my mind drifting to the Frenchman I fought – Rimaud. Warm-up fight for the British title eliminator bout. Pat had told me once that he was there for that one. Second on the card to the European lightheavyweight fight. I let my mind go – stopped resisting it. Let it go back the four or five years. Knowing I was going to win. Totally centred. Totally in control. And in the fourth round, cracking my right hand, and then finishing him in the fifth, not realising that I'd effectively finished myself. The beginning of the end. I looked at my right hand. Broke it again winning the eliminator and never made it to the title fight. It was postponed when they had to reset the hand and then they took away my licence, even before the operation on my wrist. It wasn't too bad now, but the dream was gone. Don't let them tell you that it's the taking part that counts.

'Put it in the dryer.'

'What?'

'Your washing – it's done. Put it in the dryer.'

'Oh yes, sorry – I was miles away.'

I transferred everything to the dryer and opened the paper at the jobs section. Nostalgia isn't good for me – I get morose.

Telesales and more telesales. Well, there must be money somewhere. If so many people are selling, then someone must be buying. I could do telesales, I just didn't want to. I'd done sales-repping before, when I first stopped fighting. I had a good introduction. After a while though, the driving really began to wear me out. Two years driving almost non-stop started to get to me. So I jumped ship and got into importing and wholesaling, which wasn't too bad, until about three or four months ago, when the company I worked for relocated three hundred miles out of London and I didn't relocate with them. The redundancy was pathetic; I hadn't been with them the regulation two years yet and suddenly I couldn't pay the rent on my flat. So a couple of months ago, I stuck a few bits of furniture into storage and moved everything else into my present, much cheaper hovel. Actually, it wasn't that bad, just small and shared. But affordable, at least for the moment. Sooner or later though, I would have to stop being fussy and take any job, just to keep myself going. But it's a problem, when you've had a crack at your real ambition, to start again from nothing. You need to get your motivation from somewhere. I suppose if you let yourself go far enough, it comes from necessity. I wasn't sure how far I'd let myself go, but I wasn't ready for telesales yet.

By the time the drying cycle had finished, it was gone 3.30 pm. I looked in at the fruit and veg shop, but he had nothing for me to do, so I stocked up on mushrooms, onions, carrots and potatoes and crossed the street to home. Time to think about food. Number 58 in the 101 recipes for basic vegetables. I knew that I'd have to up my living standards before I reached the end of the book, or face starting it all over again. There, maybe I'd found my motivation.

At home I read the paper properly and diligently checked

the TV page. Not a lot, but enough to see me through the first part of the evening. I'd go out later on and get a video and half a bottle of scotch. Living it up, right? Well, just now I don't need to live, I just need to keep going.

*

Friday dawned bright and early. Too bright and too early. I hadn't shut the curtains properly last night. Some insane impulse jerked me out of bed and out for a run. I was moving before I was really awake. I hate running. I find it boring as well as exhausting. I only run now if I wake up early and my legs get into gear before my brain. I ran for about twenty minutes. I don't have to be precise anymore; I'm not in training.

When I got back, Linda was in the bathroom. I sat on the floor of my room in my own sweat for about ten minutes, controlling my breathing, until I heard the bathroom door open. I waited a few moments so as not to bump into Linda. Not that I don't like her, I do like her, but she has a fairly low tolerance point first thing in the morning and a comment such as 'good morning' might just see you wearing your face back to front.

I showered and went back to bed. Yeah, I know, but what else do you do at 7.15 in the morning if you're not working?

I woke up again just before noon. A quick wash, breakfast and on to the business of the day. The newspaper, the job centre and round to see a mate, have a chat or maybe a drink. Mick perhaps, or Tony at the car lot. It doesn't matter really, anything to hang the day on. I slipped a couple of harmonicas into my pocket. Mick plays guitar and if I went to see him, we could jam a bit. I play blues harp, not great, but good enough to get by and it makes me feel good, which is all I need.

Pat called to me before I could even move towards his stand.

'Mr Garron, something that might interest you.'

'Sure, Pat,' I said.

'Couple of guys asked me if I knew anyone who'd like an evening's work.' That figured, Pat knew everyone in the area.

'Straight is it?' I asked.

'That's what I asked 'em, Mr Garron, first thing I asked 'em. They said it was straight, but cash in hand. I didn't mention you of course, Mr Garron, but I said if I found anyone I'd send 'em into the pub – I thought of you right away, I did – so if you want, just ask for Mr Smith at the bar.'

I looked at him.

'Mr Smith?' I said.

'Well that's what he said.'

'Mr Smith.' I loaded the words with as much sarcasm as I could, but Pat missed it. Him and Mex. My humour was definitely wasted around here.

'Right. Thanks, Pat. I'll think about it. Thanks for keeping me in mind.'

'No problem, Mr Garron. Anytime I can help, you know.'

I bought a paper and thought about it. Mr Smith? Well I could listen to the man. It wasn't as though I was booked up for the next half an hour. I walked down to the pub. On most High Streets I would have had to ask which pub, but here there was only one. There used to be three, but one turned into a wine bar for the yuppies and the other into an American style bar for the kids. Thankfully, I didn't belong to either of those groups.

The pub was quite full. Friday lunch-time. For the workers, a short afternoon ahead. 'POETS' day. *Piss Off Early Tomorrow's Saturday*. Not for the retail workers though, and not for the unemployed. For them every day is a Saturday. Me? I only know it's the weekend because I can't buy the evening paper.

I ordered a soft drink. It was already lunch-time, but not for me. It felt too early to drink. Then I sat in the corner and checked off as many faces as I could. Pat had said two men. I narrowed it down to two men at the bar, or two at a table near the gents at the back. It would be the two at the back. If they'd left a message at the bar, they would want to see their people walking towards them. Time for evaluation and consideration.

I finished my orange juice, got up and walked towards them. They ignored me. I hadn't asked at the bar. I took a good look as I passed them and went into the gents. Dark suits, dark ties – both quite tall, although they were sitting down, one much bulkier than the other. Both clean shaven. The bigger man heavier in his face as well as his body. Relaxed eyes, patient, watching, waiting.

In the gents, I washed my face and towelled it off carefully. I didn't want them to think I was sweating. I stepped out of the washroom and in front of the two men.

'Mr Smith,' I said immediately, addressing the slimmer man.

'That's right,' he answered. Neutral voice.

'My name's Grade,' I said, 'I understand you're offering work.'

'Where did you hear that?' He looked hard at me.

I sat down. 'Around,' I said, holding his eyes. They'd probably asked questions of more people than just Pat and there's no point in giving away your source for nothing.

He looked at me for a couple of moments, trying to con me into thinking he was making a decision. Then he said, 'There's a man arriving in London from Europe. He wants to go out tomorrow night, see the sights, I don't know what, maybe a club, maybe just drive around. We've got a driver for him. We need someone else to go along, in case he decides to get out of the car. Make sure he doesn't get lost.'

'Who is he?'

'Business client. Not too important, works for someone who is important. We want to create the right impression, make him feel he's somebody.'

'You telling me you don't have people to do this?'

He leaned back in his chair. 'We have people, we just don't have people available.'

'Why not a security firm?' I asked.

'We don't want too many people knowing he's here. You don't ask questions, we pay and we don't ask questions. Security companies can check things up. An independent can't do that so easily.'

'How much?'

'One hundred. Driver will pay you when you're done.'

'Okay, tomorrow night then.'

'Black Escort, four door. It'll pick you up outside this pub, eight o'clock sharp. He'll have the address where to pick up the man. Wear a suit.'

I got up. The heavy man said his first words. 'I know your face. Where from?'

I looked straight at him. 'I don't know yours,' I said. I held his gaze for a moment longer than was necessary and then turned to go.

'Grade,' the slim man said, 'Get a shave.'

I didn't look back. 'I'm growing a beard,' I said and walked away.

Out in the street I checked my hands. No shakes. Not that there should be, but I was a long time out of their world. At least it seemed like I remembered how to play the game.

Except I'd left the newspaper in the pub. Mistake? Did I leave it at their table, at mine, or in the gents? Well it was too late now, I'd just have to tighten up. I bought another paper, not from Pat, a few groceries and went home.

I spent the afternoon working out. Body against itself. Press-ups, crunches, squats, plus my own exercises. After a while you work out your own routine. Also a good stretching session, since I didn't want to tighten up, just work out. I finished with a series of moves, my own *kata*. Even before I'd damaged my hand, I'd learnt how to use my feet, knees and elbows. On the street you learn quickly that there are no rules. I could still hear Al telling me, 'It's not like the ring. Don't damage your hands if you don't have to. Snap the guy's knee with a kick and he won't be following you. Better still, use something else on him. Use anything. A piece of fencing, a dustbin lid, anything, but make sure you use it hard. In the end there's only one rule. Survive. Whatever it takes. Survive.'

Crazy man. 'My teacher', I used to call him. He didn't train me or advise me, he taught me. Al Shapiro. Crazy Al. Professional bodyguard, minder, 'delivery' man and God knows what else. When I wasn't making a living fighting, I worked for him. And he showed me how it worked. How to survive. It still makes me smile to remember the look on his face when they started replacing metal dustbin lids with plastic ones. You couldn't splatter someone with a plastic dustbin lid in quite the same way. He was genuinely upset.

I showered and slept for a while. I woke up when Linda knocked on the door. I grunted something and she poked her head into the room.

'TV dinner tonight?' she asked. I woke up properly.

'Aren't you out with Mitch tonight?'

'Not tonight, he's working, well, so he says anyway.' She

put on her mock sex siren voice. 'It's just you and me, honey.'

I responded with my not very convincing Southern States drawl. 'Well then Ma'am, I think I might just take you up on your kind offer. I'll cook shall I?'

She lapsed into her own voice. 'Er – no, I'll cook.'

'And what, pray, is wrong with my cooking?'

'Nothing. It's just that I have to eat it.'

'Touché. Your place or mine?' I asked. She looked with overdone distaste at the mess that was my room.

'Mine,' she said. Then she imitated my imitation drawl. 'Why don't y'all just nip out and get a six-pack, huh?'

'Condoms?' I asked, innocently.

'Beer, you dummy. You know I'm an attached woman.'

As you can see from this, me and Linda get on pretty well, even though we haven't known each other very long. Sometimes we don't see each other for a few days, but then we'll get together and have a drink, or rent an old movie. For now we were mates. One day we might make it to friends.

When I'd moved in, I'd wondered how someone like her, to use a cliché, ended up somewhere like this. Her reply was that she hadn't 'ended up' here, she was just passing through. Later, she told me that she'd been living with a man and had eventually left him. Unfortunately, she also walked out on her home, since it belonged to him and her job, since he was her employer. So she'd had to start again, almost from scratch. She once said that she had everything going for her, intelligence, personality, good looks. (I didn't argue with any of this, I just added modesty and sense of humour to the list.) She ignored me and went on to say that the only problem was that she was almost thirty and she kept picking up these self-pitying dumb ass-holes, putting them on their feet and then realising that they were only dumb ass-holes after all. This particular dumb ass-hole kept his mouth firmly shut!

So that was Friday night. A good meal, a modest amount of alcohol, a couple of dismal sit-coms and an old Bogart movie that Linda almost ruined by quoting every second line before it had been spoken. She only stopped when I threatened to do my Bogey impersonation. I never actually have to do it. The threat is always enough. We parted about half past one, after much quoting of goodbye movie lines. I've never met Mitch, only spoken to him on the phone, but he's a lucky man.

*

I slept in late on Saturday, late even for me. I wasn't sure how long the night was going to be and that's a good enough excuse. The rest of Saturday was spent waiting. I'm good at waiting. I can fill time or just let it pass. This day I filled it. I cooked and ate a marvellous egg, rice and veg brunch and then blew harmonicas to some of my old blues tapes. I tell you, Big Joe Turner and Elmore James never knew what they missed, not playing with me as sideman. Then I put on some Sonny Boy Williamson and decided for the hundredth time to quit playing altogether.

*

By quarter to eight I was dressed and ready to go. I'd been over walking and driving positions in my mind, but I didn't really need to. It was about five years since I'd done this kind of work, but you don't forget something that you learned to do automatically. It stays in your mind. The right trigger, the right set of circumstances and it all comes straight back.

I was outside the pub with a couple of minutes to spare. A black Orion pulled up. The driver opened the window.

'You Grade?' he called.

'You got the wrong car,' I said.

'Escort, Orion, does it make a difference?'

I nodded, walked around to the passenger side and got in.

'David Harwood,' he said, and put out his hand. He was very young.

'Grade,' I answered, and shook the hand.

He pulled away and carried on talking.

'You got a first name, then?'

'Yep,' I said. 'This car's a manual.'

'So what?'

'You done this type of job before?'

'What, driving? Yeah, I'm a courier.'

'No, I mean driving a man like this?'

'Well, no, but it's a good earner. I'd do more of it. Oh, I got your money.' He pulled out an envelope and handed it to me. I slit the end with a key, and counted it in the envelope. It was all there.

'What's wrong with a manual?' he asked. Amateur hour. Al always said you shouldn't work with them, they're dangerous. I could hear him saying, 'They don't know what they're doing, but they think they do. Most of them are either too cocky or too stupid to ask the right questions.' Well, Al, this one had asked.

'There's nothing wrong with a manual car, it's just that an automatic is better, certainly for a beginner, on this kind of job.'

'Why's that?'

I spelled it out for him. 'You can drive an automatic easier with one hand and one leg, just in case you have to.' He didn't answer. He'd worked it out. 'Also,' I said, 'automatics don't stall in the same way.' There can be a downside as well, but I wasn't getting into a discussion on the pros and cons of automatic versus manual cars for bodyguard work.

'Right,' he said.

We drove on in silence. He seemed to know where we

were going. We got towards the centre of town, and headed for Euston. He pulled up outside a small hotel in Gower Street.

'He's registered as "Broussier",' Harwood said.

I went in, rang the bell at reception and asked for Broussier's room. Number 22, second floor. I called him on the house telephone and he asked me to come up. His English was good, with what sounded like a French accent. When I knocked on the door, he was ready, just putting on his jacket. Tall, stylish, with thick black hair, and a good suntan, he greeted me with a big smile. I hate these good looking bastards.

'Mr Grade,' he said, 'I am pleased to meet you. I understand you are going to be looking after me tonight.'

'Well, hopefully you won't need too much looking after.'

He laughed. 'I hope not, but I think any foreigner in London needs looking after – no?'

He was still smiling as we reached the car. I put him in the back, kerbside, and took the front passenger seat. He asked a lot of questions about London and compared parts of it with Brussels and Antwerp. He was Belgian, not French. We went north through Camden Town to Hampstead, and then back through Swiss Cottage and St John's Wood into town, which we criss-crossed at his direction. I felt rather like a tour guide. He made a point of looking at the major clubs and casinos and he also stated that he had to meet someone at one of the West End clubs at one in the morning. It was a fairly sanitised tour of London, sticking to the major tourist routes, but one of the things that fascinated Broussier was the number of homeless people around Trafalgar Square and the Strand, rubbing shoulders with the theatre-goers. Somehow, social comment from this type of continental businessman was not quite what I had expected.

We hit a couple of pubs, just for local colour, and made it to the club at just after midnight. I told Harwood to be back at two and if we weren't here and he couldn't park, then every fifteen minutes after that. Inside the club, Broussier was approached by the 'Mr Smith' who recruited me. I didn't expect any recognition from him, and I didn't get any. Broussier politely asked me to wait for him and followed Smith away. I sat at the bar and waited, not drinking. I didn't feel particularly comfortable. This was an upmarket place. I'm strictly downmarket.

Broussier was back alone before two. He sat down at the bar and ordered brandy. It was his first alcoholic drink of the night. He asked me what I was drinking. He was still smiling. It must have been part of his job description. I smiled back at him. 'I'm working, remember?'

'Ah yes,' he said, 'but I am not. I am almost done for the night. But I would like to see some of East London, the Docklands, perhaps. I know there is property to buy there.'

'If you like, but it would be better to see property in the daylight.'

'Yes, but I leave tomorrow morning, I have a flight arranged. I would like to take a quick look over the area tonight, if possible.'

'Oh, anything is possible, Mr Broussier, especially as you're in charge.'

He laughed, finished his drink and we went out to the street. It was just on two, and as we emerged Harwood pulled up in the Orion. I walked Broussier to the car, opened the kerbside door and put him inside. I got in the front and Harwood clicked down the central locking system. I pulled the lock on my door back up again.

'Home?' Harwood said.

'No,' I replied. 'Wapping, Shadwell and the Isle of Dogs

for Mr Broussier, David and don't worry about taking the scenic route, he can see it warts and all.'

Harwood glanced at his watch, raised his eyes to heaven above and we moved off. Broussier restarted his questions about London and the places we were passing. There was a fair amount of traffic on the roads out of town, after all it was a Saturday night in London, but it thinned out as we got nearer to Limehouse and the Isle of Dogs. Broussier wanted to know why it was called the Isle of Dogs. I couldn't tell him. If I'd ever known, then I'd forgotten. Tobacco Dock interested him as an enterprise, until I told him that I'd never seen more than a handful of people shopping there at any one time. He really did seem fascinated by the area and I hoped he didn't want to get out and go walkabout.

I'd been shifting my position occasionally to check the mirrors, but I couldn't see anyone taking an interest in us. Then Harwood, who seemed to be concentrating very hard, touched my arm.

'I'm going to do a left soon and come back onto this road.' He gestured to the mirror.

Good lad – not only for keeping his eyes open, but for telling me, without scaring Broussier, what it was he was going to do. After all I didn't know him. If he swung off suddenly, I might think he was taking me and Broussier for a ride. Actually, he still might be.

We'd come off The Highway in Shadwell onto Narrow Street. Harwood pulled a left off Narrow Street and slowed. A few seconds later, a car swept past the turning and continued away from us. I opened the window and we heard it fade into the distance.

'Okay, David.' He looked at me and half-smiled. There is a thin line between reaction and over-reaction, but I'd rather be with a cautious beginner than a foolhardy one. He pulled away and we went around in a crescent and back onto Narrow Street. It had been too dark to see the car clearly, but I thought it was a dark four door hatchback, possibly a Cavalier or an Astra. Throughout this, Broussier had sat in silence. Now he chirped up again as though there had been no detour. We turned right onto West Ferry Road and drove past Canary Wharf. As we got into Millwall, I saw a dark four door hatchback with its rear lights towards us, stopped thirty yards up a side street. It didn't follow us. The road was empty and quiet. As we came around the bottom edge of the Isle of Dogs, towards the recreation ground, a Luton van pulled out in front out of us, from the side of the road. Harwood swerved to go around the van, but it moved out with us and sat in the middle of the road. Harwood hooted.

'Arsehole,' he said, under his breath, then settled down behind the van. As we passed East Ferry Road, the hatchback swung out behind us.

'Shit! It's a block,' I said. I reached back and pulled Broussier down flat onto the back seat. 'Brake and swerve right!' I shouted at Harwood. He was too late reacting. The van slammed on its brakes and although Harwood did too, we hit the back of the van.

'Reverse away.' I was trying not to scream at him. The engine was dead. He'd stalled. The car stopped ten yards behind us. Two men got out. The driver stayed in the car. Without hurrying they walked towards us. They were both carrying baseball bats. I pulled the gear lever into neutral and said quite calmly, 'Turn on the ignition.'

Harwood looked at me. The two men were coming to my side of the car. They couldn't see Broussier flat in the back. With any luck they would think I was him.

'David,' I said gently, 'turn on the ignition.' He'd frozen. He looked at me and then at the key. The van pulled away slightly from in front of us and began to drive slowly off. The men were almost at the car. The last thing that you want to do is get caught as a passenger in a car, you're a sitting target. I was already leaving it late to move.

'Start the fucking car, David!' I shouted, as I shouldered open the door and dived out of the car, straight into a kick in the ribs and a crack across the top of my back and shoulders. I rolled away from the car, tucking in and trying to give Harwood some time. I thought I heard the car kick into life. Then I felt a crack in the face and lost everything for a second. They were both standing over me. I don't think they were using the clubs, just kicking me. I tried to roll away and found myself on my knees with one of them in front of me. I reached up between his legs. Grabbed for his balls. Squeeze, twist and pull. He fell forward on top of me and suddenly he wasn't there anymore. I pushed myself sideways and hit a lamp-post. I turned myself round and tried to see what was happening. Everything was blurred. I blinked a few times. I still couldn't see properly out of my left eye. It didn't matter. There was nothing to see. The hatchback was pulling away, leaving the street empty. Apart from some broken glass, where the Orion had hit the van, there was nothing to show for the last forty or fifty seconds. Except for a hell of a mess sitting up against a lamp-post.

I tried to touch my face. My left arm didn't want to move. I used my right. It came away red and wet. I tried to move and heard a shout. It took a moment before I realised it was me who had shouted. I used the lamp-post to pull myself up. I don't know how I got from floor level to upright, but somehow I did. Sort of. I couldn't straighten up. I couldn't stand on my left leg. I just leaned against the post, holding on with my right hand. Suddenly my face started hurting, I felt the bile rising and leaned forward as I threw up on the pavement. I stood still for a few minutes and felt less nauseous. As the adrenaline slowed, different parts of me began to hurt – dull ache to sharp pain. In the back of my mind I knew there was something I should do. I ran my tongue around my teeth. They all seemed to be there, but my mouth was slowly filling with blood. I spat it out and realised that I had to move. I couldn't stay here. It wasn't a residential area, but I still had to get away, before someone found me and I had to start explaining things that I couldn't explain. I started to move off down the street and fell forward onto my hands and knees. I was too dizzy, too disoriented. I gave it a little while and tried again. Better, this time. With a bit of practice, I could get good at this walking stuff.

I don't know how long I walked, or rather staggered, but it couldn't have been too long. There was a payphone quite close by. I picked up the receiver and then put it down again. I had to find some change. I knew I had change on me, it was just a matter of finding it. I was working by rote. On automatic pilot. Get up, get moving, get to payphone, get change. I could do all of this without thinking, it just required effort. I put twenty pence in the slot and then realised that I didn't know who I was calling. I was suddenly exhausted. I slumped against the side of the phone box and tried to focus. I was out of touch with too many people. People I used to be able to call on if I was in trouble, or needed help. Now I couldn't think of anyone to call. Did I have anyone to call? I felt almost like crying. I had to get home. I couldn't call a cab, because then there would be a record that I had been in this area tonight and at this time. Any cab driver would be certain to remember me, the state I was in. This was better. At least I was thinking straight. Tony. I would call Tony. I could even remember his number. I dialled it and his wife answered, her voice full of sleep. I tried to speak, but my throat hurt and my voice was rasping and probably slurred.

'Marie,' I said, 'I need to speak to Tony.'

'Who is it?' she said. 'Do you know what time it is?'

'Please, Marie, wake him up.'

'Is that Garron? Hang on.'

I could hear background noises, but I couldn't make them out. Then Tony's voice.

'Garron, is that you?'

'Tony, yes, it's – '

'Do you know what bloody time it is? Can't this wait? I've got to be up in, oh Christ, three and a half hours.'

'I'm sorry, Tony – I'm sorry but – '

'Are you drunk? You sound drunk – '

I summoned up a burst of energy. 'Shut up, Tony! Please! I'm in trouble. I've got no-one else to ask.'

'What's up?' His voice was different now, listening to me.

'I'm in a call box on Manchester Road, on the Isle of Dogs. I need help. I need you to come and get me. I need you to get me home.'

'All right, mate. I'm on the way. Are you okay?'

'I'm a bit of a mess, Tony – stick some newspapers on the back seat.'

'All right. Hang on, I'm coming now – Manchester Road.'

I hung up and slid down the side of the phone box to the floor, wondering who would get to me first. Tony, a cruising police patrol, or the local skells. I was light-headed and tired. I passed out.

I came to with Tony half-dragging, half-carrying me into the back of his car. He didn't argue when I told him no hospital. Tony may be legit, but he knows how it works. I must have gone out again on the journey back to his house, where I came to properly and he tried to clean me up. Tony is no doctor, so this meant washing off the cuts, which re-opened – one badly, ice for the bruising and a lot of Elastoplast. A handful of painkillers and a drink, and I crashed out on their sofa.

*

I woke up and opened my eyes. In fact, one eye to be precise, the left one didn't open very far. I started testing which bits of me worked and which didn't. The sofa wasn't really comfortable and I wanted to get home, clean myself up properly and sleep in my own bed. I moved my left arm. It seemed to work better than it had done last night. I pushed myself up and swung my legs onto the floor. It hurt, mainly around the ribs on my left side. Marie came in.

'How's the walking wounded?' she asked.

'Walking – I hope.'

It hurt to talk. My mouth felt swollen on the left side and as I began to move the whole left hand side of my face began to throb. I shifted my jaw from side to side. It hurt, but it moved.

'Tony's at the car lot,' she said, 'he'll be back after lunch, if you want to wait. Or I can take you home now if you like. The kids are round at friends.'

I stood up and waited for the room to stop moving. I said that I'd rather get home now. Both my legs seemed to work, although I was stiff and aching all over. On the way out, I avoided looking at the mirror by the front door.

It's a twenty minute drive to my flat and Marie was almost totally silent as she took me back. Still, it can't be much fun being woken up in the middle of the night and having a bleeding, battered lump dumped on your sofa. I wasn't in the mood for talking much either, so we sat in silence until we pulled up outside my hovel. Then she said, 'I don't know what happened and I don't want to know, but I want to ask you, whatever it is, not to get Tony involved.'

I looked at her. I hadn't even thought about this. She was staring straight ahead through the windscreen.

'I know you two go back a long way, but things are different for Tony now. He's older, he's got a business and a family and I'm asking you not to – '

'Wait, wait a minute Marie,' I cut in.

She turned to look at me. I thought she was going to cry.

'It never crossed my mind,' I said. 'Honestly, there's nothing for him to be involved in. This was a one off.' I tried to smile, but it hurt too much. 'Really, I hear what you're saying and you mustn't worry. I wouldn't pull him into anything.'

She smiled at me. 'Thanks.' Then she paused and said, 'Do you need help up the stairs?'

'No, I think I'll make it. There's a rail.' I opened the car door. She looked at me with concern now.

'You'll be all right then?'

'Yeah, sure.'

'You'll probably feel a lot better after you've cleaned up properly, you know, had a bath, a shave, something to eat.'

'I'm growing a beard, Marie,' I muttered.

'What?' she said, not following what I was mumbling.

'Never mind. Don't worry, I'm okay.' I waved goodbye and shuffled to my door. She waited until I was inside and then drove off.

One day, when I'm rich, I'll install escalators to all six floors of my mansion. In the meantime, I'll continue at times like this to curse whoever invented stairs. I made my way slowly up to the first floor flat, opened the door and walked straight into Mex.

'*Madre de Christo*! What happened to you? Jealous husband eh, or the wife herself, or maybe – '

I said quietly, 'If you don't shut up, I'm going to kill you.'

'Hey, whoa, is jus' a joke.'

I realised he was waiting for me to say something. If I wasn't careful, this could develop into a conversation. He gave up waiting and looked closer at me.

'Hey, you better siddown man, come on in the kitchen.'

He sounded genuinely concerned and I was almost touched by it. I still didn't want to sit down and talk to him. I just wanted to crash out on my nice warm bed. Mex put paid to that.

'Linda, hey Linda, looka this.' Linda poked her head out of her room.

'My God, what happened to you?'

'Nothing,' I said, which was a pretty stupid answer, but then it wasn't a very original question and I didn't feel like answering it.

'You look like – '

'Please, don't say it.'

'Fine,' she said. 'Well, we'd better get you cleaned up.'

'No, really, I'm fine. I can deal with it.'

'Yes, you probably can,' she looked at me, 'but you don't have to. No, don't say anything, that is supposed to be what friends are for, right?' Her look changed to one of challenge. I'd had enough challenges recently. I gave in.

'Mex, get the medical box from the bathroom please.'

'Hey, Linda, I gotta go now, I'm late already.'

'Mex! Get the box!' The shout nearly took my head off, never mind Mex's. He got the box.

'Okay to go now, Linda?' he asked from the doorway.

'Certainly, Mex, off you go.' It was like a teacher dismissing a school kid.

The next twenty minutes or so were painful, but probably necessary. At the end of them, at least I was cleaned up and the cuts were dressed properly. Linda thought I needed a couple of stitches and I didn't think so, but she let me have my way, with the promise that if the cuts opened up again, I would go to hospital. Then, with me lying down on my bed at last, with a cup of coffee liberally laced with whisky and Linda sitting on the chair next to me, she finally asked again.

'What happened – or do you not want to tell me?'

I tried to be polite.

'Well, actually no, I don't want to tell you.'

She looked at me. I looked at my feet and wondered if that had been polite enough. Obviously it hadn't.

'You know, you are a real pain in the arse. You stagger in, allow me, just about, to put half a plaster on your face and then say nothing at all. And I'm supposed to say "okay, boys will be boys and try not to do it again". Well sod you! You tell me what happened, or that's the last cup of coffee I ever make for you!'

She had a point, so I told her, well half told her at least. I said I'd done a quick cash in hand job, a perfectly legitimate job, for somebody, but that someone else obviously didn't like the client and I got in the way. Not a lot to tell really and basically true. She asked me what happened now and I told her the truth again, which made me feel quite virtuous.

'Nothing happens now,' I said.

'No police or anything?'

'No.'

'No repercussions or revenges?'

I smiled, almost.

'No, Linda. No revenges or heroics or anything remotely stupid like that. I just take things easy for a couple of days. It's actually not as bad as it looks.'

'Good,' she said, sounding relieved. 'In that case I leave you to sleep and I'll sort something out for later on, supper and a vid, or something.'

'Well thank you but I can manage to – '

'Of course you can, but I'm not doing anything else, so that's settled. I'll wake you up later on to eat.'

And with that she left and I slept. Later, in between dozes, I heard her on the telephone putting off her date for the night. I was so tired, it hardly even registered. I wasn't really thinking straight. If I had been, I might have realised that I had been paid in full, in advance, for my troubles and that might have started me thinking properly. And that in turn might just have influenced what was to follow.

*

Monday hurt, but not worse than Sunday. I could move all right, just not too quickly, but I'd rather be moving slowly than lie in bed all day. Besides which, I'd been hurt worse than this before.

As I swung myself off the bed I thought back to the state I was in after I'd fought a Liverpool man named Duggan. I was twenty years old and he must have been in his early thirties then. For eight rounds we punched each other to a standstill. He had the hardest head I've ever come across and hard fists as well. Luckily for me, he wasn't too quick on his feet and I got the decision, although in truth it probably could have gone either way. My mouth and the left hand side of my face were so swollen, I was on liquids through a straw for I don't know how long and my body was so bruised, I looked like a patchwork quilt. Compared to that, this really wasn't so bad. My left arm and ribs hurt, but I was mobile and my face wasn't swollen up, just marked. A day or two and anybody looking would just think I'd walked into a kitchen cupboard or something. Well, almost.

Mex seemed to be out, I couldn't hear any music or manic singing from his room and Linda was at work, so I had the place to myself. I dug some change out of my jacket and headed for the payphone. I wanted to thank Tony and ask him a favour.

'M and T Autos.'

'Hi, Tony, it's me.'

'Ah, the bleeding beacon shining in the night. How're you feeling?'

'Yeah, I'm all right. Just a little sore. Wanted to say thanks for Saturday night.'

'S'all right mate, just don't make a habit of it. For your sake not mine.'

'I'll try not to.'

I could hear him take a bite of something and his voice went slightly muffled.

'Not going to tell me what it was all about are you?'

'Not if I can help it, Tony, but I could do with a favour if you've got the time.'

'Oh yeah?' Wary voice.

'No, no trouble, just if you get the chance at lunchtime, could you nip round to Mick for me? I want some info on somebody and I need to know who to ask. I'd call him myself but you know what Mick's like, he won't say anything over the phone.'

There was a moment's silence, then, 'You know I can't stand that dog of his. Gives me the creeps, the way he looks at me.'

'Ah, come on, mate, that dog looks at everyone like that, that's what he's supposed to do.'

'Yeah, all right. I'll give you a bell back after lunch.'

I made a cup of tea and thought about what I was doing, trying to find out some background on Smith. I hadn't lied to Linda, I wasn't going to do anything, I was just interested in why Smith had been asking around for the job. It was only information. No-one was going to know and no-one was going to get hurt over it. I drank my tea and went back to bed.

*

About half one the phone woke me up. I dragged myself down the hall to hear Tony, telling me to get to a pub that was about twenty minutes from me any time this afternoon and look for Charlie Nelson who would be playing pool at the back of the pub.

'Mick says you'll know him easy 'cos he's only about five foot two, sixty years old and he's got most of two fingers missing off his right hand. Mick says don't comment on that whatever you do. He says he'll call him and tell him to expect someone called Jones to play him at pool and you can take it from there.'

I almost laughed. Smith and Jones. Ah well, Mick wasn't to know. Tony was still talking.

'... says Nelson knows most of what goes on and can find out the rest. And don't ask me to go near that dog again for a while.'

I thanked him, rang off and called for a cab to pick me up in half an hour. I didn't think I was in a fit state to get on a bus and besides, I had Smith's money waiting to be used. If I'd have been obeying the rules, I would have had the cab collect me from outside the launderette and drop me off a little way from the pub, but I wasn't thinking like that. And if it had occurred to me I would probably have dismissed the thought anyway. After all, it wasn't as if those measures were necessary.

*

The cab dropped me off and I looked at the shoddy exterior of the place where I was to meet Nelson. It was one of those pubs that look dark from the outside and even darker once you go inside. There was a long bar stretching away from the door and I could see the pool tables beyond the far end with a handful of people standing around one of them. There were eight or nine men scattered around the rest of the pub in twos or threes. It was the kind of place where everybody knows everybody else and everybody notices when an outsider steps in. I was an outsider. I stepped in. I went to the bar and bought a pint of cider. I'd have got a half since I didn't really want to drink on top of all the painkillers I'd been taking, but this wasn't a half pint pub. The barman was friendly enough, after all money is money, but he clocked the bruises on me and filed my face away for future reference.

I stayed drinking at the bar for a few minutes and then ambled over to the pool tables. Both of them were in use now, which made it easier for me. Less time to wait before I got to play. I stuck a coin in line on the table's edge, there was only one in front of me, leaned back against the wall and watched Nelson play. It was obvious who he was. There was only one small man in his sixties playing pool and five foot two as an estimate was probably on the generous side. Come to think of it, there was only one man with half of two fingers missing, but it didn't seem to check his pool playing in any way. The first two fingers of his right hand, or most of them anyway, were gone, but he just curled the last two around the cue quite naturally. And he didn't miss – I mean he didn't miss a thing. When I'd leaned against the wall he'd had three reds left. Thirty seconds later, he'd cleared them and rolled the black the length of the table into a corner pocket. He nodded to the man he'd just beaten and went back to his drink on a side table whilst his next opponent put his money in and set the balls up. I didn't go over to him. We'd talk once we had a reason to be talking to each other. I'd be playing him soon and that would be the opening. Until then, nothing. People who sell information like to be discreet.

I did look him over though. A small roundish face, not too lined, topped by a bald head and a fringe of grey hair around the sides and back. A small frame, but a bit of a belly on him. Probably a drinker's gut; too much lager with his pool.

Nelson let the other man break and one red went down. The balls had broken nicely and there were three open reds. The man took off his jacket, revealing a sweatshirt with a fighting gym's name on it. The guy didn't look like a fighter, in which case he was either a hanger-on or a poser. Either way, I didn't think he'd be able to play pool.

He took a long time to study the table, then rolled a slow red into the centre pocket but lost position for his next shot, missed it and Nelson stepped forward. He snapped three yellows in, snookered the poser, got two shots for a foul and cleared up. Clinical wasn't the word. He nodded to his beaten opponent and looked at me.

'You on next?' His voice was north London cockney, but a bit high pitched, almost chirpy. Bit of a stereotype really.

I nodded.

'What's your name, mate?' he said. 'I like to know who I'm beating.'

'Jones.'

'Got a first name, Jones?'

'Don't use it much.'

I put in my money and racked the balls up.

'Want to put a drink on it, mate?' he asked.

Cheeky bleeder. He'd never even seen me play. Maybe I'd lose, but I'd played before and I'd give him a run for his money.

'All right. Who breaks?'

'Winner's prerogative,' he said, pronouncing the word

carefully. He walked to the head of the table, placed the white ball in the 'D' and top spun it into the pack. Two yellows dropped. He took the lie in with a quick glance and as he walked around for his next shot, he wasn't just a man in a pub playing pool anymore, he was someone who knew exactly what he was doing. And I knew I would lose.

He potted two more loose yellows, left a third that was covering a pocket and with a long pot into one of the baulk end top pockets, used the cue ball to dislodge the most difficult yellow which had been tucked up between two reds. About fifteen seconds later, he'd doubled the black and I'd lost without playing a shot. All seven reds were still on the table. He leaned his cue against the wall.

'I'll take that drink now, son, if you don't mind.' He nodded to one of the men sitting nearby. 'Your table, Rog, if you want it. I'll take a break.' He walked off to the bar and I followed him.

'Pint of lager here, Mike please, on this gentleman.'

The barman came over smiling.

'Got skinned did you, son?' he said, pulling the pint. I put my money down.

'Never got on the table.'

He walked off laughing and my credentials in the pub were at least partly established.

'Yeah,' said Nelson, after the barman had gone, 'sorry about that, but they expect me to do that to any new face that walks in.'

'It's all right, I was going to buy you a drink anyway. I would've liked to have hit a ball though.'

He laughed and his small round face creased up. If I ever make it to sixty, I hope my lines are from laughter and not worry. He took a long pull at his drink and then asked, 'What do you want to know, Jones, what's the question?'

'Man called Smith.'

He looked at me dubiously.

'Well, that's what he calls himself.' I described him as best I could and Nelson seemed to recognise something in the description.

'There is a man calls himself Smith, goes around with a heavy almost all the time.'

'That's probably him,' I said.

Nelson shook his head a couple of times and looked at me as though for the first time, taking in the bruising and probably everything else as well. The four day growth of beard, the old scar tissue above the left eye, even the expression in the eyes themselves. He was an observer, this man and he wouldn't miss much. For a moment I even thought he was trying to read my mind.

'Why do you want to know about him?'

'Just curious.'

He half-smiled and said, 'Didn't you hear about the cat?'

I didn't want to start talking about me, certainly not to an information gatherer like him, so I hardened the tone a bit.

'Mr Nelson, I came to you because I was told that you were the man with information. Now do you know anything about this man Smith or not?'

'Take it easy, son. I know a little bit about him and I can probably find out some more.'

'How much is this going to cost me?'

'That's between you and Mick. I'll settle with him later.'

The old boys' network, working in my favour again. I thanked Mick silently.

'So what about Smith?'

Nelson leaned forward on the bar.

'He works, or worked for, an East London firm. They own a couple of clubs there and some property. That's the legit side. They also run a certain number of prostitutes out of the clubs and they control an area of drug running.'

Christ! Had I been working for those people? That shook me up a bit, but I didn't show out.

'What does Smith do for them?'

'Oh he's quite high up. He's an organiser and he hurts people. Almost certainly kills sometimes as well. He's a professional. Probably not a psycho, he doesn't get a kick out of it, he just does it. It's his job.'

'You sound like you know him.'

Nelson shook his head again and took another drink.

'No, it's just what I've picked up and my own impression, from what people say and how they say it. If you're mixed up with him then I would get un-mixed up. I'm telling you this 'cos you're a friend of Mick's. Otherwise I'd keep out of it.'

I looked him straight in the eye.

'I'm not mixed up in anything, just keeping out of trouble, but I appreciate the word of warning.'

He looked hard at me again and I got the feeling he was weighing me up. Checking to see if I was telling the truth or not. I was. He'd not see anything else in me. After a couple of seconds he said, 'All right, but just remember, Smith is no fool and he's ambitious. Word is that he's been given permission to branch out on his own, as long as he keeps in touch and doesn't tread on his old firm's toes.'

'What's he into then?'

'I don't know everything, Jones, I'm not the bleeding oracle.'

'All right.' I took the plunge. 'What about a European connection, Belgium maybe?'

'Don't know about that. I can listen out though. Anything else?'

'No, I think that's it.' I didn't want to give him

Broussier's name, or details of what I'd been up to.

'How soon do you want something on this?'

'How soon can you get something?'

'Yeah, I thought so. Meet me tomorrow night in the caff down the road on the left, the one by the corner.'

'What time?'

'Just before the pubs close, a bit before eleven, before it gets busy.'

'I'll be there.' I turned to go, but he grabbed at my arm and stopped me.

'Hey, this hasn't got anything to do with that business down in town, has it?'

I caught my breath for a second. Did he know about the job?

'Where down in town?' I said.

'Down in central London.'

'No,' I said, relieved he was talking about something else. 'Nothing to do with that. I'll see you tomorrow night.'

'Yeah, see you there,' he said.

As I walked out he was already wandering back to the pool tables, back to where he was respected, instead of everywhere else, where he was just a small man with a damaged hand and a despised way of earning a living.

I left the pub and suddenly realised how tired I was. I got another cab home and went to bed.

*

Monday night, Linda suggested we go out for a drink. Actually, it was a bit more forceful than a suggestion, she told me it would do me good to get out, so that was that. I hadn't told her that I'd been out earlier in the day and anyway, I was feeling better. Although my ribs still hurt (that would take a while) my left leg was working reasonably well. The bruises on my face and arms looked worse than they were. The human body is an amazing machine. It has no memory. The mind has memory, but not the body. It just keeps working to the best of its ability. No matter what you throw at it, it will naturally start the healing process and get on with cleaning up whatever mess it's in.

The stairs seemed to be easier to negotiate than they had been earlier and they were certainly a lot easier than on Sunday morning when I'd had to work my way up. I was feeling quite pleased with myself when we reached the hall downstairs and I opened the door for Linda to go out. Smith walked in. His chunky friend from our first meeting in the pub came in behind him and pushed me back against the wall. He leaned towards me so that his face was a few inches away from mine.

'Hi,' he said.

I nutted him, my forehead striking the bridge of his nose. It was a purely instinctive movement and probably not very diplomatic, but very satisfying as I heard his nose crack.

'Stop.'

I thought Smith was talking to me, but I realised he was telling his friend not to smear me all over the hallway. I suppose in my condition I should've thanked him for that. I didn't, because it went out of my mind when I looked at Smith. He was holding what looked like a 9mm automatic.

Now, I've seen guns and been around guns and I've worked with people who carry guns and I've even fired and practised with guns. So while I may not be in any way an expert, I am familiar with them. But this was the first time that anybody had pointed one at me. Let me tell you, when a gun is pointing at your stomach, it doesn't matter whether you think you know about guns or not. You don't move. After a few seconds you realise that you haven't taken a breath. So you do, but it isn't easy. It flashed through my mind that Al would've stayed completely calm, at least outwardly and totally in control of himself. He once told me that a knife or stick was only as good as the man using it. I wondered if you could apply that to guns. I looked at Smith. He seemed to know what he was doing.

I opened my mouth to say something and found that my voice had disappeared into the pit of my stomach. I looked over at Linda. She wasn't moving, just staring at Smith and the gun. She seemed to be in a state of shock. Then I realised that I was too and that I had to jerk out of it. It was like a physical exertion although it was in my mind. I said:

'Is Smith your real name?'

He laughed, I think with genuine surprise and ignored the question completely.

'I just want to talk to you, Grade. Sorry, it's Garron isn't it?' He seemed totally relaxed. There was no tension in his face or eyes, or, thank God, in his gun hand.

'This whole mess is, well, really my fault. I should have checked you out properly, but I didn't. What I wanted was some local lad who reckoned himself a bit. What I got was someone who knew what they were doing. You've messed us up. Now it's just possible that you can help us out.'

'How did you find me?' I was worried that they might know I'd been checking on them, but Smith didn't seem to know about Nelson.

'That was quite easy. We only asked around for the job in a couple of places. One of them was the newspaper man. You left the evening paper at our table in the pub. We just put two and two together and had a chat with the man this afternoon. He wasn't very helpful at first, but my colleague here leaned on him a little and he told us which building he'd seen you come out of. Then we just needed to know which flat you were in. We could have rung at everyone's door, but we thought it would be quieter if we just waited for someone to come out. And that someone was you.'

I looked at broken-nose, but spoke to Smith.

'How bad did you hurt him?'

'Probably slightly more than we needed to.' His tone hardened. 'It's not a game, Garron.'

I looked at the blood covering the heavy man's suit and shirt front and wondered if I could have hit him any harder. His nose was still bleeding. He was trying to staunch the blood with his sleeve and looking like he wanted to break me up. It's a bit difficult though, to look seriously hard with your arm covering half your face. That bloody newspaper. They'd probably have got to Pat anyway, but I didn't have to make it easy for them.

'What do you want me to do?'

'We want Broussier. His business dealings are not in our interests. We –'

I broke in. 'You're not going to tell me about those dealings are you?'

Smith didn't even bother to answer that. 'We wanted to give him a message and scare him off a bit,' he went on. 'You messed that up for us.'

'Sorry,' I said. He ignored my comment again. I was just trying to upset his rhythm and get a foothold in the conversation, but he wasn't having any of that.

'Now this has got out of hand. A message is not enough. We had someone go to his hotel and he made a mistake. He got the wrong man. Now we have to find him and kill him before he gets back to his own people in Europe.'

'You're a nice guy, aren't you?' I put in with as much sarcasm as I could.

'Don't push, Garron.' He gestured to the heavy. 'I could have him beat the crap out of you and you'd still have to do what I want.'

'What do you want, Smith?'

'Broussier might try to get to you. He left the hotel in a rush, through a window and down the fire escape. He has, it seems, no money, no credit cards, no change of clothes, nowhere to go and nowhere to stay. No doubt he has contacted his people in Belgium, but they will have to come here for him and meet him somewhere. We hope to intercept whoever arrives, or get to Broussier first.

'You saved his life, so he thinks. He almost certainly spoke to Harwood about you and Harwood will probably have told him everything he knows about you. Which is nothing, except what we told him. That you were local to this area and that you'd meet him outside the pub.

'You are the only person, as far as we know, that Broussier knows in London. It's just possible he'll come here to try to find you. I can't spare somebody to sit in a pub all day, so you're going to do it for me. If he contacts you, you call me on this number.' He handed me a slip of paper. 'We will arrange a meet and you will bring him. Is that clear?'

I looked straight at him as it dawned on me what it was that he expected me to do. Throughout this little speech, his tone had not changed and his gun had not moved. He scared the hell out of me. I said slowly:

'You want me to set this man up, so that you can kill him, right?'

'That's right, Garron.'

'What if he doesn't contact me?'

'Then we will.'

'Okay.' I paused. 'How about if he doesn't trust you and won't come to the meet?'

'It's up to you to convince him. He should trust you. Tell him that we want to talk to him to sort things out. If he won't come, force him, or trick him, anything. Bring him back here and we'll come to you. It doesn't matter how or where, but you must bring him.'

I looked around at the scene. It was unreal. From the moment Smith had pulled the gun, no-one had moved. Smith was motionless, the calm in the eye of the storm. Linda was frozen, Broken-nose was furious, but held in check by Smith and as for me, I was still leaning against the wall listening to some mobster telling me I had to arrange for another man to die. And this was all happening in my own ten by eight foot hallway at the foot of the stairs.

I took a deep breath. I had to break the tableau somehow.

'Linda, sit down. On the stairs.' She looked across at me wide-eyed, as though she hadn't understood. 'Go on, sit down. There's fine.' She sat, still staring at me.

I looked back at Smith and moved away from the wall slightly. There were about five or six feet between us.

'What if I don't help you?' I said.

'Don't be bloody stupid,' he said, as though the idea hadn't occurred to him. 'We know who you are, where you live –'

'I could disappear,' I said.

Smith looked at me. He said quietly, 'And could she disappear?'

'She just happened to be walking down the stairs at the same time.'

'But you know her name.'

'What?'

'You said her name just now.'

Christ! If I carried on like this, I'd drop all the people I knew in trouble.

Smith reached down and picked up Linda's handbag. She

didn't resist. He tossed it to broken-nose.

'Go through it for ID. Check the door keys in the front door here.' He looked at me and he seemed to be enjoying himself now. The neutral voice was harder, with an edge to it. The dark eyes had become darker, almost black. He was in total control now: of himself, of the situation, of his world.

'You cross me, Garron and I can have you killed. Her too.' He gave me his hard eye stare. On its own I hoped it wouldn't have fazed me, but with a gun in his hand and everything worked out, it was quite effective.

I looked down at Linda. She had her face down on her knees. I desperately wanted to knock him off his perch, destroy his control. I turned back to Smith and held his stare.

'Suppose I was to kill you.' I had felt like shouting it, but it came out dead quiet.

Broken-nose stopped rummaging in Linda's bag. I didn't look at him, but I could hear him stop. Smith was silent for a moment. There was no flicker in his eyes.

Then he said, 'Do you think you could?'

I didn't answer him.

'I don't think you could do that.' He was speaking slowly now. 'Oh I've no doubt you're a tough man. I'm sure if we had a fight, if I was stupid enough to put the gun down, you'd take me apart, after all that was your business, but if I gave you the gun now and turned my back on you, would you shoot me, in the back, in cold blood? Or would you tell me to stay there while you called the police?'

I couldn't tell if there was mockery in his voice or not. It sounded as though he was just stating the facts as he saw them.

'Have you ever killed someone, Garron? Have you crossed that line that separates me and my kind from the rest of you? Maybe you have. But if that's the case, I'll bet it was hot blood, in a fight, in the heat of the moment, because it was you or him and that doesn't make you a killer. That's not enough for you to cross over to my side of the line.' He smiled at me, a hard smile. 'It's almost worth it, isn't it? Giving you the gun I mean. Just to show you that you couldn't do it. Of course, it would be a gamble. Killing me would certainly solve your problems. Do you want the gun, Garron?' He held it out to me. His voice began to rise. 'Can you do it, Garron? Are you a life-taker?' He was talking faster, urgently. 'Come on, it's easy, just point it and pull the trigger – now you see them, now you don't. Just switch off and do it.' He was almost beginning to shout now. I could see the sweat on his face. 'Come on, Garron, it's easy, life's easy to take away. One moment it's there and the next there's nothing, just a bag of bones. Nothing there. Just a blank, empty space, where there used to be a breathing, thinking life!'

Abruptly, he stopped and took a couple of breaths. He said quietly, 'No, Garron, you stick to your side of the line and leave me to mine.' He turned away and then, almost as an afterthought, said, 'Be in the pub from tomorrow morning. If he comes, he'll come soon.'

He opened the front door and walked out. Broken-nose glared at me, tossed the handbag back to Linda and followed Smith out. The bag landed on the second step and slipped down to the ground, spilling its contents on the way. Linda didn't look up. I leaned back against the wall and let out a deep breath. Again, I hadn't realised I'd been holding it in. His words had had the same effect as seeing the gun pointed at me. In fact, more effect. The violence, in a strange way, I could deal with, but the realisation that I couldn't hurt them, that in the end they would win because in the end they were prepared to go further than me, was a painful one. Smith was right. However much I felt like an outsider, I was still inside.

I was still this side of the line.

I went over to Linda and picked up her handbag. I put the bits and pieces back inside and sat down next to her. She turned into me, so that I couldn't see her face and I could hear her crying quietly. I put my arm around her and we sat there, each of us coming to terms with what had just happened. When violence enters someone's world, it's usually sudden, unexpected and often shattering. Linda had just been threatened with death. I suppose I was lucky; I'd been threatened before, just not in this way. What I had to come to terms with was not the violence, or even the threat, but the knowledge that what Smith had said was right. And that if Broussier came to me, I would have to lead him to his death. I don't know how long we sat there, but it seemed like forever.

With all experiences though, good or bad, if you survive them, you carry on. You have no choice. Your mind locks onto some facet of normality and uses it to drag you, step by step, back towards the real world. The stairs are there, so you climb them. The banister is there – you hold on to it. The door is locked – you find the key and open it. Each action is an affirmation that whatever it is that has happened is one step further behind you. It's over, at least for the moment. Linda had helped me downstairs. I helped her back up. The roles were reversed. I sat her in her room and made coffee for her. I also stuck a shot of whisky in the mug. As I put it down on the dressing table in her room, she said quietly, 'Thank you. Now go away, please.' She wasn't looking at me.

I started to say, 'Look – '

'Just go away.' Her voice was rising, but she controlled it. 'I don't know anything about what's going on, but I'm scared stiff and it's your fault, so please, just go away.'

She still hadn't looked at me. I tried to think of something to say, but there wasn't anything. She was right. It was because of me that she was involved. I closed the door quietly behind me and walked down the corridor to my room.

It was a couple of hours later that Linda knocked on my door.

'I'm sorry,' she said, standing in the doorway.

'For what? I'm the one that's caused this.'

She half-smiled at me, a bit more like herself again. 'What are you going to do?'

'Well, I'm going to lie here, listen to the tape and work out what I *can* do, if anything.'

'Go to the police.'

'And tell them what? That someone called Smith with a pet gorilla paid me to look after someone that they wanted to take to pieces. And if I don't pick out his mugshot, or even if I do, both you and I will have to get police protection for as long as it takes to catch up with them and possibly after that, if they really are organised crime. I can see the headlines now. "Ex-boxer involved in gangland killing." "Former contender tracked down to protective custody cottage in Cornwall." I don't know, Linda, I've got to think it out.'

There was a moment's silence. 'Listen,' she said, 'I don't want you to take this the wrong way, but I don't really want to be on my own at the moment, can I stay here a while?'

'As long as you want, Linda, all night if you want. I'll sleep on the floor, I've got my sleeping bag in – '

'No, that's all right. I don't mind, as long as you know that – '

'It's okay. I understand.'

And that's how we spent the night: lying on top of my bed, not talking much, listening to a continuous loop of Billie Holliday and Dexter Gordon and killing most of a bottle of Jameson's. Linda dozed on and off. I didn't. I worked through all the options in my head and by morning I thought I'd covered everything. I didn't really have much choice. I knew what I was going to do.

*

'The rain follows me around,' Julot thought as they approached the warehouse, 'at my age I should not have to be walking around in the rain on the docks in Marseilles. I should be leaving that to younger men.' He glanced across at Michel who was walking half a stride behind him to the left. 'What is going through his mind now? Tension, fear, excitement, maybe nothing. It looks like nothing. He is good, this boy, maybe almost too good. So why are you here, Julot, if he is that good?' He smiled to himself. He knew the answer to that and it pleased him although he was not a vain man. 'Because he does not have the authority, the experience to carry this off. Because the point here is not to perform a shooting, but to establish order and to do that you need presence. Shooting someone is not enough, you must shoot them in the right way.'

He had hoped that this would not be necessary. It could cause waves, but now there was no choice. Jean had run to London, but this man Smith, who had been so highly recommended, had made some kind of mistake. Now Jean was on the run again and all the more likely to try and sell the disc in France. He could not, must not, allow that to happen. If somebody bought that disc and tried to use it, it could be the end of him. 'I did not spend more than thirty years building a business and a reputation to lose them both like this,' Julot thought. 'Jean must not have an outlet to sell. If he is pressurised, if there is nowhere for him to run, he will come back to me. He will try to buy back his life with the disc and I will agree.'

They stopped at the main entrance to the building. Michel unbuttoned his overcoat; Julot did not. It was dark inside the warehouse except for a pool of light to the left in a gap between some storage crates. There was no-one to be seen, but an amplified voice said, 'Monsieur Julot, step inside, into the light.'

Julot half grunted to himself. 'Clever,' he thought, 'but a gimmick.'

He stepped into the warehouse and over to the lighted area. Michel followed, taking his lead from the older man. They stood in the light, a few feet from the side wall, facing back out to the darkness.

'You wanted to talk to me,' the voice said.

There was a touch of an echo and Julot realised that there were fewer crates in the warehouse than he had thought. Maybe business wasn't so good. He said, 'I don't talk to people I can't see.'

There was silence for a few moments, then footsteps and a figure emerged from the darkness and stood at the edge of the light.

'I am Clavet. You wanted to talk.'

Without the amplification his voice was thin. 'He should have stayed in the shadows,' thought Julot, 'he was more impressive with a microphone. He is too short for his weight, his face is too heavy, his clothes are too sharp. He is a role player this one, he left his guts somewhere along the road to here.'

He said,

'I was hoping to talk in a more comfortable environment, maybe with a drink, or a chair...'

'You wanted to talk to me. So I pick the place and the circumstances.' Clavet snapped his fingers and six men stepped into the light, three to each side of him and formed a semi-circle facing the Belgians.

Julot almost shook his head. 'Theatrical,' he thought, 'very theatrical.' These were muscle men, almost certainly armed, but not showing out yet. Beside him, Michel never moved.

'What do you want, Julot?' No monsieur now, sure of himself, in control.

Julot's tone was measured. 'We have not met, Clavet, but we have done some business before even though our areas of interest are different. You dealt with my secretary, Jean. He made delivery and collection arrangements with you. Jean has gone off on his own with something of mine which he will try to sell. He has limited options available to him and you are one of those options. If he approaches you I would like you to refuse to do business with him. That is all.'

There was a short silence as though Clavet was thinking this over. Then:

'*Julot, you have a reputation in your own field, but I have been working for myself now for almost five years and I will do business in my own country with whoever I want.*'

Julot took a step to the side, giving Michel room to work in if necessary. Then he said firmly:

'*No, Clavet, you will not.*'

Clavet stared at him in surprise. He had not been looking forward to this meeting. If he was honest with himself, Julot scared the hell out of him, although he would not admit it to anyone, but he had been sure the warehouse set-up would work, especially as Julot was only bringing one man with him. Now though, he wondered if he should have just met him in the office as a businessman. It was too late for that, he would have to tough it out.

'*I could have you killed now, Julot.*'

'*I don't think so.*'

'*You are crazy. You back your man against six? You –* '

'*I do. I have.*'

They looked at each other for a moment. Clavet wished that he had told his men to have their weapons drawn, but he had not wanted to be that confrontational with this man. Julot was in his element, but he did not want a gunfight, he wanted a walkover.

'*Michel,*' *he said quietly.*

And before anyone else moved, Michel had drawn a short barrelled revolver and shot the nearest man through the right knee. The shot reverberated around the warehouse. The man screamed once and collapsed sideways, his leg no longer able to support his weight. He lay on the stone floor gasping and clutching at his knee. Nobody else moved. When Clavet looked up from the crippled man and back to Julot, he found himself staring straight at the barrel of Michel's gun. He could still hear the echo of the gunshot. He suddenly realised he was sweating. He couldn't take his eyes off the gun.

A voice, Julot's voice said:

'He doesn't miss.'

Clavet knew what he should do. He should shout to his men, tell them to draw their guns, to shoot, but he didn't. Michel's gun was aimed straight at him and he didn't want to die. Julot spoke again.

'You men, kneel on the floor, but not you, Clavet.'

The five men knelt. None of them looking at Clavet. He was no longer their boss.

'Now face down on the floor, spread your arms and legs.'

Clavet found his voice.

'What do you want, Julot?'

'You know what I want.'

'It's done. I won't deal with him. Whatever he has.'

'But how do I know that? Why should I believe that, when a minute ago you were threatening me?' He started to walk towards Clavet, careful to stay out of Michel's line of fire. 'Give me a reason. It would be so much easier, so much more definite, to leave you dead.'

'Please, Julot.' Clavet's voice was shaking now and Julot could feel the fear in him. 'Please, I understand now. Whatever you want. That is how it will be.'

Julot, still standing to the side of Clavet, put a hand on his shoulder and felt him flinch.

'Good,' he said, 'I like things to be the way I want them to be. Now on the floor with your men. You are all in the light and quite visible. No-one will move until we have left. In due course, Clavet, we may have business to do again. It will be done on my terms.' He glanced at Michel and they made their way out of the warehouse into the rain. No-one moved.

Once outside, Michel asked, 'Why did you not kill him?'

'Because he will now do what I want. He cannot trace me and he may one day be a useful contact. If he was dead, someone else would take his place and we might have to come back and do this again at some time. And the next man might be tougher.'

'*So what now?*'

'*Now we get out of Marseilles and wait for Jean to come running back to us, or for the Englishman to catch up with him. Either way it will be good for us. And it will be soon.*'

*

It's an annoying but true fact that whatever you think through at night always seems ridiculous the next morning. During the night I'd worked everything out point by point. In the morning I wasn't sure if I could carry any part of my master plan through, never mind all of it. Still, I had to do something, so I thought I'd start at stage one and see how far I got. Stage one was actually going to be pretty difficult, since it involved persuading Linda to move somewhere else, permanently, and take some time off work.

'Permanently?' she said. We were in the kitchen.

'Yes.'

'No!'

'Linda, they know where you live. You have to be somewhere else for a few days, in case I screw up.'

'In case you screw up what? What are you going to do?'

'I'm going to sort things out, if I can.'

'How?'

Women have this really upsetting habit of asking very direct questions often in very direct tones. When I didn't answer she pressed on.

'You're not going to the police,' it was rhetorical, 'and you're not running because otherwise you would've said "we" have to get out of here – '

I broke in. 'I am moving, just not with you. I have to be seen to stay here for now, in case they're watching – '

'So you're not running, otherwise you wouldn't worry about that. Besides which, your stupid ego wouldn't let you run and – '

'I have no bloody ego about this, I'm just trying to do what's best!'

'And best is setting up some poor sod to be killed, is it? Don't tell me – '

'No it bloody isn't!' I shouted.

There was quiet. She was looking wide-eyed at me.

'Jesus,' she said softly. 'You're going for them!' I turned away, but she carried on talking to the back of my head. 'You're not setting that guy up, you're not running and you're not going to the police. You're going for them. What are you going to do to them? Kill them?'

I didn't say anything. I didn't turn around.

'You're crazy. You are totally fucking crazy! You can't kill them!' Her words hung in the silence. 'Kill them!' For a moment I thought there was an echo.

I broke the spell. Quietly, I said:

'Why not? Won't they die?'

'Because they'll kill you. No! No, no, no, that's not the reason! The reason is because you're not a killer. You couldn't do it. You can't do it!'

And then I felt it again. The cold heat inside. The ice burning in your stomach, your throat, your head and the cold, cold knowledge of what you are capable of. The first time I felt like this was years earlier as a teenage kid in a street fight. The first time I realised what it was, was as a boxer. And Al taught me how to reproduce it anytime I liked, anytime I needed. I knew what I looked like now. I'd seen it when someone took photographs of my first pro-fight. I destroyed the guy and the photographer caught my face on film. Cold and blank. No emotion. Blank face and dead eyes. When I saw it, I was shocked. Al said it was perfect. He was the only one who understood that that was what made me a good fighter. Not technique, not training, but that cold, dead streak, that no-one saw. I hadn't felt this in a long time, years maybe. Now it felt like an old friend had returned. Perhaps it was wrong, but I enjoyed the feeling. I turned to face Linda.

'You sure?' I said, my voice as cold as my eyes.

She looked at me and saw the difference. 'You can't,' she said, but without the same conviction. 'You're not like they are.'

'No,' I said, 'I'm not. But I can be.'

'I don't want you to be like them. That's not the answer. It mustn't be.'

'If you think of anything else, you tell me.' I let the sensation go, felt it draining away, felt myself relax. I sat down. 'Until then, we're going to take this a step at a time and the first step is to move you out.' Something was niggling at the back of my mind. If I didn't think about it, it would surface.

'Where am I going to go, then?'

'I don't know, anywhere.' I had a good idea. 'Stay with Mitch, he'd be happy for you to go there, wouldn't he?'

Apparently, this wasn't such a good idea as I'd thought. After throwing an open one kilo packet of self-raising flour at me, which hurt quite a lot as well as making a mess and calling me various names, a couple of which I didn't understand, but one that I did was certainly 'brainless imbecile', she stormed out of the kitchen and back to her room. It took me twenty minutes to clean up the kitchen and get the flour out of my hair and off my face. And I was running late already.

*

I phoned Mick, told him I needed to see him and I'd be around later. I also asked him if I could crash with him for a couple of days till I found somewhere to live. He said it was not a problem, so long as I wasn't in trouble with anyone he knew or dealt with. I told him I hadn't asked them for a CV, said I'd see him later and hung up.

I called Tony and asked him to bring a small van around to the back of the flats to pick up Linda's stuff later that afternoon. I also asked him to take whatever was boxed up of mine and keep it for me. Then I laid the lettings pages of the local paper out open on the floor in front of Linda's closed door, with a note saying to take anything short-term and that Tony would be coming over later to help her move. I told her to leave any new phone number with Tony and I would call her in the evening. Then I went off to the hospital to see Pat.

They didn't want to let me in. It was almost ten o'clock in the morning, but if I wasn't family... I told them I was and walked into ward B3. Pat was awake, propped up in bed and looking like hell. Stitches in his bald head and on one cheek, one badly swollen eye and bruises. He looked worse than I'd looked two days earlier. He could talk okay though and the first thing he did was apologise.

'I'm sorry, Mr Garron, really I am.' He'd seen the bruises on me. 'They got to you as well then. I couldn't help it, but I didn't tell them where you lived, just which block I seen you come out of – '

I cut in and told him not to worry, but he was worried already. Worried that he'd let me down and worried that the gorilla would work him over again. I tried to calm him, told him that he hadn't let me down at all and asked him for a description, as if I needed it, of Smith and the gorilla, really just to make sure they hadn't brought anyone else along. I also told him that they wouldn't be back and apparently he believed me. He said he hadn't told the police about Smith, wanting to talk to me first.

'I thought it would be better to keep your name out of it, Mr Garron, I just told the police that these two blokes didn't want to pay for their paper and then laid into me.'

'That's fine, Pat,' I said, wondering if it was, or whether I'd have been better off if the police had got themselves involved. We talked for a few minutes about when he was getting out, quite soon it seemed and I promised I'd be around to see him at the stall when he was working again, although I might be away for a few days. It was only as I was leaving that I realised I hadn't brought him anything, you know, grapes, chocolates or something. That's me though; thoughtful, but only up to a point, or after the event.

I had to be at the pub by eleven, when it opened, but I took the time to look in at a newsagent and ask him if he had a newspaper from yesterday still around. Luckily he had and gave it to me for nothing, so I bought an up to date paper as well to keep him sweet. The third page had a report on Harwood's death as 'Gangland Killing in Gower Street.' Harwood had been shot twice, once in the back from about fifteen feet and once from close range in the back of the head, execution style. Harwood had been identified (he was carrying his driving license and credit cards etc.) but the hotel room was occupied by a Monsieur Broussier from Belgium, who had apparently escaped through a window in the ensuite bathroom, leaving behind his passport, money, credit cards and all his belongings. It suddenly clicked – what Nelson had been talking about in the pub the day before. This was the incident in town with a European that he'd mentioned and I hadn't known what he was talking about, since I hadn't heard the news or read a paper about it. If I had've done, would it have made a difference? What would I have done then? There was no point in thinking about it. I hadn't known and anyway it was Nelson's business to look after himself when he was gathering information. That was included in his fee. Depending on what he came up with, I'd apologise to him when I saw him later.

The paper said that the police, naturally, wanted to speak to Broussier and also anyone who had seen the gunman entering or leaving the hotel, or walking along Gower Street. The description they issued was of a 'tall Caucasian, with dark hair, wearing a dark suit'. I felt sorry for the detective in charge, trying to get something from those details. I felt sorrier for Harwood though. He hadn't known anything about what he was getting into. He hadn't even known enough not to take Broussier back to the hotel, which obviously might have been compromised. And, come to think of it, Broussier hadn't objected either, which told me that he wasn't a field man, whatever else he did. In which case, he really wouldn't know what to do next, other than phoning home and waiting for someone to come and get him. I'd thought, in the back of my mind, that the chances were that Broussier wouldn't show at the pub; that he would be sorting himself out, but now the more I considered it, the more likely it seemed that he would arrive there. I'd told Linda we'd take it a step at a time, but instead of an incomplete stroll, this was turning into a sprint finish. I threw yesterday's paper away and made for the pub.

*

English pubs all have the same type of ambience, yet all the good ones have their own individual atmosphere. Pub drinking is a social event in England. Most people go to the pub to meet friends, colleagues or business contacts, or they go hoping to meet someone. I was desperately hoping not to meet someone.

It seemed quite likely that Harwood had told Broussier where he'd met me, since after leaving me to the dogs, even though I'd meant them to, I would have been a natural topic of conversation.

If Broussier had any sense at all, he would be watching

for when the pub opened. He would want to know who was inside before he walked in, and so did I. The High Street was very busy just before eleven and although I scanned the street and buildings from five to the hour until a quarter past, I couldn't see the man anywhere. By this time, my pretext of waiting for a bus was wearing a bit thin, since I'd let two go by already, so I thought I'd hit the pub for what could be an extended stay. I hadn't wanted to go straight in for a couple of reasons. First, I'd wanted to see if any one else was watching the pub, not that I was sure who would be, or that I would recognise them and second, I wanted to see if Broussier had brains enough to take his time and watch, rather than rush straight in. There was actually a third reason. I hate being the first person in a pub, it makes you look desperate, either for alcohol or for social intercourse. Well, social intercourse isn't the kind I would look for in that pub and I'm not an alcoholic. It's true, there was a time when I probably drank more than I should have done, but now I don't consider it a problem. I still drink, I just don't consider it a problem.

I was about to start across the road when a third bus pulled up. Talk about blowing your cover. When you want a bus, none turn up and when you want a nice long uninterrupted stay at a bus stop, which London Transport can usually be relied upon to provide, three bloody buses turn up! Roll on privatisation, comrades, that's what I say. Taking my life in my hands – from London drivers this time – I crossed the road and entered the pub.

There were half a dozen punters there already and a solitary barmaid. I bought a pint of Strongbow. Obviously, I couldn't drink all the time if I was going to be here all day, but equally, I couldn't drink orange juice all day either, so I might as well start off on the right foot. Besides which, although it wasn't midday yet, I'd been up for a while and it seemed late enough in the day for a drink. I wasn't used to mornings anymore. I took a table by the side wall of the pub where I could sit and watch the door. They had background music all the time here and I could hear Steve Harley, *Come up and see me* and yes, I smiled. It sent me back for a few moments to a different time and different people. I wasn't quite sure how I'd got from there to here, but here I was. I spread the newspaper out on the table and settled down. I remembered the Peter Sellers film where he tried to see through a newspaper by making a pinhole in it. Of course it all goes wrong. I wasn't going to try that myself; I didn't need to hide behind anything and I didn't want to stay reading the same page all day. I wondered idly if you could make holes in all the pages and line them up as you turned each one, but this ridiculous thought was interrupted by Broussier walking in and looking around, obviously for me. Gone was the smooth-dressing, smooth-talking executive. Instead, there was a rough-edged, unshaven man, wearing only a shirt, trousers and shoes. No jacket or tie and the clothes were dirty. How are the mighty fallen, I thought, as he caught sight of me and came over. The barmaid hadn't seen him yet. When she did, she'd probably want him out of the pub. He started talking before he sat down, but I shut him up.

'What are you drinking?'

'What?' he said.

'You're in a pub,' I said. 'You've got to drink something or they'll ask you to leave, or more likely, looking like you do, they'll throw you out.'

'Brandy,' he said.

'Good, back in a minute.'

The barmaid was looking uncertainly at Broussier as I walked to the bar.

'Car accident,' I said, 'went into a ditch, poor sod. Have you got a brandy for him please?'

She went from uncertainty to concern. 'Poor man,' she said, turning to get the drink. 'Is he all right?'

'Yeah, he's okay, just a little shaken up. Better make that a large one if you could.'

I paid up and with the barmaid suitably satisfied that her pub was not being overrun by vagabonds, made my way back to Broussier who was sitting back in his chair with his eyes closed. It occurred to me that if vagabonds did overrun this pub, there wouldn't be much to distinguish them from the regular clientele, but as far as the barmaid was concerned, it was probably a case of better the vagabond you know than the vagabond you don't.

'Go on,' I said to him, 'get that down you and relax for a couple of minutes. Then you can tell me what's been happening and we'll decide what we're going to do with you.'

He looked at me as though I was the last hope for sanity in an insane world, which to him, God help the man, I probably was. He took a drink and began.

After I'd unceremoniously left them on the Isle of Dogs, Harwood had taken him back to the hotel and had gone up with him to figure out their next move. A couple of minutes after they'd arrived, someone had opened the door, apparently with a pass-key, and had shot Harwood in the back, presumably thinking he was Broussier, who was in the bathroom. Broussier had known Harwood hadn't been carrying a gun and so, hearing the shots, correctly assumed the worst had happened and scarpered through the bathroom window onto the fire escape and away. Having no money, he'd spent the night in Regent's Park which he'd found by accident and which, by his account, was cold and damp. The answer to the obvious question of why he hadn't gone to the police or even to the Belgian embassy was so equally obvious that I didn't bother asking the question.

On Sunday, while I'd been recovering, he'd called home, reverse-charge call through the international operator and told them what had happened. Then, realising that he would be on his own until his 'people', as he called them, could get to him, he remembered that Harwood had mentioned where he'd picked me up and on the off chance that I was still alive, he'd gone into a newsagents, stolen a London A-Z and started walking. He spent Sunday night in the local park and Monday watching the pub in case I showed up. He'd stolen some fruit, but he wasn't really up to mugging anyone for real money. Whatever Broussier was involved in, he certainly wasn't the hands-on type. Monday night was so cold he thought he was going to die, but he didn't and today I'd arrived and now I had to help him.

I said no. Well, he hadn't said please.

'Please, you must help me!'

That was better, so I agreed. Not because he was one of the good guys, but because if he hung around here much longer Smith would catch up to him. Maybe, since I'd been hired to protect him, I felt that was what I should do.

Obvious questions first. He'd called his people on Sunday; this was Tuesday. Why weren't they here already? Answer – they had to get him a new passport, identity, plane tickets and so on. These things apparently take time, but the 'colleague' who was going to take him back was due to arrive late tonight and meet him outside this very pub. The guy was obviously a cretin. The place that Smith was most likely to cover, as he had done, by placing me here, was where they decided to meet.

I tried to think this one out. Strangely enough, it never occurred to me that Broussier might be lying through his teeth to me. I suppose since I thought of him as the victim, I assumed he was being straight with me. Stupid, right? Still, I worked it through that if Broussier left London tonight, then I might be off the hook, unless Smith asked around, for example here in this pub, where people, especially the barlady, were sure to remember him. Then I'd be well and truly on the hook again and swinging. So we would have to make sure that Smith didn't find out that Broussier had left. But even if he missed him leaving London, he'd be sure to have a contact somewhere in Brussels. Either way I was in trouble. Unless Broussier actually didn't leave until after I'd dealt with Smith. Sorry, let's use the right language – until after I'd killed Smith. That was how it would have to be. There was no way I could get organised by tonight, I didn't have the gun for a start. I could maybe use a knife, but he probably wouldn't let me get that close. Smith wouldn't buy too long a delay, it wouldn't make sense to him, so it would have to be Wednesday night. That gave me less than two days, but it would have to be enough.

I tried to explain to Broussier that he'd have to stay here another day. Naturally, he didn't want to. He just wanted to get out of this unfamiliar city where people kept trying to kill him. It was a fair point, but not what I wanted to hear. I didn't want to tell him that I planned to kill Smith. Admitting that wouldn't be too clever and I didn't really want to tell him that Smith had contacted me, since he might then stop trusting me completely. He'd worked out himself that it had to be Smith who was after him. No-one else had known he was here. I decided that the only thing to do was to get tough and as I thought this, it occurred to me that it was about time. So far I'd taken a job, been set up and beaten up, walked down my own stairs and had a gun pointed at me, been threatened, had my friends threatened and beaten up and been ordered to set someone up to be killed. This self-same person that I was trying not to set up, was being a little unhelpful to my master plan. Maybe that's unfair. After all he'd had a hard time, but then so had I, and I was bigger than he was, so he was going to do exactly what I told him to do. And what's more, if he wanted somewhere to stay and my help, then he'd bloody well smile and say thank you. Then to show there were no hard feelings, I bought him a pub lunch. It didn't matter if anyone saw Broussier now, or remembered him, since I was about to call Smith and tell him myself. First though, Broussier had to phone his 'people', which he did from the payphone outside the pub, telling them to meet him on Wednesday night, not here at the pub, but at Nelson's Column in Trafalgar Square at 10.30. Foreigner or not, I didn't think he could miss Nelson's Column.

We both tucked into lunch. He was so hungry he couldn't talk and eat at the same time, which was just as well, because I was working out what to tell Smith when I called him. I was also wondering where to leave Broussier for the rest of the day and most of Wednesday. I couldn't leave him in the park, the police might pick him up, so I decided to take him back to my luxury apartment. Linda, hopefully, would be gone by mid-afternoon and Mex was working to-day, so I could stash him in Linda's room and leave him there with instructions not to move. It might be the safest place to keep him anyway, since Smith would think I was bringing Broussier to him on Wednesday night. It was starting to look as if it might all come together. There were still some major holes though. Mick still had to get the gun for me and he didn't even know it yet and I still had to organise the exact where and when to meet Smith. And, of course, I still had to kill him.

*

We stayed in the pub for a while, Broussier digesting his lunch, me hoping that Linda would be out by this time. Somewhere around two, we strolled down the High Street and I left Broussier in the launderette while I checked to make sure no-one was watching the flat. It seemed clear, so I collected him and took him up. Linda was gone. No note or message, just gone. Well, what did I expect, a thank you, pinned to my door? The bed belonged to the landlord, so Broussier had somewhere to sleep and he looked as though he could sleep for days. There were no bedclothes, but after a couple of nights sleeping rough, he wasn't complaining. I didn't have any spare towels, so I took the one from the kitchen and told him to please take a shower. I also told him to stay put, not to use or answer the phone and not to lean out of the window. He didn't really need much persuading. I told him what time Mex would be back and to keep out of sight until I got home. He started to thank me but I told him to wait until he got my bill. It was meant as a joke, but Broussier seemed to take it seriously. Ah well, it would be nice to turn a profit as well as staying in one piece. I left him, repeating the order to stay here no matter what and went out to phone Smith. No, I didn't think my phone was bugged, I just didn't want Broussier to hear me speaking to Smith.

'Mr Smith, please,' I said.

I couldn't tell if it was the gorilla on the phone or not, since all the voice had said was 'yes' when it answered the phone. But I recognised Smith's voice all right.

'It's done,' I said. 'He's going to meet me tomorrow night. He asked me for money and I told him I'd need a day to get it together. I gave him enough for tonight, he wouldn't tell me where he was going to stay and I told him to meet me tomorrow night at the back of the Metropole hotel, on the Edgware Road. There's a disused factory and offices a street away towards Paddington and I'll bring him to you there, 10.30. I'll tell him that's where I keep my money stashed or something. I thought that somewhere like that would be better than the pub near me.'

I waited for him to speak, as though for approval. There was a pause while he considered what I'd said, looking for holes in it. Finally he said:

'Good, you've done well.' Throwing the dog a biscuit. 'You're out of it as soon as you bring him to the factory. As long as there are no hitches.'

I decided to throw in a tough guy line. It would seem in character.

'Any hitches will be down to you, mate. I'll do my bit. Also, I'd appreciate you leaving your friend at home. I don't think he likes me too much, since I bust his nose.'

There was another pause, then:

'Yes, all right. And as I said, as long as there are no problems and you're not lying in any way, then you'll not hear from me again after tomorrow.'

'I'm not lying, Smith, I just want to be out of your way.'

There was no pause this time, just a mock cheerful voice.

'Well it's been a pleasure doing business with you. Don't hang on to this number. It will be useless by tomorrow.'

I gave Smith the directions to get to the factory and said to bring a torch. It would be dark in there. He repeated the directions and then there was a click and a tone. Smith had brushed me off, now just a mechanical part of his plans.

But my plans still had to be worked on and it was about time I got moving with them. I went to see Mick.

*

Mick lives in a council flat in a block. This is sort of surprising, since he must have some money somewhere. He's been a fence for years, but he doesn't show any outward evidence of making a living. Another surprising fact is that although he lives in a ground floor flat, he's never been turned over. It's like an unwritten law. Everyone knows who he is, everyone leaves him alone. He in turn knows everybody, but never takes sides in any argument. I've known him for years. He was a contemporary of Al's, which makes him a fair bit older than me, but he has never told me what to do, unlike Al, who was always putting me right. Mick would just point out the options and let me make my own mistakes. He seems to live a very simple life, moving between the local pub and his flat in a more or less straight line. Every now and then he meets someone and she may move in for a while and then on after a while, always swearing blind that he's the most wonderful man, but...

I should point out that Mick isn't physical. He doesn't get into trouble like that. One time, someone threw a punch at him in the pub and knocked him straight over. None of the local villains could've been around, or it wouldn't have happened, but it did and the kid that hit him kicked him a couple of times when he was down and then carried on drinking, thinking he'd earned himself a reputation. Mick eventually hauled himself up and crawled out of the pub. He was hurt quite badly. Two days later the kid was found tied to the railings next door to the pub, with most of his bones cracked and his neck broken. Al had an alibi a mile long. The local police detective called it 'the miracle mile'. In truth, it might not have been Al, there were others who would have done the same for Mick, although maybe not with the same style.

Since Al's death, I'd spent a lot of time with Mick. We shared a liking for blues music and a dislike of people. I always went to see him though, Mick never went out to visit anyone.

I rang at the intercom and he buzzed me in. As I rounded

the corner from the front entrance of Mick's block, I could hear the familiar low growl of the dog. He was standing in the middle of the open doorway of the flat, filling most of it. Mick himself doesn't know which breed or mix of breeds it is. When anyone asks him what sort of dog he has, he says 'large'. As he saw me, the dog stopped growling and thumped his tail on the floor. It's a good thing that it's a ground floor flat, because anyone living underneath would have complained at the noise. It sounded like a bass beat.

The dog was well trained. He didn't move out of the way, even though I'd been going there for years and he knew me as 'friend'. After all, he didn't know who might be with me. Mick told me that he never called any woman who stayed with him 'friend', just in case they came back for any reason after they'd left him. The dog wouldn't let them in, even though he knew them. I told Mick that it was a fairly pessimistic way to view relationships, but he told me to examine my own track record before I preached to him. He had a point.

I walked up to the dog and gave him my hand to smell, fingers closed just in case he got his signals crossed, patted him on the head and pushed past him. The dog leaned into me, barring the way. This was his idea of a game and it was a regular occurrence. After a bit more pushing, he let me past him and followed me inside. I closed the front door and walked through to Mick in the living room. The dog trotted in after me and dropped in the doorway of the room. Mick was lying on the sofa, feet up, reading from a list of some sort, ignoring the TV which was talking to itself on the other side of the room.

'Be with you in a minute,' he said, 'I just want to finish with this. Make yourself a cup of tea, or something.'

I moved towards the kitchen and the dog stood up to let

me through. The kitchen was immediately on the right, but the dog made sure to move the three feet and cover the kitchen doorway. I don't know if Mick trained him to do this or not, but there was no way you were getting out of any room if the dog didn't want you to. And he always knew where you were. I suppose I should have been flattered. At least when I was in a room the dog didn't watch me the whole time. With someone who wasn't a 'friend', he would track them the whole time, eyes pinning them wherever they went, daring them to put a foot, a hand, or an eyelash out of place. I knew my way around the kitchen.

'You want something?' I called.

'No, I'm fine thanks.'

'What about him?' I asked. The dog was looking at me expectantly. The tea bags were next to the dog biscuit tin.

'Yeah, if you like,' Mick answered. 'Keep him happy. Just one though.'

I opened the tin and the dog stood up. I looked for the biggest biscuit and picked it out. After all, it pays to know who your friends are. I threw it to the dog who jumped back and let it land on the floor. I've never caught him out yet.

'He's waiting,' I said.

The dog looked towards the living room and Mick gave him the word. The biscuit, about the size of a Weetabix, disappeared. I went back to the main room with my tea and the dog resumed his position in the doorway.

'Got you somewhere to live,' Mick said, putting down his 'work' and throwing me a set of keys. 'No, don't thank me, I just couldn't stand the thought of you staying here. It's a dump, but it's yours if you want it.'

'What's the rent, 'cos I'm pretty low at the moment and it's going to get worse before it gets better.'

'Rent free.'

I had to laugh. Rent free in London is a contradiction in terms.

'There's a catch, right?'

'A minor one. The landlord has some property around London. All the tenants pay cash and some of them can be a little difficult. There's a high turnover rate. You collect the rent each week and he gives you this place rent free. Guaranteed privacy. You don't even have to meet him. You bring the money here and he collects it. I've told him you're honest and that's good enough for him.'

'No rent, no extras?'

'That's right. Also no phone, no furniture and no gas, but there is hot and cold water and electricity. You have to pay the bills. You can put them in whatever name you like.'

'You've worked it all out, haven't you? What makes you think I wouldn't want to use my own name?'

'Son, whenever you say you need to see me, it means some kind of problem, especially if you say you have to crash somewhere for a few days. I'm just, er, thinking logically.'

'You know, it really pisses me off when you're right.'

'So what is it?' he asked.

'I need a gun,' I said.

There was a silence.

'You sure?'

I started to speak, but he waved me silent.

'I don't want an explanation of why you need it, I just want to know that you're really sure that you do.'

'Yes I – '

'Uh uh, no comments, 'cos I don't want to know. I certainly don't want to know who, when or where and why I already know. Remember, I know you and I know who taught you. You don't pick up a gun to scare someone, you don't pick it up at all unless you're going to use it. And if you're going to shoot someone, you better make sure they're dead, or they'll be coming back for you. So I know you're going to kill somebody, or at least try to. I don't want to know anything else.'

There was another silence. 'What kind of gun and when do you need it for?'

'Er, any kind I suppose, but I need it for tomorrow.' He looked at me like I was nuts, which I probably was.

'For tomorrow? And I suppose you'd like it gift wrapped and hand delivered by Michelle Pfeiffer?' His tone went from incredulous to sarcastic. 'Are you familiar with any kind of firearm?'

'I've fired 9mm semi-automatics and .22s before.'

'Right. Well. I'll see what I can do. How much cash have you got?'

I looked at him.

'Oh come on, son,' he was almost annoyed now, 'If you want hire purchase go to New York.'

There was a third silence.

'Mick,' I said, 'this is really important. I don't have a choice. Get whatever you can as cheap as you can and I will pay you back as soon as is possible.'

This was getting to be a conversation of silences. He looked at me and I looked at him. The TV carried on at the side, a sort of background noise.

'What's the matter?' I said, 'You don't want to sub me?'

'No, it's not that, mate,' his voice was resigned. 'It's just that I'm realising that you're serious and I hope you know what you're doing.'

'You don't think I can shoot someone, kill them?'

'No, I do think you can. In fact I'm sure you can. Al always said that you could... you could kill It's just a bit bizarre, sitting here discussing the fact that someone you've seen growing up is going to murder somebody.'

He was picking his words carefully, making me realise what it was that I was actually thinking of doing. Kill. Murder. Plain words which left no room for disguising what I was talking about.

'Come on, Mick, I'm sure these four walls have heard far worse than this, all – '

'Not from you they haven't.' He'd cut in quickly and his voice had hardened. The dog heard the change in tone and lifted his head, looking from one to the other of us.

'Look, it's not my way to get involved, but I hope your doing this for the right reasons.'

'What would the wrong reasons be?'

He swung his legs off the sofa and sat facing me, leaning forward. It had been a sudden movement and I glanced at the dog, who had immediately reacted and was now sitting up and watching him intently.

'You come in here marked up with bruising, looking a little rough to say the least. You haven't shaved for a while, so maybe you haven't been home for a few days. Yesterday you wanted information on something or somebody and today you tell me you want a gun. So what is it? Revenge? Hurt pride? Got your head kicked in, something like that?' I started to speak but he waved me quiet. 'I don't want an answer, but if it is some kind of revenge, then you know as well as I do that it's not worth it. Doing time for a matter of pride is not worth it.'

'It's not pride, Mick. It's necessary. If I don't do this, then one or two other people might get hurt and I might have to keep looking over my shoulder.'

'You kill someone, son and you'll always be looking over your shoulder and you won't even know who you're looking for. You'll have stepped over the line and once you do that, there's no going back.'

There it was; that line again. Smith knew about it, Mick knew about it and I was apparently getting closer to it. Maybe you had to be in the life to know it was there. I hoped I'd recognise it fast enough not to trip over it. Mick was still talking.

'Do you owe these people, the ones that might get hurt?'

'One's a friend. The other, I sort of feel responsible for him. It is complicated and I don't... you don't want me to go into it. I have thought it through and this seems to be the way that things will work out best.'

'How far have you thought it through?'

The dog had settled down again, satisfied that nothing untoward was going on. Only a discussion of murder, I thought to myself, nothing serious.

'Have you thought about what happens afterwards?'

I thought that was a pretty dumb question.

'I can cover my tracks, Mick, get rid of the gun, lie low. Believe me this guy is hardly likely to have told the police about me. There's not much that can connect me to him.'

He shook his head. 'I didn't mean that. I think you're quite capable of working out the practical bits and pieces. I meant personally.' He paused like he was trying to find the right words to use and I realised that he was genuinely worried about me talking like this. That made two people in one day. I wasn't used to it.

'It worries me that you might be trying to do what Al would have done. Walk straight through this guy, do whatever you think has to be done and walk away. But you're not him and you're not the same as him.'

'I know that, but I can do this. I know I can do this.'

'No, I don't mean that.' He got up and turned to the window. 'I know you can shoot somebody, I know that's in you. I've seen you in the ring, blank off and just do the man, but fighting is different. There are rules. Not just rules, but understandings. You know the risk and he knows the risk. Whatever happens in the ring is not your fault. It's understood.' He turned back to face me. 'But if you shoot a man, you're going to take his life. Now, I think you can do that, you can do the mechanical part of it, the pulling of the trigger, but that's not the difficult part for someone like you. The difficult part,' he sat down again, 'is living with it afterwards. Knowing what you've done. I don't mean the famous "urge to confess" or anything like that, I don't think that'll get you, but you have to live with it. You have to live with what you've done, taking another human being's life away from them. And you're not like Al and you're not like these guys who run around blowing people away. It's not you. It's not in you, not yet anyway and it's better to be like you are now, 'cos once you get like they are, things stop having any value. And if things don't have a value anymore, if people don't have any value anymore, then you're lost.'

He sat back and watched me. What he'd just said went around in my mind; 'you're lost'.

'Was Al lost?' I meant it as a genuine question, but Mick took it as a challenge to what he'd been saying.

'Yes, he bloody was!' he shouted. The dog was on its feet again, looking at the strange scene being played out in front of him. Mick gave him the command and he lay down once more, but watchful.

'You don't get it, do you,' he said, standing up again. 'You are not like Al, you can't do the things that he did. You're not made the same way, you're not driven by the same things. Listen, I know you, I know the way you think. If you kill someone, you're going to have to live with it every day and every night. It's going to haunt you. It's going to hound you. It's not going to give you any peace. You're not going to give yourself any peace, because that's the way your mind works. It's going to turn it over and over. Yes, you can kill this man if you decide to, but I don't think you can survive it if you do.'

He sat down again, lifted his legs back onto the sofa and lay back. I don't know if he expected me to say anything, but I didn't. I was almost in a state of shock. I don't think I'd ever seen Mick as worked up about anything as this. As upset, yes, but not as angry.

'You can move into the flat whenever you like.' His voice was flat.

'Yes, thanks.'

'I've got the address here somewhere. On the table.'

I got up and looked among the mass of scraps of paper on the table for one with an address on it.

'This one, in Camden?'

'Yeah, that's right, above the shops. There's another list there of the tenants and their addresses and the rents they owe. Collect on whichever day it says. Bring the money to me here on Sundays.' With anyone else I would have said I'd phone first, but Mick would be here. I put the address and the list in my pocket.

'I still want the gun, Mick.'

'I know.' He wasn't looking at me. He lit a cigarette, closed his eyes and stretched out further on the sofa, blowing out a long stream of smoke.

'Come round tomorrow morning about ten. I'll try and have something sorted out by then. But just think about it, you don't have to do things Al's way.'

'No,' I said, 'but maybe it's my way now. I'll see myself out.'

The dog followed me to the door.

*

Mick had definitely put the wind up me. I wondered if he was right. I've always thought that I knew myself pretty well. Rule number one, in the ring or on the street. Know your limitations. Keep pushing them, but know them. I knew I could take Smith, but the more I thought about it, the more I thought that Mick might be right. If I killed Smith in cold blood, I was going into uncharted waters. Did I know how I would react? Mick was certainly right in one respect. I was worrying about it. Not about killing Smith, but about my reaction to it. That in itself put me way behind the people I was dealing with. I'd never had this problem before, but then I'd never gone this far before and certainly not on my own. I'd always had Al to check with. Now here I was, more than four years out of the life, jumping straight into the deep end. I knew I could swim, but how much stamina did I have? Maybe Mick and Smith both knew what I didn't. That I belonged on this side of the line.

I'd been walking from Mick's block to the bus stop. Now I stopped, as though in order to think this out I had to concentrate, as if the act of walking would disturb the thought process. The fact is, I thought, that I'd always been to one side of living 'the life'. I'd always been semi-legitimate. I could have ended up going down the same road that Al and Mick had taken, although they both ended up at different destinations, but I got sidetracked into boxing and became, well, maybe not a citizen, but certainly something that was at least a step away from the street. I started walking again, the bus stop was only around the corner and I didn't want to be standing here as the bus whizzed past.

Growing up out of school in north London and without what you might call 'parental guidance', I could easily have become another Smith, but I didn't. I found boxing and something to aspire to. I found people to look up to and they, including Al, pushed me away from the street and into the legitimate world. And after the years of boxing, the opportunity to get a job, have a career and I thought I wanted it. Al telling me to take it, to take my chance, so I did. And then I lost contact, slowly but definitely, with the people I had known. I was moving in a different direction. Some of those people I was glad to leave behind, but some of them were diamonds and we just drifted apart. I tried to keep in touch, but eventually we had nothing to say to each other and I felt guilty about it. Guilty about earning money and leaving them behind. Not a lot of money, just enough to make a difference and it was a difference that embarrassed them and therefore me. Only Al, Mick and Tony stayed the same. Tony, because he'd dragged himself up and wanted to leave the street behind him, Mick, because he had too much sense to break a friendship and Al because he was Al. And as he said: 'Sod 'em, son. If they don't want to stay mates, then sod 'em. Besides, they're only jealous of you.' Yeah, I thought, jealous and just a bit disappointed. It might not have been my fault, but I hadn't made it to the championship. Funny that. They wouldn't have been jealous of me being British or even World Champion, if that could ever have happened, they'd have loved it, but they couldn't take me being gainfully employed with a company car. Maybe they thought I'd sold them out in some way. Still, the fact was that I saw less and less of them and even of Al, out of necessity and about a year or fifteen months later, he was killed.

It threw me completely. For all the problems of his trade, I never thought anything could happen to him. He'd get hurt, yes, but never die. And mixed in with it, although I could never say this to anyone, was a feeling of guilt. Like if I hadn't have been working my day job, I might have been with him and somehow made sure he was okay. It wasn't true, I knew that, but I couldn't help the feeling. Mick never told me all the details of what happened, he was worried I might go on a rampage or something, I think. I remember at the funeral, at the Jewish cemetery in Waltham Abbey –

'Hey! You getting on or what?'

I jerked upright from where I'd been leaning against the bus stop. The driver had the bus door open and was looking at me like I was nuts. He was right of course. You don't stand at a bus stop for twenty minutes and then let your bus go by. I got on and paid the fare. Automatically, my mind still on the past, I went to the back seat of the bus, downstairs and sat next to the emergency exit. I cleared my mind of old thoughts and noticed where I was sitting. I almost smiled. A full view of everyone getting on or off the bus and an instant exit. The subconscious obviously still knew how to play the game.

It was the truth. I knew the rules. I'd learned them. I'd studied them. I'd grown up with them. I'd just never had to live them full time, right on the edge. But now I did. And I was four years out of practice.

Was there any other way out? Only to cut and run. Leave Broussier to find his own way out and clear out of London. And what about Linda and even Pat? They might be left alone, but they might not. No, there was no other way. I leaned back and closed my eyes. It's funny how stray thoughts just arrive in your mind. There must be a connection, but you don't notice it, just the end result. I was remembering a girl I knew when I was just starting profighting. She said that you can't escape what is meant to be. I think she was talking about us at the time, but fortunately I'm no fatalist. However, it did seem that I was being dragged back into a life that I thought I had left behind me.

Maybe I should stop questioning and just accept that was where I was headed. And maybe it was where I belonged.

I got off the bus up the road from my room and walked the last quarter of a mile, looking for anyone sitting in a parked car, standing at a bus stop, reading a newspaper, anyone static with a view of my flat. It seemed clear, but I walked past the flat and up the road for a stretch to check the other side of the High Street. I bought a paper at the farthest newsagents and wandered back. Pat's stand was being manned, if that's the right word, by a young woman. She was the only person who was out of place that I could see. If anybody was watching my flat, then short of renting a place above the shops near my corner, she would have to be the one. I went over.

'Where's John today then?' I asked.

'oo's John? This is Pat's stall.' She had a London cockney accent you could cut with a blunt squeegee.

'What are you doing here then, if it's Pat's stall?'

'ee's me grandad inn'e and ee's not well.' I'd never thought of Pat as having any family.

'Oh, right, sorry to hear that. Hope he gets better soon.' I started to walk off, then said, 'By the way, what's your name?'

'It's Angie. Aint'cha buyin' a paper then?'

'Nah, sorry Angie, got one already.' As I walked off, I heard 'stingy git' from behind me. I walked on to the nearest payphone, called one of the dozen Directory Enquiries Services that now exist and got the number for the hospital. Enquiry calls used to be free from payphones. Now they're not. So I had to go to the fruit and veg shop to get some more change. Back to the payphone, which was in use for several minutes and finally, I managed to get through to the hospital.

'Ward B3, please.' I got the obligatory, 'hold for one moment please' and then mediaeval chamber music to keep me company which was a bit out of place really. It should have been the Eagles' *The last resort* or Motorhead's *Too late, too late*. That started me thinking and I'd got as far as Lynyrd Skynyrd's *The needle and the spoon*, which I thought was pretty funny for the spur of the moment, when I was put through.

'B3, can I help you?'

There was a silence as I realised I didn't know what Pat's second name was.

'Er, I'd like to speak to Pat, please.'

'Pat who?'

'I'm sorry, I don't know his second name. He's the newspaper man, in his sixties, was the victim of an assault. I wondered if I could have a word with him, I'm a friend of his.'

'Ah, yes. I know who you mean. Hold on a minute.' Well, he had to be better if he was coming to the phone.

'Ello?'

'Hello, Pat, how are you feeling? It's Garron here.'

'Oh, 'ello, Mr Garron, I'm all right. They're letting me out tomorrow.'

'That's great, Pat. I just wanted to check you were okay. Have to get you back out here soon though, some young girl's nicked your pitch.'

He laughed. 'No, Mr Garron, that's my granddaughter, Angela, she's looking after it for me 'till I'm back on my feet proper like. Didn't want to just let it go empty. People'll go elsewhere if you do that.'

'Don't believe it, Pat. They'll be straight back to you, soon as you're out there.' We chatted for a couple more minutes and then I said I'd see him in a few days as I might be away for a while.

When I hung up I felt safer. Angela had been cleared. I hadn't been so worried about a seventeen year old girl since I was thirteen and Stella from next door said she'd cut my tongue out if I told about her and the supply teacher from the local high school. I walked back to my block and went up to the flat.

I opened the front door and took my time walking through the hallway. I checked the bathroom and the kitchen and also my room before coming back down the hall to stand in front of Linda's door. If Broussier was in there alone, as he should be, then I ought to knock. I didn't. Slowly, I turned the handle. It took a long time, millimetre by millimetre. When I'd released the catch, I threw it inwards, took a quick glance and jerked my head back behind the wall.

The door turned through 180 degrees and crashed against the inside wall. There was a shout and then as I walked into the room, a stream of French or Flemish which, from the tone and accompanying facial expressions, I took to be swearing. I'd seen before I'd pulled back behind the cover of the wall, that Broussier was on his own and lying on the bed. Now he was standing up and as the swearing slowed, I could see that he was shaking. Ah well, he should have picked a safer business. Actually, I'd been 99 percent certain that no-one was at the flat, but it pays to be careful. Or maybe I just wanted to scare the hell out of him. When he'd calmed down, I got us both something to eat and showed him to my room, which Tony had cleared of all my gear. I told him that I'd see him the following afternoon and sort him out for getting to Nelson's Column later on Wednesday night. In the meantime, he was to sit tight, as before. I warned him about keeping out of Mex's way if possible and left a note for Mex, telling him that I had an old mate staying here for a couple of days. Then I checked over my room, to make sure I hadn't left anything and, after finding a quarter of a bottle of Jameson's under the bed, went off to Tony's car lot.

*

'You really growing that beard, or you just hiding the bruises?'

'I'm really growing it,' I said. He sort of grunted and gestured to the van.

'I don't want any damage on this, okay. I got a possible buyer at the weekend, so no damage.' Tony looked at me like he wasn't sure I understood. 'Not a scratch, okay?'

'Yeah, right. Listen, it's only 'till tomorrow, just so as I can shift my stuff around.'

Reluctantly, he gave me the keys. 'I got eighteen hundred cash coming for that.' It was an accusation.

'It'll be fine. What do you think I'm going to do with it, stock car racing?'

'Okay, just get it back here tomorrow.'

'Yeah. Hey, just in case I can't get it back by tomorrow, Thursday would be all right, wouldn't it? I mean just in case.' I wanted it for Wednesday night.

He looked at me. 'You stitching me here, Garron?'

'No, Tony, I'm just saying, you know, if I get stuck late at the storage or something, can I drop it back Thursday morning instead of tomorrow night?' It was my most innocent voice. He gave in.

'All right, Thursday morning, by ten at the latest. And tell me you're not using this van for anything that I don't want to know about.'

I looked him straight in the eyes. 'Tony, I am not going to tell you anything that you don't want to know about, regarding the van or anything else.' There was a pause.

'Is that what I asked you to say?'

'Near enough.' I changed the subject. 'What's Linda's number?'

'I don't know.'

'You what?' I said.

'I don't know it. She wouldn't tell me what it was.'

'Well why not?'

'Well –'

'But you know where she's living now, right?'

He looked at me uncomfortably. 'Yeah, I helped her with her stuff, but she asked me... well, made me promise, not to tell you where it is.'

'She did what? What does she mean by that?'

'I don't know, mate, but she was pretty pissed at you. Which is strange, 'cos I'd say that she's also sort of attached to you, or thinks she might like to be anyway.'

I thought about this. The two things that Tony knows about are cars and women. Not that he's a womaniser in any way, he just seems to know how they're thinking, and he always has done. Five minutes after he met Marie, he told me that he was going to marry her and he did. He also told me that my old Chrysler Avenger would pack up within two days and he was right there as well. Women and cars. He's amazing. He can't work it with men though, always saying the wrong thing or winding someone up. I once walked into a pub in Fulham to meet Tony and found him underneath a pile of four guys trying to punch his head in. He'd only been there five minutes and he'd managed, unintentionally, to rub everyone up the wrong way.

So now I listened to him. If he said Linda was getting attached to me, then it was almost certainly true. I suppose I wanted to think that we'd been sort of drifting that way for a while, but I hadn't really let myself consider it. Partly because she'd been seeing Mitch and partly because I don't see the signs until they are up in ten foot neon letters, right in front of my face. There were a couple of things, though, that didn't ring true.

'If she's so keen on me, then why won't she give me her telephone number, or let you tell me where she is?'

'Ah well, that's 'cos she's really upset with you about something.'

'How upset?'

'Very upset. And nervy as well. I don't know what you've done to her, but if I was you I'd undo it as soon as possible.'

I thought about saying that I hadn't done anything, but I reckoned that dropping someone in trouble, getting her threatened by pro killers and forcing her to move home with four hours notice, probably amounted to something. Anyway, I was trying to sort the mess out as best I could.

'I'm doing the best I can, Tony, as fast as I can. How am I supposed to get in touch with her?'

'I gave her the number here in the office, but she said if you wanted to see her, she'd be in the cafe at the National Film Theatre at half eight tonight, you know, by the Festival hall on the South Bank.'

'At the NFT? Why there? Is she living near there?'

He shook his head. I swear he was enjoying this. 'Uh-uh, that would be telling. I think she picked there 'cos it's central and she can walk away without you getting any idea of where she's going. So I'd tread carefully tonight mate.'

'Yeah, cheers. That's just what I need.' I took the keys and opened the van door. 'Advice from a married man with two kids, a mortgage and a pension plan.' I got in and started the engine. Tony leaned in at the window.

'That's a happily married man, with two wonderful, bright kids, a successful business and a manageable mortgage 'cos he bought at the right time.'

I hate it when someone has a better exit line than me. I drove off.

*

'If Paris does not seem to be the way that it was, then maybe I really am getting old.' Julot drank some more of his coffee. 'Or maybe,' he thought, 'it was always like this and I never noticed. Or maybe I just can't remember it properly. Or maybe I should just drink my coffee.'

Michel came into the cafe and sat down opposite him.

'Jean called Sabine,' he said. 'He left a message with one of our people. He will trade his life for the disc. 10.30, Wednesday night in Trafalgar Square in London.'

'Good, but why wait until then, why not sooner?'

'I don't know, but there is another problem.'

'Go on.'

'Smith called. He says he has someone bringing Jean to meet him on Wednesday night somewhere else at almost the same time.'

Julot sat and thought about that for a while and Michel did not interrupt him.

'Smith does not know about the other arrangement?'

'No,' said Michel, 'he does not seem to.'

'And Jean did not mention meeting Smith?'

'No.'

Julot shook his head. 'Someone is playing a strange game here. Who is this person that is bringing Jean to Smith?'

'He is an ex-boxer. His name is Garron.'

'How does he know Jean?'

'Smith said he hired him to protect Jean, as a set-up.'

Julot grunted. 'He protected him too well then.'

He finished his coffee and carefully put the cup back on its saucer. 'Everything has its rightful place,' he thought, 'and something is badly out of place here.'

He looked up at Michel.

'I don't think I trust this Smith too much. Find out the where and the when and tell him to go ahead, but don't tell him anything else. At the same time, get anything you can on this Garron, who he is, who he mixes with. If he was a boxer we might find a connect to him, someone *who knows someone. If we do, then I want to try to set something up so that I can get a look at him. If he works protection then find out who he works for. And this has to be done quickly, there is not much time now. Jean cannot be in two places at once and somebody knows what is going on. I don't like it when somebody knows more about my business than I do. I can't trust Jean, I don't trust Smith and I don't know this man Garron. I think also, Michel, that you had better book us onto a flight for London.'*

*

It felt good to be mobile again, but I didn't have too much time to enjoy it. It was going to be a long evening. If I hurried, I could probably get to my lock-up and then down to town by 8.30. I also had to get out to West London to meet Nelson by 11.00.

I share the lock-up with an old friend of mine, Pete the musician. He lives up north now, but before he went, we split the cost of a small garage near Finsbury Park and each dumped some stuff there. Nothing you would hate to lose, since anyone could break in past the two padlocks and the Yale if they wanted to, but it's a useful place to leave things.

I wrestled with the padlocks, swore to bring some WD40 with me next time and finally got in. I get the same feeling every time I walk in here, because nothing ever changes. I get a sort of ache for the things that I've left here, like I've abandoned them. It's lucky I don't own much.

It was pitch black inside, but amazingly, the light still worked. I walked past the box of books and tapes and dragged out one of the armchairs and then one of the straight backed chairs. Somewhere there should be a folding table. I found it behind three boxes of bits and pieces, debris from a former life. One of the boxes had my scrapbooks of the fight cuttings, reports and pictures in local papers and some nationals of me and some of my mates from the gym.

There were also a couple of packets of personal photos. I grabbed the table and ignored the boxes. The past wasn't going to help me right now. I thought of taking the second armchair, but left it. I wasn't expecting company. I did take the second straight chair to stand the TV on and I went back for the books and tapes. I couldn't get the padlocks to close and it started to rain. Someone once wrote 'the blues ain't nothing but a woman'. He obviously hadn't spent twenty minutes getting soaked, dropping keys and fumbling in the dark, trying to close two ancient padlocks in a back street in Finsbury Park.

I drove down towards Waterloo and the NFT with the uncomfortable knowledge that most of what I owned was in this van and I was about to leave it parked in central London. Still, it was either that or take it to Camden now and be late for Linda. Everything in the van was replaceable. She wasn't. End of argument. Of course, if I had thought about it, I would have realised that there was in fact something irreplaceable in the van. Me.

I could have driven right down to the South Bank, but I didn't. I parked by the river near Embankment station and walked across Hungerford Bridge. It's a pedestrian walkway next to the train line from Charing Cross and it's one of the best places in London. I don't know why. It used to be old brick, noisy from the nearby trains and smell terrible, but now they've built a new bridge and it's clean with straight lines. I always loved it and it still has something for me. Years ago, I would always make a point of stopping at the little semi-circle that jutted out over the river near the south end of the bridge and look out at London. Now that little semi-circle has gone, but it's still the right place to look out and think. It was nearly a quarter past eight, so I had a few minutes.

People hurried past behind me. There were a couple of boats working their way down the river. But most of all there were the lights. A lot of people would have left their work by now, but there were still lights, hundreds of them, dotted around the office buildings north of the river. And behind each light, somebody. Doing something. A life. With all its own highs and lows, problems and pleasures. Totally unaware that someone else, unconnected, was thinking about them. And the lights of the cars, moving it seemed at random, yet each one with a purpose, to a destination, the people inside wrapped up in their own lives, not really caring about anyone outside of them and theirs. If that car there, moving down the Embankment, crashed and burst into flames, how many would stop and how many would carry on to their journey's end with a 'thank God it wasn't me' attitude and a ready made tale to tell? All these lives. All these delicate lives. So easy to damage. So easy to break. All it takes is luck. An accident, an illness, a few seconds here or there. But these are chance happenings. We may not care about each other, but how many of the people behind the lights that I'd been looking at would actively take another's life? How many would kill? I didn't have an answer. Maybe in the right circumstances all of them would. Maybe none of them. It didn't matter. I wasn't asking myself about them.

*

She was already there when I walked in. I sat down opposite her and said 'hi'.

'Hello,' she replied.

'What are you having?' I asked.

'I've already got coffee, thanks.'

There was a long pause. Whatever it was she wanted to say, she wasn't ready to say it yet. I tried to lighten the mood.

'So, do you come here often then?'

She looked sharply at me to tell me it wasn't funny. 'Don't,' was all she said.

'All right. I'll wait for when you're ready.' I got a cup of tea from the counter and we sat in silence. Eventually she said, 'Did that Belgian man turn up?'

'Yes, he did.'

'And?'

'And at the moment, he's in my room at the flat. I've moved out.'

'What's he going to do?' She didn't ask where I'd moved to.

'Get out. Back to Brussels, tomorrow night.'

'And you're doing what?'

I didn't answer straight away. Maybe I was looking for the right way of putting it. Then I said:

'You know what I'm going to do.' There was silence for a few moments.

'I've been thinking,' she said, 'you're helping this guy, he's going to owe you. Can't he arrange for something to be done about Smith when he gets back to Belgium? Instead of leaving you with the mess. I mean, he must owe you that.'

I thought about this. It hadn't crossed my mind before.

'There are two problems with that, Linda. First, we have to trust Broussier, which we might, but only might, be able to do, but second, that sort of thing might not be his decision to make, whatever he said now. It might be out of his hands once he got back to Belgium.' I smiled at her. 'Nice try though.'

She looked daggers at me. 'Don't be flippant. I'm trying to find a way out of this.'

I reached across the table and took her hand. 'I know you are and I shouldn't be flippant about it, but I've found a way out and I think it may be the only way.'

She took her hand away. 'I'm not sure you've tried hard enough.'

'What do you mean by that?'

'Nothing... I'm sorry. It's just that I thought, well, I thought we...'

'You thought we were what?' She didn't answer. 'You thought we were getting to be maybe more than just friends?'

She looked up at me.

'Yes,' she said.

'Well, maybe we are.'

'I don't know, Garron, I don't think I like what I'm seeing in you now.'

I sat back. 'What are you seeing now?'

'I can't... I don't want to say it to you.'

'Go on. Say it.'

'It seems like you want this. Like you're not looking for another answer. This morning and now, you look like you want to do this.'

'I don't,' I said quickly, 'it's just that I can only see one way out.'

'Are you sure that's not what you want to see?'

'Christ, you're right, you shouldn't have said that to me. Do you think I want to kill people? Do you think I'm going to enjoy it? Do you think it doesn't scare me? Do – '

'I think you want to prove something.'

There was a silence. Some of the people in the cafe were looking at us. We'd been getting louder. She went on quietly.

'I think you want to show that you're as tough as you used to be, that they can't push you around, I just don't know who you're trying to prove it to. To yourself maybe, or to them. Or perhaps me. Or somebody else that's in this that I don't even know about – '

My thoughts cut across what she was saying. Was I trying

to prove something? To myself? Well, who else was there? Yes, I wanted to shake Smith up, but was that it? Was there anyone else? A crazy idea came into my head. Could it be Al? Was I showing Al that I could do it? Was he talking to me from somewhere, testing me, asking whether I'd learned well enough? The thought was too much to deal with then. I pushed it away.

' – understand if you don't want to go to the police, but we could get away, just leave here.'

'What about Pat?' I said, 'and Harwood, the guy they shot in the hotel, don't I owe them something?'

'Don't you owe yourself something?'

'Maybe this is what I owe myself.'

As soon as I'd said it, I knew I shouldn't have done. I said so. 'I'm sorry, that was a stupid thing to say.'

'But it's true, isn't it?' Her voice was hard, edgy. 'It's what you feel. You think you owe it to yourself and I don't know why. All I know is that you look like you want this and that is scaring the hell out of me. You think you can do what they do, you think you're like them, but you're not. You're kidding yourself and you're going to end up dead!' She paused for a moment. I didn't say anything, but she hadn't finished yet.

'And if you do carry it off, what are you going to do then? What happens then? A steady nine to five in an office, when you've just murdered someone?'

Hers was a different angle to Mick's, but maybe she was also right. I find it easy to take when people are wrong about me, but I can't handle it when they're right. She had more to say.

'If you kill him, who will you be when it's done? Because you won't be the same person and I don't think that I'll want to know you then.'

She pushed her cup away from her, across the table and

picked up her bag.

'I don't know where you are,' I said. 'I can't get in touch with you.'

'I don't think I want you to get in touch with me.'

She got up to leave. I didn't want her to go, not like this. I wanted to say something, anything. Of course, it was my night for saying stupid things.

'I can find you, you know.'

She looked down at me and I couldn't read anything in her eyes.

'So you can find me,' she said quietly. 'Then what?'

She turned and walked out. Every head in the place turned to look at her go. Except mine. I wasn't looking at anything.

*

I crossed back over the river, but this time I didn't notice any lights. I didn't collect the van, just went walkabout, up Villiers Street to Charing Cross and Trafalgar Square and then on to Leicester Square and beyond. I wasn't taking any account of where I was going, I just went. I didn't even think that much about what she'd said, just let my mind wash over the sights and sounds. Somewhere along the Charing Cross Road, someone moved towards me, but I slipped one hand in my jacket pocket and hard-eyed him and he swung away. I stopped at Oxford Street and tried to focus. I didn't know what I was going to do now. Linda had given me an ultimatum. Stop what I was doing or lose any chance with her. I might have lost her already. Mick thought I was a fool. Tony, if he'd known, would have thought the same.

I turned round and started back down towards the van. There were people in doorways sleeping rough, although sleeping is a misused term. A lot of them don't sleep at night. It's too dangerous. They end up snatching dozes during the daytime in between moving on, or being moved on. One guy, maybe in his forties, but it's difficult to tell, stood up as a group of tourists in front of me walked past him, asking them for spare change. They looked straight ahead, carried on talking to each other, carried on walking, not making eye contact, not wanting to know he existed. He was still standing as I reached him and he turned to me, hesitating as he saw the old clothes, the tears in my jacket and my unshaven, marked up face. He didn't know if he was talking to one of his own or not. I looked at him. The clothes, even the hair and dirt can be faked, there are plenty of professional beggars around, but it's more difficult with the eyes. Besides, those of us close to the edge tend to recognise each other. He was genuine.

'It's all right, mate,' I said, 'I've still got a roof over my head.' I gave him a pound.

'Haven't got a cigarette, have you?' he asked.

'Sorry, don't smoke.'

'Well, cheers anyway. God bless you.'

I doubt it, mate, I thought as I walked away. About ten yards further on, I swung round. He was about to settle himself back into his doorway.

'Hey,' I called, ' – you mind if I ask your opinion on something?'

He looked at me with surprise. 'No, not if you want. What's it about?'

I walked back to him. 'If someone put you in a bad situation, a dangerous situation and the only thing you could do was something that everybody else thought was wrong, maybe you did as well, but it was all that you could think of that would work, would you do it?'

'Well, I don't know,' he said. Perhaps I hadn't explained it too clearly. 'Depends on the details really,' he went on, 'but in the end, don't worry about what everyone else says, it's what you think that's important. It's got to be.' He was looking at me earnestly. 'It's down to you in the end.'

'Yeah,' I said. 'Yeah I suppose it is, really.'

'Doesn't matter what anyone else says,' he repeated, 'Matters what you say.'

'Yeah,' I said again. 'Thanks.' I put out my hand. He looked surprised for a second time. Not many people shake hands with the homeless. He took it though.

'Take care,' I said.

'You as well, mate, you as well.'

I carried on down towards the river. Everybody has things they can't handle. It might be something that has happened, or something that might happen. An event or an idea. I learned a long time ago how to deal with them. If something is too big or too difficult, you break it down in your own mind. Break it down into smaller pieces and think them through one at a time. If you still can't handle it, then break it down even more. Filter it. Sooner or later there will be some part of this monster that you are able to look at and say 'I can deal with you' and then you're on your way. It works. Well, it works up to a point. There are some things that you can't do anything about, except get angry or philosophical. The problem with most people is that angry doesn't get them anywhere and by getting philosophical about something they mean resigning themselves to it. It's not the same thing.

There's another category to contend with. The things you've locked away in your mind because they hurt too much. Things that have happened. Things you wish you'd done and things you wish you hadn't. Sights, sounds and memories. You can't get rid of them, you can't clear them out, so you shut them away in the back of your mind and hope that they'll give you some peace. But every now and then, maybe for no reason, one or other of them reappears, sliding into your conscious thoughts and giving you that stab of pain, like the physical act, until you can catch hold of it and throw it back into the dark corner that it came from. Everything that happens to you, good or bad, marks you. And every mark has a place in your mind. Forever.

This was marking me. Linda didn't understand. I could disappear, but if Smith wanted to, he could always find her. Surely, though, he wouldn't bother. But I wasn't so convinced. If he thought I'd helped Broussier, he might just take the time to track her down. Al would've said that if you've thought it out and not got an answer and you've got to do something, then go with your gut reaction. But right now, Al was just confusing the issue. How much of my gut reaction was a reaction to him? Besides, his attitude was great if your instinct was almost always right, which his was. Mine might not be so good.

The thought suddenly came to me that I wouldn't have to tell Linda what happened. She wouldn't know what I did or didn't do. It would be a monumental lie, but I ought to be able to think of a set of circumstances to cover it. This cheered me up a bit, until I realised that she might not contact me now anyway. She was also far too perceptive to be taken in like that, certainly by me. Maybe I could work something out though, a sort of half-truth, tell her that it was self defence, that Smith came for me, or that Broussier killed Smith himself. It was something to think about.

I walked past one of the big nightclubs, but I didn't recognise either of the two bouncers on the door. Not that I should now, but I might have done three or four years ago. I worked it myself a few times, mainly as favours to Al, when he had to find someone quickly. I was a bodyguard though, not a bouncer. At my height and weight, I wasn't really big enough to work as a bouncer. Often, in those situations, it's not what you can do, it's what you look like you can do. If somebody is smashed out of their head on drink or drugs, then you can't always stare them down, because it's odds on they're not focusing on you anyway. What may put them off is sheer physical size. They might have a go at me. They might not have a go at someone three inches taller and three stone heavier.

It's the same thing on the door. If you turn someone away in front of his mates, or worse still, his girlfriend, then he's lost face. If he thinks he can take you, he'll probably try. And the fact that you can take him out, maybe without even breaking sweat, is irrelevant. The club wants you to prevent trouble, not get into it.

I learnt an invaluable lesson working the door of one club. Watch out for the unexpected. I'd refused entry to one young man. I'd seen him slip a blade from his outside to his inside pocket and he wasn't getting in with that. He wasn't happy about it though, so he moved closer to me and squared up. I was okay with it though. Too close and I'd take him. And if he moved his hand anywhere near his inside pocket, his testicles would be visiting his brain via the internal route. He looked at me and I looked at him and he decided against it. Just as he was moving away, his girlfriend stuck her foot out from behind him and rammed her stiletto heel through the top of my shoe, taking off the skin between my first and second toes. I didn't do anything about it. There wasn't any point. They were leaving and I don't think the man even knew what she'd done. But she taught me an important lesson. Be aware of what's going on around you, or buy shoes with steel toe caps. The guy called something out at me as they left, but I wasn't going to react to that. Besides which, my shoe was filling up with blood.

But while bouncers aren't necessarily trained, most of them are hard men. One or two of them though, may be there just for the ride, like the one I came across with some of the lads from the gym, when we were just teenagers. There were two bouncers outside this club, dressed up in the monkey suits and the bow ties. A queue of people were waiting to get in. One of the bouncers looked like he knew what he was doing, the other was pure Neanderthal. We weren't going into the place, just walking past, but little Cliff, who was only a bantam-weight, looked up at this guy, all six foot four and sixteen stone of him and said:

'You know why they call them dicky bows, don't you?'

'Ugh,' said Neanderthal.

"Cos they're wrapped round pricks,' says Cliff.

Well, that was it. Neanderthal was out of the doorway and grabbing for Cliff, we were trying to pull Cliff away, he was trying to thump the guy and the other bouncer, luckily for us, was trying to pull his colleague away. Meanwhile, the queue shortened as people snuck into the club. We laughed about it afterwards. Well, all of us except Cliff. He was being held by his ankles over the side of Waterloo Bridge.

I grabbed something to eat on Villiers Street, taking a window seat to watch the world go by. A woman on the next table was reading a newspaper, holding it open in front of her, so that I could see the front and back pages. Manchester United winning again on the back, another government scandal on the front, but that was two or three days old, a sure sign that there was no real news. I'd had one or two small write-ups on the back pages before. I wondered whether I'd be head-lining the front pages in a couple of days.

The van was still there and intact when I reached the Embankment. It coughed a couple of times before starting.

Eighteen hundred pounds. I smiled. At least Tony was making a living.

It was getting late and I had to get to Nelson before eleven. I turned the van west and headed for the meet, my mind bouncing from thought to thought.

*

I had to drag my mind away from Linda and what she'd said to me, back to Charlie Nelson and his information on Smith. I had to focus again. What Nelson had to tell me might give me an edge over Smith, or it suddenly occurred to me, it could even open up another way of dealing with him. To me, it made sense for Smith to be working on his own now, rather than for anyone else. That's why he'd pulled me in for the job. He knew a lot of muscle, but he didn't want to use anyone he knew or had worked with in a set-up, even if they knew what was going on. If they didn't know, they might get hurt, which would be embarrassing for Smith and if they did know about it, they wouldn't be acting naturally.

The traffic into west London was heavy and I was running late. By the time I reached the cafe where I was to meet Nelson, it was gone eleven o'clock. I parked up a couple of hundred yards away and started to walk towards the meeting place. I hadn't got too far when I saw a big man forcibly walking a small man out of the cafe and into the back of a saloon car. I couldn't see their faces from where I was, but from the size of them, the small guy was almost certainly Nelson and the large man could easily be Smith's gorilla. It was too coincidental to be anyone else. I wasn't sure what to do. The car doors were closing and they were too far away to reach before they drove off, so I turned and raced back to Tony's van, swore once as it coughed and then thanked whoever as it started second time. I still didn't know what I was going to do, but I couldn't just let them drive Nelson away, without doing anything at all. Thinking about it on the drive from town, I'd stopped looking at Nelson's possible information purely as background. The more I thought about it, the more I realised that he might come up with something that I could use against Smith that would mean a different kind of confrontation. Now, for whatever reason, it looked like Smith was snatching that possibility away from me and the only chance I had of getting it back was to try and stay with that saloon car wherever it went, without getting caught by them myself.

It's not easy tagging a car on your own, really you want more than one vehicle so that you can switch the tail between you and keep changing the image, but maybe here I'd be lucky. Al once told me that the most important fact about following somebody is whether or not that person is expecting the possibility of being followed. If he is then he'll be looking out for a tail and it becomes nearly impossible for one person to track him. Smith, if it was him in the car ahead, couldn't know that I was going to be following him. The only questions now were whether he was security conscious enough to routinely check for a tail and whether I was good enough to stick with him.

Why had they taken Nelson? Was it because of me? Nelson didn't know who I was, so he couldn't have told them that I'd been asking questions. But they obviously wanted something from him, or they wouldn't be taking him to wherever they were going. Where were they going?

We were heading through Acton towards Ealing, not too fast and with a fair amount of space between us. There were a good number of cars on the road and I didn't want to get caught out by them shooting a light and me getting stuck with cars between us and unable to follow. The dark helped though and I made sure not to be the car directly behind them when we did have to stop at lights. I was as careful as I could be. Once when the road was clear between us and also behind me and I reckoned I'd been in their mirror too long, I indicated and turned left, did a quick U-turn and came back onto the main road a hundred yards further behind with only my side-lights on, not the main lamps. Changing the image again. We'd been travelling on main roads, but after a while the saloon pulled off into a residential area. Small houses, two up two down style. No garages. They did a couple of lefts and a right and then turned down a smaller side street that led nowhere and pulled up. I drove past the turning and tried to find somewhere to park. Not easy late at night in a road without off street parking. I ended up a couple of hundred yards further on up the road, but then I didn't want to be too close either.

I'd been checking the mirror and no-one had come back up from the side street. I still didn't know what I was going to do, but I'd come this far, so...

I jogged back down the road and when I reached the corner peered cautiously around it. Nothing. The car was gone. At the far end of what I now saw was a cul-de-sac, there were a few houses, but the car had stopped here. Then I noticed the double doors in the fence that ran down at the side of the pavement. The garden or yard behind it belonged to the corner house on the main street. I looked through a crack in the fencing and saw the car parked on gravel. I could also see that the curtains were drawn over French windows in the back room of the house, but there was a glow at the edges that showed that the lights were on. I pushed gently at the double doors, but they were bolted now from the inside as well as having the slam lock on the front. I stopped to think for a moment.

What was I doing here? I couldn't see how I could help

Nelson. I was unarmed and not exactly in the best physical condition. But I had to know what was going on. I had a quick look up and down the street and then jumped up, grabbed the top of the fence and pulled. The fence wobbled and so did I. I wasn't really ready for fence vaulting yet, but I got one leg over the top and swung myself down to the ground. I landed on gravel. Noisily. If you want to hear somebody walking towards you, put down gravel. I stood stock still and waited for the curtains to move and someone to look out. They didn't. I crept as quietly as I could to the French windows. There was no gap at the centre of the curtains, but at one edge I could see past to the room inside. It was a double through room and almost empty, save for a few packing cases and a small side table. The first thing that came to mind was an interrogation room; a place to ask questions and get answers. Nelson was sitting on one of the packing cases almost side on to me. He wasn't tied or cuffed and he didn't seem hurt in any way. Standing over him were Smith and his heavy. It didn't look pleasant, but it seemed as though it could have been worse. From where I was, I could see, but I couldn't hear. If this was a question and answer session I wanted to know what was being said.

I moved along to the back door of the house and without much hope of success pulled down on the handle. It opened. It wasn't locked. Well of course it wasn't. There was no-one that knew they were here, they hardly needed to lock the door behind them. It would only slow them up if they did need to get out in a hurry. The back door led into a dark kitchen, which led to a hallway. The door to the main room wasn't closed all the way, probably so that Smith could keep an ear on the rest of the house. It also meant that I could keep an ear on him. I squatted down and put my eye to the crack on the hinged side of the door. I was feeling quite calm now. All I had to do was look, listen and stay quiet.

From my angle, I could see most of the back of Nelson's head, the right hand side. Smith was in full view, facing me to Nelson's right and the bruiser was hidden from me to the left. At the moment, no-one was saying anything.

'I'm waiting.' Smith.

'He was just a man, Mr Smith, just an ordinary bloke.' Nelson's voice was nervous, but not out of control. I couldn't see his hands, if he was fidgeting or not.

'How did he get on to you?'

I felt my stomach lurch. Oh Christ, Mick. Don't give him up, Nelson, don't give him up.

'I don't know. He had my name, he came to the pub. You work as long as I have and people who need you, get to know who you are and where you are.'

I thanked Nelson silently and realised that I was sweating. My sense of calm had vanished. It's a fragile thing, self-control.

'Isn't that a bit dangerous, Charlie, people knowing that you're a – well, an information distributor?'

'I'm an honest man, Mr Smith, it's well known. I don't take sides, I just give out what people want to know and I don't talk to the police.'

Smith was on the move, pacing around in and out of my view and I could see Nelson's head turning to follow his movements.

'Regular public service, aren't you, Charlie? So what did you tell him about me?' The voice had softened now. There was even a hint of a smile in it. Just a mate asking about the local gossip.

'I couldn't tell him anything. I don't really know anything about you. Only that you were well known, you know, re-spected.'

A soft laugh from Smith, almost friendly.

'Respected, is that what you said to him.' He'd turned away from Nelson as he said this and now he was walking away from him.

'But you told him something else as well, didn't you, Charlie?' He was at the far end of the room now, by the long windows. He turned round to face Nelson again. The voice still soft, but somehow with an edge, with some indefinable hardness to it.

'You told him you would find out more about me. That you would "ask around" about me.'

He was moving nearer again now, straight towards his prisoner. Nelson was like a rabbit caught in the headlights. Hell, so was I and Smith didn't even know I was there. It was pure manipulation. Psychological manipulation. Using his own reputation, Nelson's fear of him and not even a threat, just an implication, the suggestion of a threat. I suddenly knew that Nelson was going to die.

'I know, you see, Charlie, I know. I've got people out there with their eyes and ears open looking for someone, but instead they came up with you showing an interest in me.' He'd reached Nelson and was standing over him. 'Now,' the word was snapped out, 'What did you tell him?'

'Nothing, Mr Smith, honestly. I – '

'Don't give me a – '

'No, I mean it, I never got the chance. He was going to phone me at the pub where I play pool in a couple of days.'

Thank you, Nelson, thank you.

Smith stared at him for a moment or two and then turned away.

'Yes, I believe you, Charlie. I don't think you did tell him anything.' Then a change of attack. 'How did you lose your fingers, Charlie?'

'I don't want to talk about it.' Almost a note of defiance in his voice.

'No, I don't suppose you do. But that's all right, because you see, I know already. Once I knew we were going to have this talk I checked up on you. Resources, Charlie, I have resources.'

There was a break as Smith walked out of my view again and then came back.

'Which brings us back to the question of who it is that was asking questions about me.'

'I don't know, I honestly don't know.'

'Oh come on now, Charlie, we're nearly done here, this is the last question.' He leaned closer to Nelson. 'Did he have a name?'

'Jones,' said Nelson. 'Said his name was Jones.'

'Jones?' Smith stood upright, surprise in his voice. 'Bloody comedian. Jones.' It was an aside to his muscle man, or maybe just to himself.

'That's not good enough, Charlie,' like telling off a small child, 'you know that's a false name.'

Nelson gave a sort of short half choked laugh. 'Funny that, he said the same thing about you.'

'What did he say?'

'That he thought your name was a moody.'

Smith stopped still for a moment and I knew that the words flashing through his mind were the same ones that had stuck in mine. What I'd said to him in the hallway, facing his gun and his eyes. *Is Smith your real name?*

He leaned closer to Nelson again.

'Describe him, Charlie, describe this man Jones.'

So Charlie did. Just in general terms, probably not thinking that he was giving enough away to drop anyone in trouble. But I knew, I knew, that Smith already had me in mind.

And the description, general though it was, fitted. I wanted to run, but I couldn't, not yet. I might still find out something that could turn things my way.

'Was he marked up, Charlie, was he bruised?'

'Yes he was.' Nelson was surprised by the question and answered it, I think, before he even realised that he might have said something important.

'Garron.' It was the gorilla's voice, speaking for the first time. I still couldn't see him, but he'd been playing his part in the session with just his physical presence in the room.

'No, I told you,' said Nelson, trying to recover some ground, 'his name was Jones.'

But Smith was ignoring him now, speaking to his sideman, or maybe again just to himself.

'Yes, yes it is Garron, almost certainly, but…,' his voice slowed as he worked things out, '…that's not necessarily a problem. You,' he said, looking back to Nelson, there was no more Charlie now, 'When did you first talk to him? The truth now.'

There was no point in lying.

'Monday,' said Nelson, his voice tired and his body beginning to slump. 'It was Monday afternoon.'

'Before we talked to him at his place.'

'What's the difference when it happened?' The gorilla again.

'Oh, there's a lot of difference. He wanted to know about us before we started to put pressure on him. Before he knew we were responsible for the attack on Broussier, for beating him up. He didn't know we were going to walk back in on him. He was just interested in us. Even you might be interested if you'd just been worked over. Somehow, maybe from one of his old boxing people, he's got hold of Nelson's name and gone to see what he knows. Putting a little bit of adventure back in his life again. But then things change. We walk in and show him that it's not an adventure after all. It's real life and it's tougher than he ever was. This isn't a problem. Garron probably won't even try to call him,' he gestured towards Nelson, 'to hear what he's found out. There's no need to. It's a different situation now.'

'Maybe we should go see him anyway.'

Smith laughed. 'You're just sore because he broke your nose. No. Garron's set. What we need is Broussier and Garron's going to bring him right to us. This – '

'I ain't hearing this.' Nelson speaking again, this time more nervous, losing control. 'I don't want to listen to this, any of it.'

Smith turned to face him again.

'It doesn't really matter what you hear now, does it, Charlie? You've been listening for a lot of years, to a lot of things that mattered. But what you hear now doesn't matter. Not this time.'

They were going to kill him. I was right. Nelson was going to die. Probably here and now and I was going to see it happen. I had to stop it somehow, but I didn't know how.

'Mr Smith, I'm not going to say anything to anybody, honest I'm not. I – '

'I know you're not, Charlie, because I'm not going to give you the opportunity to. I'm working for myself mainly now and it's difficult to build a clientele when someone is running around asking questions about you. You see, it's not even really what you know, it's the fact that you've been asking.'

'But if I turn up dead, people will know.' Nelson's voice was desperate now. 'People must know it was you, 'cos I've been asking about you.'

Smith left Nelson's words hanging in the air for a moment. When he spoke, his voice was smooth, gentle even.

'Yes, Charlie, but you're not going to turn up dead. You're not going to turn up at all.'

He gestured to the heavy. 'Do it.' As an afterthought, 'Quietly.'

I could still see only half of Nelson, just his right hand side from behind, sitting down, but I saw the large pair of hands that closed around his throat and neck and began to squeeze. I couldn't see the face that belonged with the hands, but I thought it would be showing some enjoyment of the act. This was what people like him lived for. Smith, though, didn't seem to be taking any pleasure from seeing Nelson die. There was nothing in his face at all. It was just something that had to be done.

Me? I was crouching down behind the door, not twenty feet from where a man was being killed and I could do nothing about it. If I burst in, they'd just deal with me first and go back to Nelson later. I thought of making a noise, causing a distraction, but I didn't think I could do that and get out in time. And even if I did, they would just come back and finish the job. So I stayed where I was, knowing I should do something, but that I could do nothing except watch Nelson die. I kept willing him to resist, to fight somehow, but he couldn't. All he did was half raise his right arm and crippled hand in a kind of stop sign, a final plea. And as the life was choked out of him, the last two fingers and thumb curled over until they were level with the two stumps of the missing fingers and the arm fell to his side.

The killer didn't let go though. He kept his grip in place for maybe another ten seconds, before releasing it. The whole thing had happened in silence. Not a sound. Nelson hadn't been allowed to make a sound. His body fell backwards across the packing case he'd been sitting on and rolled off it onto the floor. He didn't even make much noise when he hit the ground. Just enough to make you realise that he wasn't getting up again.

'Let's clear him out then.' Smith, back to business.

I had to move, which wasn't easy. I'd been squatting for some time. My legs ached as I crept back through the kitchen and opened the back door. I didn't think I'd made a sound, but from back in the house I could hear Smith saying, 'What was that?'

'What?'

'I heard something. Check it out.'

I was gone, closing the door behind me and across the gravel to the double doors in the fence. If I unbolted them, they'd know that someone had been here, so I had to go over the top again, but I didn't think there'd be time to get over and away down the street, so instead I scrambled under the parked car, working my body low into the gravel to give my-self room. I could only just get in there and I couldn't move my head, or hardly breathe.

Almost immediately, the back door opened and he came out. He took a quick look around and then walked over to the car. I could see his shape moving towards me, but I knew he couldn't see me. It was too dark for that. He stopped near the car and all I could see of him were his shoes and ankles and I realised I was scared. It wasn't something I was used to feeling. I suppose I had been scared when Smith pulled the gun on me, but things were happening then. I hadn't had time to think about anything, just to react. But now all I could do was wait. There was no reacting. There was no ac-tion of any kind and I had the time to recognise that I was scared. Scared of being discovered. Scared of being dragged out and taken into that empty room, of being sat down on one of those packing cases and of being asked questions, probably not in the same way that Nelson had been asked, but almost certainly with the same end result. I was scared and I didn't like the feeling and I silently cursed Nelson for getting himself killed. And I cursed myself for sitting there and letting it happen. But most of all, I cursed Smith for putting me in this situation and the fear turned to anger. So I lay there and thought about what I could do. Now. To give an outlet to the anger. And I thought about going for him there and then. About grabbing one of the heavy's ankles and trying to tip him up. Scrabbling out from under the car and taking him out. Picking up his gun and going back inside after Smith. But I didn't think I could do it. It was too risky.

And then the moment was gone. The feet moved away out of reach towards the double doors and I heard them open as he checked the street. Obviously nothing there as he closed them again, bolted them up and went back to the house.

I took a deep breath and let it out slowly, but I couldn't afford to wait around. They'd be moving Nelson's body soon and I had to be out of here. I slid out from under the car and went back over the fence. It was a lot easier getting out of the back yard than it had been getting into it, because this time I could use the wooden support that ran across the middle of the doors on the inside.

On the pavement outside I stopped for a moment. There was no-one around. I thought about knocking on someone's door and asking to use the phone, calling the police, but by the time they got here Smith would be gone and Nelson's body with him. I didn't know who held the lease on the house, but it wouldn't be Smith. The car I didn't even bother thinking about. There was only one thing I could do. Track them to wherever they dumped the body and then go to the police with the location. That might work. I ran back to the van and turned it around, parking it back in the same place, but facing the way I'd come from. When Smith turned out of the side street, I'd be ready to follow. I switched the engine off and waited, trying to think of anything except the sight of Nelson's arm falling to his side and the sound of his body falling to the floor. And while I was sitting there thinking about anything else, Smith's car came into sight. But instead of turning left on to the road, back the way it had come, allowing me to slot in behind it, the car turned right towards me. I dropped sideways, below the level of the dashboard as it swept past and then, as the tail lights faded behind me, switched on the engine and had to turn the van round again. By the time I'd got going after them, they were out of sight. I wasn't sure where they'd gone.

I reached the end of the road. Left or right? I couldn't see them either way, so I tried left, for no particular reason. I saw tail lights on a road to the right and swung after them, but it turned out to be a couple going home after a night out. I criss-crossed the local area for about fifteen minutes, but I couldn't see them anywhere. I pulled up for a moment. My last chance of leverage on Smith, my last chance of avoiding a confrontation, had gone. And mixed in with the frustration and the growing anger was a feeling that I didn't want to recognise or even acknowledge. A feeling of guilt. Nelson had died because of me, because I had spoken to him and he had been looking for information for me.

'It was his game son, he knew the risks, he knew what he was doing.' Al's voice, absolving me, giving me a way to live with it. He was right and it helped. But not much.

I turned the car eastwards and headed for my new home. There was nothing else to do.

*

We have a connection. He is not in the boxing world anymore, but we found someone who knows someone.'

'Okay. You can get hold of this connection now?'

'Yes.'

'If it is possible, I want Garron to look after a man in London tomorrow, take him to a meeting.'

'Is the man important?'

'He is just a technician, but his employer is important. I made a deal with him and that is one of the reasons why we must find that disc. If you can set it up, discreetly, I will be at the pickup. It is not a dangerous job, but I want to see this Garron, I want to see how he moves. That will be enough for me.'

*

When I reached Camden High Street I parked up a side road. The flat was the last one in a row above the shops. There were two floors, mine was the lower one, a fire escape at the back leading to a service yard for the shops and a small walkway in front, overlooking the road. Not a great place to get out of in a hurry. I'd just have to make sure no-one knew I was there. I had three boxes, two bin liners and a travel bag, plus the furniture and the TV, which I left in the van. I took the boxes and bags up to the front door in three lots. I was glad of the movement after sitting in the van. It stopped me thinking about Charlie Nelson.

There was a time when Camden Town never seemed to sleep. Obviously, Tuesday nights at somewhere past one was the time when everyone caught up on their rest. I looked out from the walkway over the High Street. It was almost quiet. There was still some traffic around, but the streets were empty of people. There was litter everywhere. A couple of doorways that I could see were occupied. Well, the rent's good and there's an en-suite toilet. I used to know Camden well, but it had been a while. We used to come down to see Shaky Vic's blues band at the Caernarvon Castle, but that was gone now. I made a mental note to check out what was going on at which corners, so I'd know what to avoid. It could have been worse though. The market is still here and enough business to keep a certain amount of money flowing. And at least the police still got out of their cars. When that stopped, it would be time to have moved six months earlier.

There were two keys for the front door. I unlocked and went inside. First thing was, it was dark. The second thing was, it was cold. I switched on Tony's torch and panned it around the room. As it lit up the far corner, there was a flash of eyes, a hiss, a snarl and a shout. The shout was from me, as I jumped two foot in the air and backwards. I think I shouted 'Jesus', but I don't know why, since I don't believe he was the son of God and I certainly didn't expect him to help me. It didn't matter though, since what I was shouting at wasn't human.

The cat was backed up in the corner of the room, against the far wall, almost underneath the window. At least I knew why it was so cold. There was one pane of glass, about ten inches by eight inches, missing. I looked at the cat and the cat looked at me. Now, I don't mind cats, but this was not the sort of animal that was instantly likeable. It was a big, ugly, black cat, with splodges of white on its face, chest and two paws, one front and one back. Its back was arched, its tail was up, its ears were back, its teeth were showing and it was growling, snarling and hissing, if cats do all those things. But most of all, its eyes were holding mine. Like it wasn't scared of me. Wary, but not scared. It had been startled, but it was getting over that and it wasn't going to be frightened off by this human, who had entered what it clearly thought was its own territory. Neither of us moved. In front of the cat was a half eaten rodent of some kind.

'Okay, cat,' I said, 'you can eat your, er, dinner, but then out, all right?' The cat continued to look at me. I checked my pulse rate. It was returning to normal, now that I realised that it wasn't Smith or his heavy lying in wait for me, nor was it Nelson's ghost back to blame me for his death. I flashed the torch around, looking for a light switch. It was by the front door. I flicked it, but nothing happened. I shone the light onto the fitting in the centre of the ceiling. No light bulb. I flicked the switch to off again and looked for a plug socket. There was one by the doorway in the right hand wall. The front door was still open. I dragged the boxes in and put the bin liners and travel bag on top of them. I pulled my lamp out of one of the plastic bags and shone the torch back to the cat. It hadn't moved, but it did seem to have relaxed slightly. It no longer looked as though it was going to attack me. Of course, I hadn't moved towards it yet.

I walked diagonally to the right hand wall, the space between me and the cat remaining about the same. The room was a big square, about eighteen feet by eighteen. As I was walking, I thought, 'this is stupid, it's a cat. Why am I being so careful not to disturb it?' The only reason I could think of was that since I'd been forced to move out of my home and I knew what it was like, I felt bad about evicting the cat. I plugged in the lamp and the 25 watt bulb sent a dull glow across the room. I sat down next to the light with my back to the wall. My favourite position. The cat seemed to take this as a cessation of hostilities. Keeping its eyes on me, it half sat down as well.

I looked around the room. It was completely empty. Not a chair, nor a table. Nothing. There was a carpet on the floor. I made a mental note to throw it out as soon as I could. Opposite the front door, there were two windows in the back wall, overlooking the service yard. One of them, as I said, had a customised cat flap. I glanced back to the cat. He looked tough enough to have broken the glass himself to get in. The wall I was leaning against had a doorway, but no door, leading into the kitchen. Without getting up, I turned round and manoeuvred myself into a long thin room. Well, it gave the impression of being long, but that was just because it was thin. It was actually the same depth front to back as the main room, but only about eight feet wide. At the front end was a cubicle. I suddenly realised that I hadn't stood up so as not to scare the cat. I stood up. This was my home; he was just squatting. I walked through the kitchen to the cubicle and looked inside. Toilet, small sink and shower. I crossed my fingers and switched the shower on to hot. It worked, but it was cold. I counted to fifteen and found that the age of miracles was not dead. Hot water. Switching it off, I flushed the toilet. It also worked, although it was possible, I suppose, that I'd just flooded the shop underneath me.

I turned back to the kitchen. Luxury. A sink unit, an electric cooker and a fridge, with a freezer section built in. I plugged the fridge in and the light went on. All I needed now was my furniture up from the van and some food and I could throw my house-warming party. True, I had no guests, but me and the cat could probably polish off a bottle of whisky and the odd rat or two. I sneaked a look around the doorway. The cat immediately looked up. It had been eating whatever it was that was supper. Now it had stopped and was looking up at me again. I picked up the lamp and took two steps into the room. The cat picked up its food in its mouth, jumped up on to the window sill and exited through the broken window pane. It stood on the window ledge outside, above the metal stairs of the fire escape, looking in at me. I don't know if it was my movements, or the lamp moving and with it the shadows, but when he saw me put the light down in the middle of the room and stand still, he dropped his food on the ledge and, tail twitching, carried on eating.

With the light in the centre of the room, I could now see the flat in full, including the corner that the cat had occupied. The walls were relatively clean. The carpet was not. The cat's corner was scratched up and littered with half a dozen small-ish dead creatures, in various stages of decay. Cats may be clean animals, but this one hadn't worked out the social values of throwing away your leftovers. I looked at him again. It was slightly unnerving. Every time I looked at him, he was looking at me. I thought cats had a short attention span, but maybe not when they were being evicted.

I looked at my boxes and bin liners. Now was not the time to start unpacking, especially as there was nothing to unpack anything into, or even onto, except the carpet, which I was going to chuck out tomorrow anyway. I got out my toothbrush, soap and a towel and took them to the bathroom. At least there was a hand-rail for the towel and a soap dish above the sink. I brushed my teeth and went back to the room. I pulled my sleeping bag out of one of the dustbin liners and unrolled it into a corner of the room, the one diagonally furthest from the cat's corner. Just in case any of its meals weren't quite dead yet. I found my clock radio and looked around for another plug socket. There was one, but of course it was in the cat's corner and the lead on the clock was very short. I unplugged the lamp instead and replaced it with the clock. Reset the time and set the alarm for 8.30. Another early start. Making a mental note to buy a multi-plug unit, I closed my eyes. The sleeping bag would be warm in no time. I opened my eyes again and yes, the outline of the cat was still there, outside the window.

Thoughts crowded in. Whilst you're moving, you don't always have time to think. Once you stop, you do. I thought of Linda, Smith, Nelson, Linda again and of murder. I pushed everything away, closed my eyes and let my mind go blank. I had to clear it all out, or else this would be a long night. After about half an hour of struggling not to think, I realised that this was going to be a long, long night.

*

Smith's fist crashed into me and I woke up in a cold sweat. I'd been in a ring and Smith was my opponent, but I couldn't hit him. All I could do was back away and try to cover up. Smith was advancing on me, smiling, hitting me at will and with each punch I became dizzier and dizzier. Out of the corner of my eye, I could see Linda in the crowd, screaming at me to get out of the ring, but I couldn't do that. This was my place. Mick was there as well, only half watching, shaking his head. I could hear Pat shouting that my legs had gone. In my corner, Charlie Nelson with a towel round his neck, was mouthing at me that he knew how to beat Smith, but I couldn't hear him. I looked for the referee. He looked like Al, but older, balding, with a beer gut. His shirt was covered with flecks of blood. I realised that it was my blood. His expression was one of dislike, disgust even. For me. For the way I was performing. I started to say something, some excuse, 'it's not my fault', I wanted to tell him, when I realised he was counting. I was on the floor. I had to get up. Everything was moving slowly, except the numbers. Suddenly he'd reached seven. I pushed myself onto my knees and up. I couldn't feel my legs. Al was still counting. He couldn't count me out on my feet. It wasn't fair! He reached ten, fifteen, twenty. 'How much longer do I have to count for?' he asked me, his face inches from mine. I turned my head and saw Smith advancing on me. He was small, puny, but I couldn't stop him. I couldn't move. I watched his fist slam towards me, felt it connect, felt my head turn, lights at crazy angles, disoriented, falling away...

I shook my head, ran my hand over my sweating face and

through my hair and looked at the clock. 3.35 am. Another five hours before the alarm went off. The dream was gone, only Smith's smiling face remained as an after image. I sat up. It was freezing cold. I got up and padded naked into the bathroom to wash my face off. I stood in the doorway of the kitchen, sorting my head out. I hadn't dreamed anything to do with boxing for a long time. I'd thought the images were out of my system. Maybe they'd just been lying dormant. I looked for the cat, but he was gone. I'd have to close that gap in the window soon, before I froze to death.

I put on a T-shirt and sweatpants and opened the back door from the kitchen. It was a cold clear night. The sort of night that London does so well. I took a few deep breaths, looked at the night sky, felt myself easing off. I wished, not for the first time, that I could recognise individual stars, but the only constellation that I know is Orion and I wasn't sure if he was even visible at this time of the year. I went back inside and got the end of the Jameson's that I'd rescued from oblivion in my bedsit and my jacket. Sitting on the steps of the fire escape, I finished the bottle, not wanting to try sleep again, wondering how we'd ever managed to put a man on the moon, when we couldn't usually get him to work on time and toasting Orion, wherever he was. Someone once told me that there's a constellation called 'Lepus', the hare, who is supposed to crouch below Orion's feet, although I've never seen him. I wasn't sure who I felt more affinity with at that moment, the hunter or the hare, so I raised my bottle to both of them and went back to my sleeping bag some time after four, suitably relaxed.

*

I got up at a quarter past nine, having woken at 8.30 and switched off the alarm. This was it. Today was the day.

I tried not to think of it as I showered and dressed. I

looked out of the window and saw the kind of day that London does better than anywhere else. Something was familiar about that thought, but I couldn't work out what it was. I gave up trying and concentrated on the weather. Dull and wet. Cloudy and raining. And that particular sort of London rain that is so familiarly depressing. There are only two places that I've known to be more depressing when it rains. One is Tenby in South Wales, where I spent a week in a training camp before one of my bigger fights and it rained solidly for the whole week, day and night, or so it seemed. The other place is Manchester. Only in Manchester does it rain as much as London and that is really depressing. It's pouring down and you don't even have the consolation of being in the big city.

I found my cereal bowl and cursed the fact that I hadn't put my carton of milk in the fridge last night. It was still drinkable though. It was cold enough in this flat not to have gone off. I ate breakfast standing up in the kitchen and then went down to the van to bring up my furniture. There was no parking ticket on the windscreen, but there could have been. I scribbled a sign saying 'Loading' and propped it on the dashboard. It might work, or it might not. Camden was already well up and running, but I didn't meet any of my new neighbours. That was fine by me.

When I finished the second journey, I noticed that the cat was back, sitting on the window ledge outside. He regarded me with a kind of curious hostility as I arranged my bits and pieces around the room and emptied out some of my belongings from the boxes and bags. I spent some time going through my tapes, wondering why I had left them in storage and not kept them with me. I stuck one in my pocket for later – the van had a cassette player – and stacked the rest on the floor. Throughout my home improvements, the cat kept his eyes on me, probably working out which of my *objets d'art* to rip to pieces, or pee on first. Alternatively, he could be waiting for me to leave, so that he could come inside and have breakfast. I felt rather guilty at that, since I'd swept up the remains of his previous dinners and thrown them out. I really didn't want to have to do that again later on. I certainly did not intend to cohabit for any length of time with anyone right now, especially not a hostile vicious cat with dodgy table manners. I finished what I was doing and thought about the cat problem.

I couldn't evict him until I'd replaced the pane of glass or boarded the hole, neither of which I could do at the moment. As soon as I left the place, he'd probably come straight back in, bringing with him whatever breakfast would be. I had visions of me chasing half dead blackbirds around the room, trying to catch them and put them out of their misery.

'All right, cat, here's what I'll do. I'll give you something to eat, provided you don't bring anything back with you while I'm out.'

I went to one of the boxes and pulled out a tin of tuna. I couldn't put it in a bowl, since I only had one and I wasn't giving him mine, I wasn't sure what might end up in it, so I just drained the brine and dumped the fish in the middle of the corner where he'd been eating the night before. I was going to throw the carpet out later anyway. Then I started worrying that I had nothing to put water in for him. What if he choked on the tuna? I mean, there's no blood in a tin of tuna, like there is in a rat. So I gave up, filled my one bowl with water and left it there for him.

I walked back to the kitchen entrance and leaned against the wall, surveying the room. The cat didn't come in for the food, just sat there watching me from the ledge. I promised myself not to look at him again. I closed my eyes and made a mental list of all the things that I would need for this place. Plates, cutlery, saucepans, food, light bulbs, a new carpet; it was too long for a mental list, so I got a pen and paper and started writing things down. These would have to be bought with what was left of the money Harwood had given me. There was about seventy pounds left. If everything went according to plan, I'd want to sit tight for a few days, so food would be the priority to buy. I'd have to owe Mick for the gun and Tony for the use of his van, until I could get myself sorted out. I had some money saved, my emergency fund, but that was stashed with somebody on the coast. It wasn't that much, hopefully enough to cover Mick and Tony, but there was no way that I could get to it at the moment. I checked the back door was locked and bolted, even though I knew it was, took my shopping list and went off to see Mick. I called goodbye to the cat without looking at him, telling him to enjoy his breakfast and went out of the front door, closing it on the Yale lock behind me. He'd be on that tuna like a flash. He'd probably never had tuna before, especially dolphin friendly tuna. That's something that puzzles me. Why are people so worried about the dolphins, but eat the tuna quite happily? I'll bet if dolphins were ugly or stupid creatures, a bit more like humans really, no-one would worry about dolphin friendly tuna. Just like they don't worry about being friendly to people.

I counted to thirty. He'd probably be halfway through it by now. I slid the key back into the door as quietly as I could, turned it silently, then threw it open and jumped into the room. The cat was looking at me. Sitting outside the window on the ledge, its eyes locked on mine, obviously wondering what this strange human was doing, jumping around his home like a pratt. He had a point. I felt like an idiot.

I told the cat he was a sneaky little sod and exited with as much dignity as I had left. Behind me, I swear I could hear little sniggers of feline laughter. I closed the door behind me, double locked it and moved on to the business of the day. No parking ticket on the van. I took this as a good sign.

*

I got to Mick's a little before eleven. I wasn't sure what to do, whether to tell him about Nelson or not. I didn't know how well they knew each other, if Nelson was a friend of his, or just someone he knew professionally. Although Mick seemed to know everybody and everybody seemed to know him, he didn't socialise with anyone that I knew of and the only funeral that I'd ever known him to go to was Al's. Not that Nelson was going to have a funeral anyway. In Mick's world, people getting hurt is something that happens and he's the sort of person that takes bad news in his stride.

At the moment though, no-one knew that Nelson was dead. The only way that I could know was if I knew something about how he died and I didn't want Mick, or anyone else, to know that I was there when it happened. And that I didn't do anything to stop it, even though I couldn't.

So I decided to say nothing. If everything went according to plan, maybe I'd tell Mick about it, or at least some part of it, at a later date. I had enough to worry about for the moment. I knew Mick wouldn't bring the subject of Nelson up himself. That was yesterday's news.

I rang and he buzzed me in. The dog was, as ever, in the doorway. I gave him the back of my hand to smell, fingers closed as usual and he allowed me to push past him. Mick was in the kitchen, I could smell food. Actually, it smelled bad. I hoped it was for the dog. When I looked into the kitchen, I found Mick emptying out a can of dog food into the bin.

'Left it out for a while by mistake. Don't like giving him

stale food.' He lifted the plastic liner out of the bin and tied it. 'Got to throw this outside, it's not fair to him to leave it here. He won't try and eat it, but he can still smell it. Go in and sit down.'

I sat in one of the armchairs. The TV was again, or perhaps still, playing to itself at the side. The dog moved to its customary position in the doorway. We stared at each other. They say if you lock eyes with an animal, it will look away. This one just grinned at me, tongue lolling. It knew who was in control. I thought I should have brought the cat from my new home with me. It would have been an interesting staring contest. I heard Mick come back in and close the front door. The dog never moved. It knew his tread. Mick pushed him out of the way with his foot and sat down opposite me, lighting up a cigarette. He didn't offer me one, he knows I don't smoke.

'How's the flat?'

'It's great. Cold, but I can fix that. Needs a new carpet, but I can fix that as well.'

'Good. So you'll be okay there?'

This was unusual. Mick doesn't go for small talk. If there was something wrong with the flat, he'd expect me to tell him, otherwise there'd be nothing to talk about.

'Yeah, I'll be fine. Soon as I get rid of the cat that thinks it lives there.'

'Oh, right.' He half laughed. 'Got to watch out for those squatters.' I said nothing and waited for him to get to the point. After a few seconds he said, 'You're determined, are you?'

'I think I have to be.'

'Okay.'

He got up and went to the table, which, as always, was covered with papers. Handed me a scrap with the name of a shop, a street and a time written on it. I looked at it and gave it back. I've always been pretty good at addresses and numbers.

'Man called Castle will pick you up there. You tell him you're from me. Go with him. I've arranged for you to try it out on a private range. I've told him a double action revolver. It's probably better for you than a semi-automatic, won't jam as easy and you don't sound like you'll need rapid fire. Don't pay him. That's between me and him and you and me. Don't use too many bullets on the range, they cost money.'

'What does he look like, this Castle?'

'He's a small black man, dresses nice, but not flash, blends in. He's a pro, so whatever he says, you do.'

'Okay, I understand.'

'You be outside that shop at that time. He'll pick you up. Don't be late, he won't be there. Don't be early, it's not a good place to be hanging around.'

'I appreciate this, Mick, really. I'll square with you as soon as I get myself straight.' I started to get up.

'Hold on a minute. I've already started to get you straightened out. I've got you a job.' He held up his hand as I started to interrupt. 'Just let me finish, all right?'

I sat down again.

'You've been scratching around for a while now and you're not getting anywhere. I can get you bodyguarding and minding work, maybe not all the time, but fairly regularly. And you can do it and do it properly. You're not going to let me down if I recommend you. So I've got you a short job today, just a couple of hours.'

'Mick, I can't do it today, I'm really rushed –'

'Yes, you can do it today. You're to meet him at Euston station at half twelve. He's got a meeting at half one and you put him back on a train at three. That gives you an hour to get to the East End to meet Castle. It's now quarter past eleven, so you've got the time to go home and change.'

'You've got it all worked out, haven't you?' I stood up again. 'It's a little tight, isn't it? And I don't have a clean shirt, I bled on mine on Saturday night. And my suit's dirty.'

'Hey, I'm doing you a favour, now you can do one for me! I've told the man you're picking him up and that's that. You can take one of my shirts. Think of this as paying me back the first instalment on the gun.'

Put like that, I didn't have much choice. I asked Mick for the details.

'His name's... oh, hang on...' he went over to the table. Mick writes everything down, he doesn't remember things, deliberately. That means though, that he's forever burning scraps of paper, or trying to remember which phone number applies to which set of initials. He found a yellow scrap.

'Vincent. That's Mr Vincent, not Vincent something. He's an electronics wizard. Bringing some sample down to show some people at a private meeting. High powered people. They're not necessarily friendly to each other. You just keep him out of trouble and make sure he doesn't lose anything. Here's the place you're going to.' I took this piece of paper. It wasn't incriminating. Yet.

'Got you a driver as well. Black cab.'

I wasn't impressed. 'I hope he's better than the last driver I was given, or he might get me killed as well as himself.'

Mick was a bit put out by my comments. 'Garron, this is me you're talking to, not some cowboy.'

'Yeah, sorry.' I meant it. Mick knew what he was doing. If he gave me a driver, then he'd be a good one.

'It's McGuire, you remember him?'

'Yeah, of course. He came to a couple of the fights.'

'You'll be all right with him. He's looking forward to seeing you.'

'Mick,' I asked, 'how did you get this job? I mean, it's a bit out of your line, isn't it?'

He looked at me hard.

'Yeah, sorry,' I said. There are some things you don't ask some people.

'Vincent will know you as Jones, Castle as well.' I would've laughed, except that Nelson flashed into my mind again. Smith and Jones once more. The only thing that would have been funnier would be if Mick had told them my name was Wesson.

'Okay, Mick, you've talked me into it. I'd better get moving now. What else do I have to know?'

'McGuire will be outside the station at 12.15, on the side street on the west side, you know –' I nodded, ' – and Vincent will be inside under the underground sign, by the tube entrance at half twelve.'

He followed me and the dog to the front door, when I asked him, 'Mick, is this a minding job, or a bodyguard job?'

'Ah, minding, mate. He's not paying enough for a bodyguard.' Then, as an afterthought, 'Check in when you're done, all right? Oh, hang on a minute.' He disappeared into the bedroom and came back with a white shirt for me. The dog had stayed where he was.

'Thanks,' I said, 'I'll try to keep it clean.'

'By the way,' he said, as I was leaving, 'are you seriously going to keep that beard?'

'Yeah, why not?' I waited for the sarky comment.

'No, no reason... just if I was you, I'd keep it trimmed short, not much longer than it is now.' He was looking at me carefully.

'Oh, you think it looks all right?'

'No,' he said, 'I just think that if you grow it out the grey bits will show up more.' And he shut the door on me, the dog still grinning by his side.

*

I'd asked Mick the minding/bodyguarding question for a good reason. There's a big and not very subtle difference between the two. If you're minding somebody, then you're looking after him and maybe his property. But only up to a point. If anyone points a gun at him, you are not going to get in the way. There may be other things you can do, but in the final analysis, you're not going to get yourself shot for this man.

If you are a bodyguard though, you are. In fact, if the situation arises, you must. That is the contract between you and your client. If somebody points a gun at the man, then you have to put yourself in the way of that gun. That's what you are. A bullet-catcher. And if you're not prepared to do that, then you shouldn't be doing the job. Of course, you are paid more money as a bodyguard and there are things you can do to lessen the risk.

Bullet-proof vests are good, unless you get shot in the head, or even in an arm or a leg, if it's with the wrong calibre bullet. The shock and blood loss can finish you. Nowdays, the ammunition has outstripped the defences and some bullets will go straight through a vest. The fact is the deck is stacked in favour of any attacker. A bodyguard can only do so much. Al used to say that what you were doing was making your own luck. He had three watchwords for bodyguarding. Preparation. Anticipation. Avoidance. You should prepare properly and find out about your client, his possible enemies, the site that you are using, be it a meeting place, or his home and any travelling routes that he might be using. You should anticipate any problems and prepare escape routes from places and safe rooms in buildings. Above all, you avoid trouble, side-step it before it arrives. If you do all of these things and more, then you are shortening the odds for your client. Of course, the bottom line still stands, you are there to protect him, if necessary with your life and it takes a certain kind of psychosis to be prepared to do that.

When I started working with Al, I took to bodyguarding completely. I got a real buzz out of knowing when I began a job that whatever happened in the next few hours was down to me. If I made a mistake, or dropped my concentration, that could be it. And it might just come down to a few split seconds. The time it takes to get out of a car, cross a road, or come out of a building. You have to get it right the whole time and you can't. There are always gaps, mistakes Al would call them, but he used to say that the trick is to make the mistakes, or leave the gaps, when they don't matter. Nobody notices a good bodyguard's mistakes, because nobody gets hurt when they occur. And that comes down, once again, to making your own luck. If there's a real threat to your client, then you're working on an edge the whole time. It's not exactly a high that you get from it, but it is addictive. You get to need the edge. It's exhausting if you're doing the job right, but also stimulating. You feel alive. Doing anything else becomes stale, boring even. And it's like that right up to the moment that you burn out. Or get taken out.

I thought about the Vincent job. I didn't like taking anything at the last minute. I couldn't prepare for it at all. But in the end, most jobs are a compromise between your principles and necessity. In the end, you can't always prepare, you just have to do the best that you can and rely on experience and common sense for the rest. If Al had turned down the jobs that he couldn't prepare for, he'd have starved. Besides, Mick had said that this was a minding job, not bodyguarding. That suggested that Vincent wasn't really in danger, more likely his 'sample' was, although you couldn't be sure that if someone went for his briefcase, they wouldn't take him out to get it.

I hadn't asked Mick how Vincent was getting to Euston. That wasn't my problem. My job started at 12.30, by the underground sign. The address we were going to was a hotel in Harrow. An hour was long enough to get there in the middle of the day from Euston. I'd been driving back to Camden and I realised that I'd been hunched up over the wheel. Everything had tightened up. I sat back, relaxed and switched on the radio. Flicked through the channels, looking for anything with a bit of substance to it, but no, just disposable pop music. I couldn't classify what sort of pop it was; there seems to be a new term for each type of sound, rhythm, beat or screech every two minutes. It's not that I don't appreciate some of the hard work and effort that goes into making these records, I just don't like them. I felt the tape from my old collection in my pocket. Slipped it into the deck and slipped back maybe eight or nine years. Let the music wash over me and felt myself easing up.

It was a bootleg, taped in the basement of a pub near Soho. A London blues band. Not R'n'B, but real blues. Bass, drums, lead guitar and a piano, soft-peddling in the background. All of them playing like it was what they were born to do. Never going to make any money at it, but that wasn't what it was about. As John Lee Hooker said, if it's in you, it's gotta come out. I glanced at the tape's box for the band's name: *The Alcoholic Blues Band*. Sounded like they didn't take themselves too seriously, but they took the music seriously enough.

I remembered the gig now. I was with Lisa and Pete and somebody else, but that name had gone now. I remembered the place as well. Nearly full room, dark for the most part, with smoke curling up from the groups of people, just like in the old jazz clubs. We'd stumbled on this place by accident, but these people knew what they were coming to. I was right back there now, hearing the song in that room. The music so laid back, it was horizontal. Drums and bass locked together like they were one thought. Not loud, just steady. The piano, rolling around the edges, the top hand picking out the highlights and the lead guitar cutting through, making it's point, colouring the story. And the singer. Maybe he didn't have a great voice, but he felt what he was singing.

Times are changing, oh so fast,
I dreamt of you once, long ago in my past,
Now I don't know what I'm going to do,
'Cos it looks, as though, I lost you.

Feels like I left something, somewheres down the track,
Don't know how to start, getting it back,
Maybe it's just, that I'm on the wrong line,
But I can't tell, anymore, what is and isn't mine.

Abruptly, I realised I was almost in Camden High Street. I pulled myself back to the present and switched off the cassette player. Left the tape in for later. I found a parking space round the back of my block and went up to the flat.

The tuna was gone. So was the cat. He also appeared to have kept to his side of the bargain. I couldn't see any dead animals anywhere, although there was, perhaps, a faint smell of 'cat' hanging in the room. He'd probably marked all of my stuff as his own.

I got changed into my suit trousers and shoes and Mick's shirt. The trousers weren't clean, but they were wearable. The dirt from the street on the Isle of Dogs wasn't too noticeable and there wasn't really much blood on them. My tie had been

ruined, I'd already thrown it out, so I'd have to wear my second and now only tie. I would have to do something about
that. I'd never been a one tie man before and I wasn't sure I
liked the feeling. Of course, I'd never been a three tie man
before either, so I suppose it wasn't that far a fall. My suit
jacket was unwearable. I hoped it could be cleaned, but for
now it was useless, so I picked up my imitation leather jacket
and put that on instead. Now I looked like a plain clothes
policeman. Well, no harm in that for this job. The jacket isn't
imitation leather out of any moral convictions. It was just
what I could afford. I debated whether to take any kind of
weapon with me: a knife, my extending car aerial, or a sharp-
ened piece of plastic, but I decided against it. Today of all
days, I didn't want to be stopped by the police and have to
explain anything. More to the point, though, was that I might
not be able to get back here before going to meet Castle and
I'd want to be clean when he picked me up. If he was a pro
he'd check, never mind whether Mick had vouched for me or
not.

So I just put a dozen pennies in each of my outside jacket
pockets, each set wrapped in a twist of paper. Useful as a by
product for throwing at people while they're still wrapped,
but mainly for use as a diversion. If someone is approaching
you with a knife, try throwing a dozen loose pennies in his
face. It causes a certain amount of confusion. As you throw
them, take advantage of the split second advantage that
you've given yourself – step in and kick him in the groin. It's
not foolproof, but it might just give you an edge. It would be
nice if this worked on guns, but, as a general rule, it doesn't.
Throw coins in someone's face when they're holding a gun
on you and it will probably go off. As an afterthought, I took
my small Mini – Maglite torch and a cloth to wipe any prints
off the gun if I left any. Just in case I didn't get back here

before meeting Smith.

The underground. Not my favourite place, but I'd be stupid not to use it to go to Euston, since it's only a couple of stops. I just don't like sitting in a closed tube, in a tunnel. I don't think it's claustrophobia, just paranoia. There are more and more nutters in London now and they all seem to ride the Northern Line. The safest time to ride the tube now is probably the rush hour when everybody is doing their sardine impressions. You might get your pocket picked, but you're less likely to be physically attacked and you've got to be really unlucky to get stuck right next to a nutter. Of course, if you are, then there is no getting away from them, since everyone is so jam-packed together.

At other times, anyone can roam up, down and through the carriages. Cases of 'steaming' are on the up and although we're not anything like New York here, the basic fact on a tube train remains: there's nowhere to go. I just naturally try and avoid that situation. I suppose I could have waited for a bus, but I thought the train would be quicker. So I took a deep breath of what passes for clean air in Camden and went underground. I'd bought a newspaper outside the station, but not because I wanted to know what was going on in the world. A tabloid newspaper, rolled up tightly, has a devastating effect if it's smashed into someone's temple. No, not very friendly, but legal to carry, unlike everything else in this country. I didn't bother reading it at all. If I'd wanted the news, I'd have bought a different paper.

Waiting for the south bound train, I thought about how long it had been since I'd seen Sean McGuire. The last time was maybe four, nearly five years ago, not counting Al's funeral, when I wasn't really talking to anyone. McGuire was a big bear of a man, with a surprisingly soft Dublin accent. He'd always been a cab driver, since soon after he'd come to

London and Al had used him quite often for driving work. Apparently, he could drive. Properly. Offensive driving, defensive driving, support car, blocking car, VIP driving, he could do the lot. He'd drive whatever vehicle Al gave him, but he could always get hold of a black cab, which was useful. In the centre of London, a taxi is the most inconspicuous thing you can drive. Everyone expects to see them, there are hundreds of them around and they can stop almost anywhere. On top of that they've got a great turning circle; they can do a U-turn almost standing still.

But McGuire was one of those people that I'd lost touch with, one of the ones that had seemed to resent my change of career. Mick had said he was looking forward to seeing me. Maybe he was pleased to see me back where I belonged, or perhaps I was just being uncharitable. We'd been fairly friendly. He came to one of my first pro fights, against an Irish lad. We'd joked about who he'd be rooting for.

The train arrived and I got on. Sat in the last seat at the end of the carriage. There were half a dozen other people in the compartment. A couple of them glanced at me as I got on and looked away, back to their books and newspapers. No eye contact on the tube. We're not that different from New York.

No, McGuire was all right, even if he did play a nasty little trick on me once in Dublin. I was over there for a couple of days, partly as a break and partly to see a mate of mine from the gym fight. McGuire was visiting his mum in Dublin and suggested we meet for a drink. We met up by the Liffey and he took me to a pub somewhere on the North side. Probably not a pub I would have walked into if I had been on my own. But I was with McGuire. He knew what he was doing, right? Right. We walked in and he said he was going to the bog and could I get him a Guinness. So the naive young

Englishman walks up to the bar and asks for a double whisky and a pint of Guinness.

'I'm sorry, son, could you say that again, please?'

'Sure, mate. Double whisky and a pint of Guinness,' I repeated.

The barman leaned towards me. 'You from England are you?'

By now, three or four people sitting nearby at the bar were looking at me. The barman gave me a friendly smile. 'If I was you, son, I'd have my drink someplace else.'

I looked left and right of me and I could see what he meant. I was becoming the centre of attention. I looked around for McGuire, but he was nowhere to be seen. I turned back to the barman.

'You're right,' I said, 'I'll be off.'

He nodded at me. 'Don't worry,' he said, 'You'll be all right leaving.'

'Thanks.'

As I was half way to the door, McGuire came striding out of the toilet, turned me back to the bar, put his arm around my shoulder and demanded to know where his drink was and why I was sneaking out without him. Everyone relaxed except me.

'Why didn't you tell me you were with Sean?' the barman asked. Everyone was smiling and joking. I had no option but to join in. Besides which, it was infectious. I was never quite sure whether McGuire set me up for that or not. I think he did. As it was, I loved the time I spent in Eire, except for those two minutes. The people were friendly and the booze was flowing. No, it was cascading. If you think you can drink, try a session with the Irish. I once went down with Al on Christmas day to meet McGuire in one of the Irish pubs on the Willesden-Kilburn border. I thought I could drink. I thought Al could drink. But neither of us could stay with Sean and his group. It took me a day and a half to recover. Still, it was worth it though, to see Sean and Al, an Irish Catholic and a Jew, trying to sing *Good King Wenceslas* to the tune of *Ha'va Nagilah.*

We'd arrived at Euston. It was almost 12.15. I wanted to check where McGuire was before I brought Vincent out. The underground exits into the mainline station at the exact point that I was to meet Vincent. I hoped he wasn't early. First, though, I had to get out of the tube station. I'd been folding my ticket without realising it and now it wouldn't go through the electronic machine. I had to get a ticket inspector to let me out. He scrutinised the ticket.

'You've bent it in half, see? 'Course it won't work,' he said accusingly.

'Sorry,' I said, feeling like a school kid. He muttered something to himself and let me out with his master ticket, looking at me as though I'd committed the most grievous sin possible. No, I thought, as I passed through and walked to the escalator, that's later tonight. I stopped short, the person behind me nearly crashing straight into me and glaring at me as she walked past. I had to stop thinking like that. I had to. If I didn't, then I'd never be able to go through with it. Just blank it out. It was an effort, but I collected myself together and walked onto the escalator. It took me up to the mainline station. I looked around, but didn't let my eyes rest on anybody. All right, anybody except the blonde woman in the short skirt. I didn't see anyone who might be Vincent, but I didn't stop to search him out. I didn't want to find him until I'd checked with McGuire.

I walked through the side exit, past the ticket and information offices, onto the concourse and out to the street. I looked around for McGuire. If I was going to do this regularly, I'd really have to get myself a mobile phone. There was a hoot from a taxi on the right. The door flew open and McGuire unfolded himself from the inside. He shouted the moment his head was visible. So much for discretion. Well, it didn't really matter here.

'Garron, you little bastard, how've you been?' It was okay for McGuire to call me little, given the size of him, but he was the only one. 'Bastard', I was used to.

As always with McGuire, his enthusiasm was infectious. He ran up and threw his arms around me like we were long lost brothers. It probably wasn't quite as bad as a strait-jacket, but if he ever gave up cabbing, he could get a job in an institution without a problem.

'Ah, it's good to see you, son, it really is.'

'You too, Sean,' I said, 'you don't look any different.'

'No, I don't change, but you! Have you had that scrub on your face long?'

I laughed, you had to with Sean, he just had that effect on people.

'No, not long, but it's here to stay. How're you doing? How's Grace and the kids?' He has about half a dozen kids or something like that. They were always having friends round and people staying over and I never managed to work which kids were theirs and which were just passing through.

'Oh, they're grand, grand. Well, Grace wasn't too well, but she's over that and – hey, I'm a grandad. Can you believe it? Dougie's wife had a little girl, almost a year ago now. And you wouldn't even know that he was married, would you?' He was bubbling, his face was alight.

'No, I wouldn't, Sean, but I can believe you as a grand-dad, Lord knows you're the age for it.'

'Hey, that's enough of that. I can still give you three rounds any day. But not now, eh? Now is for work. We'll talk later. Do you have the address for me?'

I gave him Mick's scrap of paper.

'Ah, I know the road. It's off the main centre in Harrow. This hour of the day, we'll get there in good time.'

'Well, I'll leave that to you, Sean.' I glanced at my watch. 'I should go and get the man now.'

'Do you want me to come around the front for him?'

'No, I'm happy to bring him out the side. It's longer to the cab, but quicker once he's in. You can do a U, and be off straight away.'

'All right son, I'll see you in a minute. Oh and next time,' he said, pointing to my bruised face, 'you should duck quicker.' He was laughing to himself as he went back to his cab.

Yeah, right. I turned back to the station. I'd lied to McGuire. He didn't look the same, he looked older. He must be in his late forties now, but he'd aged since I'd last spent any time with him. The manner was the same, but the light brown hair looked thinner and the face was drawn and lined now. Maybe Grace's illness had been more serious than he'd made out. And maybe it had taken its toll on him as well as on her. I wondered how much older I looked to him.

Still, it was good to see him and it flooded my mind with memories and feelings for times past. I suddenly realised I felt good. Really good. And I hadn't felt like this for a while, not just the last four or five days. I knew it would pass, as the present muscled its way back to its proper place, but for the moment I felt a stupid grin all over my face. All down to Sean. He just made you feel that life was there to grin at. It wasn't until you left his company that you started to wonder if his attitude was just surface dressing. Then you bumped into him sometime and you were away again enjoying his company. I used to wonder if he ever took anything seriously in his life. Now I'd seen the drawn lines around his eyes. If he never used to take anything seriously in the past, it looked as though he'd learned to since I'd last seen him.

I was back in the main station concourse. I dropped my newspaper onto one of the seats, it wouldn't look too professional to approach Vincent with a rolled up newspaper in my hand. I would have thrown it away, but since the bomb scares, all the rubbish bins have been removed. Now you just throw your litter on the floor. I hope some good has come out of that though, I hope they employ more staff to keep the station clean.

I moved to the side to get a view of the entrance to the tube, the underground sign and the people standing underneath the sign. There were two businessman types waiting there. One had an overnight bag and was reading a newspaper. The other carried a briefcase and was looking around him. Odds on that was our man. The blonde woman was still there, waiting for somebody. As she looked around, her eyes caught mine for a split-second and moved on, dismissing me, not what she was looking for. As I walked towards Vincent, her face opened into a smile, a beautiful, genuine thing, as some man rushed up to her and they threw their arms around each other, only slightly more fervently than McGuire had done to me a few minutes earlier. I thought of Linda and felt like smacking my head against a brick wall. But that's not the kind of thing a client wants to see his minder doing and Vincent was now looking straight at me, so I resisted the temptation and forced Linda out of my mind.

'Mr Vincent?'

'And you are...?'

'Jones,' I said. 'I'm to take you to your meeting this afternoon.'

'Good, good. I thought you might be late.' It was bang

on 12.30.

'No, Mr Vincent, we keep perfect time.'

He was a smallish man, in his fifties, beginning to develop a bit of a stomach on him and he had a worried, earnest look on his face, not helped by the fact that he kept adjusting his glasses as though he wasn't used to wearing them. Glasses give some people an air of authority. They made Vincent seem nervous. It was a bit difficult to imagine him as an electronics wizard. He was more of a lay preacher type in some small local parish. His case wasn't chained to his wrist as used to be the fashion, but he was gripping the handle tightly. His knuckles were showing white in places.

He was the talkative type, so I altered my walking position to accommodate him, my eyes scanning the areas around us. To a casual onlooker, we wouldn't look like minder and client so much as business colleagues. I wasn't too worried about the station though. If anyone had wanted the case, they could have taken it from him before I'd arrived.

He was saying that it had been a while since he'd been in London, although he was born here. Now he lived and worked up north and rarely made it down to the capital. Was it still noisy, dirty, vulgar and violent?

'Yes, I'm afraid it is, but then so is every other major city in the world.'

'Oh,' he said, 'I wouldn't know about other cities.'

'Well,' I carried on, 'it's the downside of being in a place where everything happens. If there are pros, there are cons somewhere.'

I don't think he got the pun. He was also a bit put out that I hardly looked at him while we were talking, but I couldn't help that. I could work, or we could down tools and go for a drink, but he was paying for me to work. He couldn't have it both ways.

'It's the pace that gets me,' he said, as we exited the station at the point where Cardington Street joins Melton Street, 'everything is so much faster here.' As he said this, McGuire, who had pulled out from where he'd been parked up the road, came to a stop in front of us. Perfect timing. Vincent didn't even have to break stride.

'Our transport, Sir,' I said, opening the door for him.

Vincent sat on the main seat, facing forwards and I sat opposite him on the tip-up. McGuire did a quick U-turn and headed north. He was right, we made good time. Vincent kept up a running commentary on London as we drove. I wasn't sure if he was nervous, or just talkative by nature. It certainly seemed as though he would have preferred to be back home and not in the big, bad city. Everything was wrong about it. Well, some people love London and some hate it. A lot of Londoners do both at once and they're probably nearest the truth.

Harrow is not quite London, but it's too close to call. The postcode may be outside, but the feeling is of outer London. McGuire hadn't said anything throughout the journey. He knew how to do the job and now he reached back and tapped the glass panel between us, behind my head. I checked my watch: we were in good time. The panel was already open slightly, in case we'd had to talk to each other. Now I asked him to do a quick circuit. That way I could check the area. He nodded and slipped a card over his shoulder to me through the gap. It was a business card with his mobile number on it. Good man. At least one of us was thinking straight.

The road was just off what seemed to be a main street. There was restricted parking along the road and the small car park at the front of the hotel was full. McGuire would have to drop us and park up elsewhere. It was a semi-residential street, with a couple of offices amongst the houses. It seemed a strange place for a meeting, but perhaps it was a central point for the others. Vincent started to protest as McGuire drove past the hotel without stopping, but I told him not to worry, we were just doing the job properly. Nobody in parked cars, no shadowed doorways, it looked good. We slipped into a one-way system and made our way back to the hotel in a circle. This time McGuire pulled in to the front car park and stopped right outside the main entrance. I got out and held the door open for Vincent, who had gone quiet and he got out of the cab, clutching his case to him.

At the desk I let Vincent do the talking, he knew who to ask for. The meeting was in a room at the rear of the hotel. I walked him through to find an ante-room with four men in it. As we entered, the two that had been sitting down, stood up. These weren't the people Vincent was to meet, these were the bodyguards. Looking at them, I realised what sort of men would be waiting in the main room. High-powered men. Not necessarily crooked, but probably ruthless in their dealings. I had the immediate impression that Vincent was out of his league. Glancing at him, I think he knew it. I felt sorry for the guy. Whatever he'd come up with was pushing him into areas that he might not be able to handle and he was beginning to recognise that. I walked him over to the connecting door to the main room. One of the guards was there first, knocking and entering ahead of us. The other three followed us in. None of them took the chance of staying behind.

There were three men inside the main room, which meant that one of them was important enough, or thought he was important enough, to have two bodyguards with him. Each of the men greeted Vincent and he was asked to please sit down. I looked around the room. It was obviously a conference room, small, but kitted out with the boardroom table and chairs. Someone had closed the curtains. Good security, but was it really necessary? I glanced at Vincent. What did he have that was so important? Or maybe the security measures were for one, or all, of the other men. All three of them looked like hard businessmen and prosperous. One of them looked around at the others and then spoke to the hired help.

'Thank you, gentlemen, if you'd like to wait outside, I think we can take it from here.' It was a dismissal. The other bodyguards filed out. I stayed a moment, leaned close to Vincent and said quietly, 'You need anything, you shout, okay? I'll be right outside, I'm not going anywhere.' I didn't really need to say it, but he looked so intimidated that I wanted to make him realise someone was on his side. He looked at me with a slightly nervous smile.

'Yes, thank you,' he said.

I took one more look at the three men, who were waiting for me to leave and then without hurrying, left the room. Not much of a protest, to walk slowly, but the best I could do. They'd put my back right up, which is unfair of me, since I didn't know any of them, but they, and their clothes and their manner, exuded money and power and I felt like I was leaving Vincent to be slaughtered, like the proverbial lamb. I noticed as I left the room that three of the other four guards were still watching me, eyes not leaving me until the door was closed behind us. Even then, I wouldn't say anyone relaxed. It was a very strange atmosphere in that ante-room. These were professionals and everyone was watching everyone else. There were straight backed chairs in the room and all but one of us took one and moved it to a position we were comfortable with, somewhere that gave a view of everyone else and of the connecting door.

Whichever of the businessmen had brought two men with him had got it about right. One to take care of him and one to deal with any trouble, if it occurred. The rest of us were at a disadvantage. One of the team of two remained standing by the connecting door. They changed over after about twenty minutes. It was a bit of an odd scene, although with a serious side. Five suited men, sitting or standing around a smallish room, each with a view of the others, waiting for the possibility of trouble. I'd been in situations like this before, but often there'd been some small talk, or some kind of lessening of the vigilance, but not here. It wasn't exactly tense, just watchful. It suddenly struck me that, illegal or otherwise, I was probably the only one in the room without a gun. Cheers, Mick! If anything did happen, they would all pull their various weapons and I'd be there holding my mini torch and a Bic biro. I wondered if Vincent knew that I wasn't carrying. Maybe he just didn't realise that everyone else was.

It was getting pretty warm in the room, but I couldn't take off my jacket. No point in showing them that I had no gun. So I just relaxed on my chair and made a subtle show of shifting an imaginary bulge under my left arm. Well, they weren't to know there was nothing there, were they?

The meeting lasted about forty minutes. It must have been scheduled for that, since Vincent had a three o'clock train to catch. I spent the time staying alert and making value judgements about my four colleagues from their appearances. These were definitely pros. Only one of them fitted the stereotype that people have of bodyguards; the big, beefy, square-jawed guy, with his chest bulging out of his jacket. The others were my sort of height, two of them perhaps a little heavier, all of them with that recognisable watchfulness and an ease of movement that comes with experience and the knowledge that you know what you are doing. I hoped they saw the same thing in me, but I wasn't really sure. I was doing everything right, but I was out of practise. I suppose I should have been flattered that Mick had put me into this kind of job straight away, but I wasn't relaxed enough yet to pat myself on the back.

At a little before a quarter past two, the phone in the ante-room rang and one of the team of two, the one sitting down, picked it up. A few seconds later there was a 'yes, Sir' and he looked up to us. 'They're finished,' he said, getting up. The rest of us followed him to the connecting door and into the main room. All the briefcases were closed and the table cleared. No sign of any 'product' of any kind. The businessmen were all standing, two of them shaking hands with Vincent and moving off with their guards. One of the team of two said something into his jacket. An inside brooch mike for his radio, telling the car they were coming out. They moved off with their man. The second businessman's guard didn't contact anybody. I wondered if he was driving the man himself.

The third client stayed talking to Vincent in the main room for a while. I moved to the phone that was on the table and, keeping my eyes on the men in the room, dialled McGuire's mobile number. He picked it up immediately.

'Coming out soon,' I said, 'okay?'

'Yes,' he answered, 'but they've put down the barrier across the car park entrance, 'cos it's full and I can't get in. You'll have to walk him to the road.'

'Understood.' I put the phone down. It wasn't ideal, but I couldn't really see a problem. A lot of the work is like that. A compromise between how you'd ideally like to do things and the circumstances that you have to deal with. If any of the people that Vincent had met wanted to relieve him of his 'product' or plans, they would be unlikely to do it here. They'd all seemed to be individuals and, as individuals, anything that they might plan to do would be attempted away from the others. McGuire would have to make sure we weren't tailed back to Euston from here and I would have to get him on the train without any tags. After that, he was on his own. Our job would be over. Vincent wasn't hurrying though. He appeared to have relaxed more, but he still kept fidgeting with his glasses and the way he was talking now, we might not even make it to the train by three.

The two men started walking from the room, through the hotel to the front entrance, still talking to each other and shepherded along by the other bodyguard, slightly ahead and to the right of his man and myself, slightly to the left and almost level with Vincent. We'd automatically moved into a two man team formation, on a diagonal, although in reality we were each only interested in our own client. At the hotel doors, the other guard took the lead and signalled us through. I brought up the rear. The two clients seemed oblivious to their surroundings.

As I walked into the car park area, I looked around. At one end of the street, maybe a little over a hundred yards away, a policeman was checking some parked cars. He didn't notice us, but it was a reassuring presence. A couple of kids, teenagers, were passing in front of the hotel, left to right. McGuire was waiting in front and just to the left of the car park entrance. It looked like the other bodyguard was also the other man's driver and they seemed to be parked on the street as well, but to the right. Our two clients were standing on the pavement now, but still talking to each other. Not the best situation to have them in, standing in the open, but it looked clear. Vincent was maybe ten yards from our taxi. I was closer, to his left, the other guard to the right of his man.

One of the kids, he looked about sixteen or seventeen, turned back to face us. He was, perhaps, fifteen yards away.

'Got the time, mate?' he asked, walking towards the other bodyguard, who was closest to him. The man was good. He didn't look at his watch. It's a basic rule. You never take your eye off a possible opponent. It's a fact that most people, if you ask them the time, will know more or less what it is, within say a quarter of an hour, without checking. What the kid had done was a standard trick. Ask someone the time and as they look at their watch, you've got them. Another one is to ask somebody for some change. They put their hand in their pocket, look down to see what they've got and the next time they look up is from the floor. The kid hadn't got this one quite right though. He'd been too far away when he'd asked the question, but the response was correct.

'About 2.15,' the guard said, in a neutral voice. He knew how to do it. Non-confrontational.

The other kid was moving as well now, to the right, a flanking movement. It looked like they'd done this before. I gave McGuire a hand signal and he rolled the cab up. I stepped in front of Vincent. The kid was fronting the other guard.

'How do you know, mate, you haven't looked at your watch?'

'Don't need to, son,' he said quietly, 'I looked a couple of minutes ago.'

'Well in that case,' said the kid, 'you'd better just give us whatever money you've got.' As he said this, he pulled a knife from inside his jacket and flicked it open.

He was about two or three yards away from the guard. If it hadn't have been a serious situation, it would have been funny. Whatever Vincent had, it was obviously worth a lot to somebody and now we were being mugged for our loose change. It was the sort of stupid incident that some people call coincidence and I call God having a good laugh.

The bodyguard wasn't really worried about the blade. He started to reach inside his jacket, going for his gun. I didn't think for one moment that he was going to shoot the little bastard, just show him the gun and scare him off, but the policeman picked that moment to look up and take in the scene. He couldn't see the knife held by the kid, who had his back to him, but he would certainly see a gun. Legal or not, I didn't think the policeman would make a distinction at this stage.

Now I had a problem. The correct move was to throw Vincent in the back of the cab, and take off. There would be no problem doing that and my only concern should be for my client. But if I did that and the kid went for one of the others, or the guard pulled the gun, the policeman would be on it in a flash. He wouldn't get to us in the cab, but he might get the registration number and he'd want us for statements at the least. We might or might not get intercepted before getting out of the area, so we'd have to change transportation, which would waste time and we were already late. The second last thing that I wanted was to have Vincent miss his train and be stuck baby-sitting him for hours until the next one, when I needed to be off on my own business. I could hardly take him with me. The last thing I wanted, though, was to spend the next few hours in a police station answering questions.

So I didn't move Vincent anywhere. Instead I said, 'Hold it.'

I was speaking to the bodyguard, although everyone stopped moving. The guard turned his body side on, so that he could see both me and the kid. I nodded down the street to where the policeman was still looking at us. I knew what

Al would have said. 'Take control of the situation. You can be in a bad position, but still be in control of what's happening.' I thought as quickly as I could. What I wanted was to get out of this without losing time, without getting arrested and, of course, without getting knifed. So I took control. I spoke to the kid. Friendly voice. He didn't look like he was high. He looked like he could be talked down.

'Nice little situation, isn't it?'

'You're the ones with the problem here, not me. I just want the money quickly.'

'Listen,' I said, 'if you go for one of us with the knife, that policeman is going to see it happen.'

'Yeah.' He gave a short laugh. 'But that old sod'll never catch me. I'm not local and I'll be way out of here before he gets anywhere near me. But you, you can't go anywhere, not with those two with you. And I saw the gun, but I'm not stupid. If it was legal, he'd have pulled it, but he didn't, which means he can't touch me with it, not in front of the police.' He paused and looked from one to the other of us. 'Now, I want the money, or I will use this knife. I will use it.'

He was lowering himself slowly into a semi-crouch without, I think, even knowing it. I spoke to Vincent.

'Get in the cab, Sir.'

'Don't move,' said the kid. 'Don't get in that cab.'

Vincent looked at me. Funny thing was, he didn't look any more nervous than he had done since I'd met him. Maybe that was his normal expression.

'Go on,' I said gently, 'get in the cab.'

The moment he was in, McGuire would get him out of the immediate area, although given the nature of the threat, random rather than actually targeting the client, McGuire would probably not go too far, circle back and pick me up. If it had been a specific threat, he'd leave me behind and just take Vincent well away, as Harwood had done for Broussier, only better.

Vincent started to move to the cab and I moved towards the kid with the knife. His friend, off to the side, was not moving, watching the interplay, not sure which way to jump. I was still three or four yards away from the knife.

'I think you've got the problem, son,' I said. 'In case you haven't realised it, neither of us are particularly worried about the blade.'

With the two of us standing closer to him, the kid was beginning to sweat, no longer in control.

'I'll use it, I swear I'll use it.'

'Yes, perhaps you will,' I said, 'but how well will you use it.' I was now standing about six feet from him.

'Have you ever killed somebody? Have you ever put that knife deep into somebody, not just a cut, or a slash, or a threat, but a killing? 'Cos if you come at me with that knife that's what you're going to have to do.' My voice was no longer friendly. Now it was hard. I had that ice cold feeling again, conjured up out of nowhere. I wasn't looking at the kid, I was looking through him. And he could feel it.

'If you cut me, you're going to have to kill me. Because if you don't, I'm going to take that knife off you and slit your throat with it, police or no police. I'll have witnesses that it was self-defence and if I go down for it, then I go down. It's not a problem. I can do time standing on my head. But I don't think you can. And if you do kill me, with a policeman fifty yards away, then you will go down for it.' I paused for a moment, then asked him, 'How old are you?'

He looked at me uncertainly.

'Eighteen,' he said.

There's a point sometimes in a confrontation, when the pendulum swings. This was it. As he said 'eighteen', he stopped being a hard case and turned back into a common rat-bag again. He'd lost control. He'd handed it to me.

'Eighteen,' I said. 'Old enough to do time.' I heard McGuire pulling away from the kerb and driving off. Saw the cab go past in front. He flicked the hazards on and off telling me he'd be coming back for me. I hadn't taken my eyes off the kid.

'You ever been inside before, son?' He didn't answer. He wasn't supposed to. I had the advantage now and I was using it.

'New piece of meat like you, in for manslaughter, on the bad boys block, they'll have you six ways before breakfast, you don't stand a chance, you're not that hard.'

He looked from me to the other guard, who was now half-smiling at him.

He knew it was over as well. Then he glanced around for his mate. He couldn't see him and he didn't want to take his eyes off me for long enough to look properly. I helped him out.

'Your friend's gone, son. Crossed the street and walked away.'

'No,' he said, 'he wouldn't.'

'He has.'

He risked a glance to his right. His partner was gone.

'Now,' I said, 'that policeman is thirty yards behind you and coming this way. Put the knife away, cross the road and walk off.'

He still wasn't sure, something was stopping him. Pride maybe, or stupidity.

'Go on, son,' I said, still not raising my voice, 'that will end it.'

'Yeah... yeah,' he said, straightening up. The knife disappeared, back in his jacket. The other guard spoke for the first time.

'You are one lucky little bastard,' he said, "cos if I had my way, you'd be bleeding and dying right here on this pavement.'

The kid looked at him and saw it was the truth. He blinked a few times. Then he turned and jogged across the road, following the direction his friend had taken. Maybe there'd be a knifing here today anyway.

The policeman was still strolling towards us. The other guard looked at me and nodded. Then he walked his man the few yards to their car, put him in the back, got in the driver's seat and sped off. The policeman approached me.

'Everything all right, Sir?' he asked.

'Yes,' I said, smiling, 'absolutely.'

I turned and walked away from him. When I reached the corner and turned, McGuire was pulling in to wait for me. He'd worked his way around the one-way system and back. As I got in the back, McGuire nodded to me. It was a 'well done' nod. I sat opposite Vincent again, on the tip-up seat. He wanted to know what had happened, so I told him. He went quiet and didn't speak much on the journey down to Euston.

McGuire made excellent time back down to town and we arrived at the station a few minutes before three. As I got out of the cab, I signed to McGuire that I'd call him. He wouldn't move from here until I did, in case I had to bring Vincent out again for any reason, possibly in a hurry.

Vincent was still quiet as I walked him into the station. It was only a couple of minutes to three. I hoped he wasn't going to want to buy a book or something at this late stage.

'Got your ticket ready, Mr Vincent?'

'What? Yes, yes I have. Sorry, I was miles away.'

He showed it to the man at the gate and I explained that

I was putting him on the train. Maybe I should have had a platform ticket, but he let me through anyway. We walked down to the train. He seemed to be the last passenger to board. As he was getting on he said to me:

'That boy, if he hadn't have given up, what would you have done?' He looked worried again.

'I'd have taken him out.'

'Yes, but what would you have done? You wouldn't have hurt him badly, would you? You wouldn't really have killed him?'

This was a little unusual. Most clients don't care what happens to someone who threatens them, as long as they themselves end up in one piece and unhurt.

'I hope it wouldn't have come to that,' I said. I tried for a sincere voice. For once, it wasn't too difficult.

He looked at me and for almost the first time since I'd met him, the worried look left his face and he stopped fidgeting with his glasses.

'Yes,' he said, 'I believe you do mean that. Good.' It was a strange thing to say, or maybe it was just the way that he said it. He closed the carriage door behind him. The window was open.

'Why is it good?' I asked him.

He looked straight at me.

'Because killing is wrong,' he said.

The train moved off.

*

I started to walk back through the station towards McGuire. Suddenly I realised that I didn't want to see him now. I didn't want the smiling face or the big, cheerful thump on the back. Bloody Vincent! 'Killing is wrong.' What did he know about killing? Maybe he'd once washed a spider down the plug hole in the bath, but that would be about it. I made for the public telephones and called McGuire's mobile number. I think he was a bit put out that I hadn't come back out in person, since it was only a few minutes walk, but I explained that I was really pushed for time.

'Don't worry about it then,' he said, 'we'll talk again soon. You can always call me on the mobile and Mick's got my home number. We should get together and have a drink and a talk.'

'Yeah, we'll do that, Sean. I'll call you in a little while, I might be away for a few days. And thanks for your help today, it's good to have someone who knows what they're doing.'

'Don't thank me, son, you're the one who dealt with the situation and dealt with it very well. Anytime you need a driver, you get in touch.'

We said our goodbyes and rang off. I called Mick. He answered the phone the way he always does, just a terse 'yes' and nothing else. Mick is convinced that there's a tap on his phone almost all the time, so it's very difficult to get him to say anything on it at all. And if he thinks that you are being indiscreet, he'll just cut you off without a word.

'Everything's fine,' I said.

'Good.'

He didn't ask if there had been any problems, if there had, he would expect me to tell him. That would normally have been about the extent of the conversation. He'd asked me to check in and I had, but today we were actually going to talk to each other.

'What we were discussing,' he said, 'this thing that you have to do, it's soon, right?'

'Yes,' I said, 'it's soon.'

There was a pause.

'Well you take care of yourself,' he said.

'Thanks I – '

'I mean it. I can't afford to lose any more people out of my life. You'd leave a gap, so be careful.'

I started to answer him, but I was talking to a dead line.

*

I made my way to the underground to go home. Linda and Mick, even bloody Vincent telling me I was wrong, it was beginning to do my head in. I knew what I was doing. I'd thought it out. 'Killing is wrong!' Tell that to the warmongers and the arms dealers and the drug barons and the pushers and the religious nuts and the nationalist fanatics and God knows so many other groups. And that's without thinking about the individuals. The psychos, the freaks, the ones who feel 'society' owes them, the ones who just don't care, the petty thief caught in the act, the jealous husband or wife, the ordinary person in the street – they, we, have all thought about it at some time. Killing is a multi-billion pound industry and it's been happening ever since Cain sneaked up on Abel. Maybe it's wrong, but it's one of the things we do so well that we've developed it into an art form. We can kill in so many different ways, primitive to sophisticated. We can kill singly or in hundreds and thousands, precisely or indiscriminately and we're constantly developing better and more devastating ways of doing it. And we've developed the justification for killing into an art form as well. We can justify anything now and frequently do, unless we're so powerful that we don't need to because we're unaccountable. Killing has become part of our culture and even if it is wrong, it seems to be natural for some people. They don't even have to shrug it off, it just doesn't seem to affect them at all.

So what is it that makes people not kill? Perhaps that is the real question. And yes, I could list some of the arguments, the breakdown of society, certain religious teachings, but in the end, the main idea was that it is wrong to take away another's life. Everyone has a basic inalienable right to their own life, whether God-given or not and it is wrong to take away that life force for your own personal gain. It's the basic right of humanity without which there is nothing left. Killing is wrong.

So where did that leave me? It left me in Euston station, trying to justify my decision to take another's life by invoking the images of Harwood and Broussier, Nelson and Linda and myself, all dead or dying and still wondering if I could live with cold blooded murder.

'Mr Garron.'

The low voice from the left cut across my thoughts and triggered instinct. Foreign accent, French. Or Belgian, like Broussier and he'd called me by my real name. React or blank it. Blank it. Don't look up. Don't follow the sound with your eyes. Keep walking.

'Okay, Mr Jones, then.'

This time I stopped and turned to the voice. Calling me Jones meant that this man knew something, maybe about Vincent, or even about Nelson.

'I'm Jones,' I said, looking at him. What I saw didn't reassure me. He was a big man, wearing a belted overcoat. Probably in his mid fifties with grey hair cut short. A heavy man with a stance that was both deliberate and relaxed. This was what unnerved me. This air of quiet confidence and the friendly look in the hard eyes. It was the same look that Al had. It meant a pro.

'Mr Garron, I know you are not Jones and I know that you have been looking after Mr Vincent and I should add that I am very impressed by the way that you – ' he paused for a moment, searching for the right word, ' – carry yourself. He was in good hands.'

I stayed silent, my mind racing, trying to work out who this man was and what the hell was going on. There were a lot of things I could say, but it's always a good idea to stay quiet in the company of professionals, so I kept my mouth shut.

The man seemed to expect me to say something, to acknowledge his compliment, but when I didn't he almost shrugged to himself and carried on.

'Mr Garron, do you know where Jean is?'

Jean. Was that Broussier? It must be. Otherwise it was too much of a coincidence. Play it down. I smiled at him, with, it must be said, an effort.

'My name is Jones and I don't know anyone called Jean.'

He smiled back at me. I hoped the cameras in the station were trained on us. It probably made for quite a nice picture, all smiles.

'Jean,' he said, 'is the Belgian man that you were looking after a few days ago. My problem, Mr Garron, is that I don't know where Jean is and I don't know if you know where he is. I really would like to find him. I am a friend of his.'

My brain was flying again. This could be one of Broussier's Belgian contacts, though God knew how he'd got hold of me. Or it could be an enemy of Broussier and a friend of Smith. I really didn't know what to think, but this man knew too much about what I'd been up to, so I allowed him the fact that I'd been protecting Broussier. I looked straight at him and said:

'I don't know where Jean is.'

He looked back at me and I didn't like it. He was weighing me up.

'If you are a liar, Mr Garron, then you are a good one. If you do see Jean, tell him that Julot is looking forward to seeing him.'

He turned away from me and walked off. I stayed rooted to the spot. I'd just lied straight out to one of the hardest men I'd ever meet in my life. It took me a minute or two to get myself together and then I made my way shakily down to the underground. I was sweating like hell.

*

On the northbound platform of the Northern line, I sat on one of the bench seats, at the end, trying to work out if I'd made a mistake or not. 'Tell him that Julot is looking forward to seeing him.' Was that a threat, or was this Julot the one Broussier was going to meet? I couldn't know. Either way it didn't change my problem of Smith. Unless Julot was connected to Smith. I didn't want to think about that at all. Stick to the game plan, I told myself, stick to the game plan.

There was a small, elderly, white-haired lady sitting at the other end of the bench and no-one in between us. I glanced across at her and she smiled at me. That was when I made the mistake. I don't know why, I didn't feel like it, but I smiled back at her. She picked up her handbag, stood up and shuffled down the two seats to the one next to me.

'So nice to see someone smiling,' she said, sitting down. 'You don't see many people smiling nowdays in London, do you?'

The typical ploy of the unwanted conversationalist. End the sentence with a question and the other person has to answer otherwise they're being rude, which, surprisingly enough for a people who are extremely capable of being rude, we English don't like doing. Especially not to little white-haired old ladies. What I should have done is come out with one of my two lines of French, '*pardonnez-moi, Madame, je ne parle pas l'Anglais*', but I didn't think of it quickly enough. Instead I made my second mistake and said, 'No, I'm afraid not.'

'Well,' she carried on, 'I suppose there's not much to smile about really, is there?' She looked up at me appealingly, willing me to join the conversation. She'd ended with a question again, hadn't she? I'd been out-manoeuvred. I sighed silently to myself and gave in to the sort of dialogue that you can only have with a certain type of little old English lady whilst waiting for a train at Euston underground.

'Well at least it's getting warmer,' I said.

'Ooh yes,' she picked up on that, 'it'll soon be summer, then everyone will be smiling again. Still the summers don't seem to be like they used to, you know, they used to seem hotter and last longer. Bit like my first husband!'

She rocked backwards and forwards laughing. I laughed with her, although not quite as loudly. A couple of our fellow passengers standing nearby gave us sharp looks. I suppose we were an odd couple. They probably thought I was trying to con her out of her life savings.

'You're not married are you?' she said.

I shook my head and she carried on. It's a skill really. With the right facial expressions and the odd 'yes', or 'really' thrown in, I could let her have this conversation all by herself.

'I can always tell, you know. You don't look married. I've been married twice. My first husband was killed in the war, in the infantry he was. Ooh, he was a handsome man.'

She smiled again, this time to herself and I began to feel sorry for her, as I'd been fairly sure I would. She wasn't a nutter, just lonely and in need of some kind of human contact in this cold city. People used to talk to each other in London, but we've forgotten how. You reach out to someone in London now and they want to know what's in it for you.

'Got a girlfriend, have you?'

I suppose I could have lied, cut the conversation short again, but some people need honesty, even if it's nothing to do with them and this little old lady was one of those people.

'That's a good question,' I said, 'I'm not sure right now what the answer is.'

'Had an argument, have you? Ooh, that's no good. You'll have to work that out, you know. She didn't do that to you, did she?'

She meant the bruises. I said she hadn't.

'A lot of young people now seem to give up when they have an argument. What was it about then, or is it personal?'

'Er, no... no, it's not personal,' (what was I saying, how did I get into this conversation?) I closed the subject. 'She just doesn't think I should do something. It's, er, work re-lated.'

For one terrible moment I thought that the next question would be what did I do for a living, but somehow she missed that one. I wondered if being interviewed by the police would be as difficult.

'Well, if she's worth it you'll have to compromise.' I started to point out that I wasn't married, but I gave up. She was off again.

'I compromised on my second marriage,' she said, 'I think I compromised from the very beginning.' She laughed again. 'Anyway, he's dead as well now, these past six years.'

Any minute I thought, the grandchildren photographs would come out. I glanced at the train information board. Three minutes to the next train. She started rummaging in her handbag.

'I've got some photos here somewhere, of the family, if you'd like to see them.'

I mumbled something vaguely in the yes category and out came the snapshots. We were like old friends now, huddled over family photos.

'That's my daughter and son in law, they live in Canada now. They asked me to go out there but I didn't want to, you know.'

A list of names and children went past me and I realised that she wasn't just lonely, she was hurting. Maybe it's worse to be old and lonely than young and lonely. When you're young, you might have a future. When you're old, all you've got is a past. If you're lucky.

The train came in suddenly and caught us by surprise. There wasn't time for her to get all the photos away, so I picked up her bag for her, while she held on to the pictures and we boarded the train and sat down next to each other. At some point this lady would have trouble. She'd let me pick up her handbag and one day she would lose it to someone. She didn't seem to be worried about me though. Maybe she was naive. Or maybe she'd seen something in me that told her I was all right. I wondered what it could have been. I almost asked her, but I didn't think it would be fair.

'How far are you going?' she asked me.

'Just the two stops,' I said, 'Camden Town.'

She seemed quite disappointed. As we pulled into Camden she said to me, 'Now you make it up with your young lady, otherwise you'll regret it later, believe me.'

I smiled at her. 'Yes,' I said, 'I probably will.' And I meant it.

As I got off the train I could hear her starting on the lady opposite her. 'Such a nice young man,' she was saying. She was only partly wrong.

*

I didn't go up to the flat, there was no reason to and I was running late. I wanted to talk to Broussier about the Frenchman or Belgian or whatever he was, but there just wasn't time. I had to make it to the East End by four and it was tight already, so I got straight into the van and drove straight off. No tapes this time, I stuck to the local radio for the traffic news. All I needed now was a traffic jam down City Road or Old Street and I'd be in real trouble.

I was supposed to meet Castle outside a shop on Cannon Street at four and I struggled to get there in time. There's nothing more frustrating than sitting in a London traffic jam when you need to be somewhere else. At least it wasn't the rush hour. I somehow managed to reach Whitechapel at about ten to four and made my way through the streets of wholesale fabric shops and warehouses 'till I found a place to park up, on a road near New Street. Cannon Street was the other side of Commercial Road. I left everything in the van, the torch, the coins, even my pen, crossed over the road and started down Cannon Street. I could see why Castle had picked this place to collect me. It's a Bengali neighbourhood and I wasn't the right colour to be hanging around. Back on the main road I would have been fine. There are plenty of whites working the businesses there, but a hundred yards down this road and I was on my own. I wasn't a trader and I wasn't a local. It wasn't the worst place to be, but it wasn't the best either. I'd probably be okay if I kept moving, but if I stood still for too long I'd be loitering. Castle was no fool. One white man standing around for no good reason for just a minute would get away with it, but if I'd brought anyone with me we'd be thought to be a threat by the local community. If I had someone follow me he'd stand out a mile unless he was an Asian himself. Given the number of racist attacks the Bengalis had suffered, I didn't begrudge them their attitude, but it didn't help me much. Being dressed smartly didn't help in this place either. I didn't look official, but I looked like somebody.

I remember once, in Notting Hill, I was supposed to meet Al and I couldn't find the place. In those days there was a lot of dealing going on there. I'd walked around the block and the eyes on the street had followed me. I was dressed in a suit and I don't know whether they thought I was old bill or easy prey, but I learnt a lesson that evening. I still hadn't found the place, so I took another turn around the block. Same route as before. This time the eyes didn't just follow me, the people did. I'd been around twice. That spelled trouble. They just didn't know which kind yet and I wasn't about to hang around until they decided. I was going to just keep walking, but for once I got lucky. A cab went past and I waved it down. Forget meeting Al, I just drove out of the area. Since then I've been pretty careful about avoiding patterns and making sure I blend in, wherever I am.

But not this time. Castle had seen to that. The meeting place was opposite a council estate half way down Cannon Street. Again, perfect for him, not for me. I checked my watch and slowed down. I didn't want to have to walk past and double back. A couple of lads were sitting on a wall by the estate on the other side of the road, checking me out. Three minutes to four. As I slowed and looked at one of the few shops there, one of them slid off the wall and disappeared. Not good. I hoped my watch was slow.

I'd reached the meeting place. There was nowhere else to go. The Bengali youth on the wall kept his eyes on me. I flicked my gaze at him and then away again, not challenging, just showing him that I wasn't scared of him, which I wasn't. It was the fifteen other teenagers that would arrive any moment that worried me. I'd really had enough of teenagers today.

A minute to go.

The youth was joined by a couple more Bengalis, older,

neither of them the one that had been there before. He'd still be gathering the recruits. We locked eyes for a second and I looked away. If Castle didn't come, they might not want to let me leave without telling me not to come back.

From further down the road I saw a black taxi approaching. It was twenty seconds to four o'clock. The cab pulled up in front of me, obscuring the growing group of Bengalis. A huge West Indian man opened the passenger door.

'Who you waiting for?' he called.

'Castle,' I said.

'Who are you?'

'Jones.'

He motioned for me to get in the cab, but I held back.

'Wait a minute,' I said, 'who sent me to you?'

The man's head disappeared inside the cab and then reappeared.

'Mick.'

I nodded at him and he moved back and made room for me to get in the cab. It was moving before I'd shut the door. Remembering to keep my hands in view, I sat back in the rear seat and glanced behind me through the back window at the group of Bengali youths. They were all looking at the rear of the cab. The message was clear. They would remember my face. It was the sort of message I wouldn't have to write down to keep in mind.

Aside from the big guy, who was sitting opposite me, there was a small black man in the cab, sitting next to me. He looked me over carefully.

'I left a message for you not to be early.' His voice was soft, almost at odds with the strong face. No accent.

I didn't try to argue that I'd only been two or three minutes early. It wouldn't cut any ice with this guy. Besides, I was still working on relaxing the tension that had built up in my mind and body.

'I misjudged the length of the street,' I said.

He didn't smile. 'You shouldn't misjudge things, it's a dangerous thing to do.'

There was a short silence. The driver, also a West Indian, was heading East. The big man was looking at me with total indifference. If he had to, he'd break me. If he didn't need to, he wouldn't. It didn't matter which.

I wasn't going to break the silence. Mick had told me that Castle was a pro. Rule number one when dealing with professionals is no idle chat and no questions. You speak if there's something to say and at the moment there wasn't. Castle knew what I was here for and when he was ready he'd start the ball rolling. Eventually he said:

'Okay, this is how it works. I don't know you. I know what you say you want, but I don't say anything until I know that we're the only ones listening to the conversation.'

Now I understood the silence. He was waiting to see if I initiated a conversation on guns or buying weapons for the sake of a wire. The fact that I hadn't didn't make me genuine, but it showed I wasn't stupid. I could still be wearing a wire, but good enough to leave it to him to start. I felt pleased with myself. I knew I was genuine, but I could be genuine and still not have the man's respect and for some reason, I wanted him to respect me. Mick's recommendation would only get me so far. The rest was up to Castle's assessment of me. I'd scored maybe half a point by keeping my mouth shut. I'd score another half for not complaining about being searched for a wire and by not making any stupid comments when the search got personal.

'Take off your shoes and your jacket and loosen your belt.'

'Sure.' Not friendly, not resigned, just neutral.

The big man took my jacket and shoes and went through them. Checked the lining of the jacket and the heels of the shoes. Castle just watched, one hand inside his coat. That made sense. If I wasn't for real and they were going to find something, now would be the time that I'd have to move. If I had wanted to get away, I don't think I'd have got too far.

When he'd finished with my shoes and jacket, the big man put them to one side and asked, no, told me to lean forward. I didn't have to lean very far, since he was on the tip-up seat across from me and he was such a size that there wasn't a lot of distance between us. He knew his job well. He didn't start with my clothes, he started with me. He checked through my hair and behind and just inside my ears. Worked his way down from there very thoroughly, paying special attention to my collar and tie, and to the waistband and belt on my trousers. I just sat still and let him do his job. Off the top of my head, I could think of other people I'd rather be bodysearched by, but they probably wouldn't suit Castle's requirements as well as this man. Finally he sat back, handed my jacket to me and nodded to Castle.

'Okay,' said Castle. 'Now usually we could do business here and now since you come recommended, but I'm told you need to try the product out.'

He was avoiding the words gun or shoot. I suppose it was force of habit and not a bad habit to get into either. He was still talking.

'That means we have to go to one of my centres and I don't like people knowing where they are.'

'What do you want to do,' I asked, 'blindfold me?'

He almost smiled. 'Nothing so crude, friend, this isn't the middle ages. You just put these on.' He handed me a pair of dark glasses with side eye-pieces. 'These will be enough.'

I put them on and the world disappeared. They weren't

just dark glasses, they were blacked out glasses. Clever though. From outside the cab, no-one looking in would think twice about a man wearing sunglasses.

'Just sit back and enjoy the ride.'

That didn't make me feel any better. The last time I'd heard that line was in a James Bond movie and that was just before they tried to feed him to the sharks or something like that. I'm no different from most people. I like to know where I'm going and how I'm getting there, just in case I have to find my own way back. If Mick hadn't sent me to this man, I'd be worried by now, although as I sat back I realised that he was just protecting himself. He wasn't doing anything that I wouldn't do in his position. The only difference was that he was doing it to me.

I began to relax a little, but I felt totally disorientated. We drove for maybe twenty or thirty minutes, but I have no idea where we went. We didn't seem to be going around in circles, but a good driver could have doubled back on himself without allowing me to notice. I thought we crossed the river, but I can't even be sure of that. The end result was that we could have driven miles away, or been just around the corner from where we started.

When we stopped Castle said, 'Don't take off the glasses yet, Jones, we'll help you out.'

I heard the door open and Castle moved out. I went to slide over to his side and follow him, but I hadn't been helped yet and 'help' was the operative word. A grip like a vice took my arm and it bloody hurt. It was the same arm that had been kicked half to pieces on Saturday night and it wasn't quite ready to be seized like this. I was very good though I didn't make much of a noise. The big man had taken my arm just above the elbow and now made sure that I moved at the pace that he wanted me to move at. No faster and no slower. I should introduce this guy to Smith's gorilla. They might know each other already of course, from attending the same charm school.

'Mind the step, Jones,' Castle's voice, but too late, I'd tripped over it. I didn't hit the floor though, just stayed in mid-air as I regained my footing, suspended by my left arm from this huge man's grip. He was definitely strong. He'd held my weight up, all eleven stones and five pounds of it, in one hand, with only a little help from the edge of my right foot on the floor. The other reason I knew he was strong was because my left hand was slowly going numb as he cut off the circulation to it. I mentioned this to him and he eased off a fraction. After all, I was a paying customer.

I heard a door close behind me.

'You can take off those glasses now, Jones.'

I did and blinked a few times. I was in a dimly lit hallway at the top of a steep flight of stairs, a few feet inside the door. Castle was half way down the stairs in front of me. There was another flight going up. I followed Castle down. The heavy followed me. Either he trusted me now, or he was making his first mistake. His distancing behind me was wrong. All I had to do was reach behind me on the stairs and I could hook his leg with my arm and bring him down. I didn't do it, just contented myself with a tactical victory.

At the bottom of the steps, we entered a small room where Castle told me to take off my jacket. I threw it on a chair. We then went through a door into a long empty room, partitioned at one end with glass or clear Perspex sheets. The room had thick walls covered with cork on the inside. Sound-proofed. This was the range. We were in the partitioned section. Castle opened a locker by the wall and took out a revolver and a couple of boxes of ammunition. He turned back to me.

'Okay, Jones, rules. At no time do you load any gun in here unless I tell you to do so. If you do, he'll shoot you.'

I glanced at the big man. He'd taken off his jacket and he had a gun tucked into his waistband. It seemed tiny against the bulk of his body. Castle continued, looking me in the eye while he spoke.

'That's my protection, okay, so you never hold a loaded gun on me. When you fire, we'll be standing behind you on this side of the screen. When you finish, you put the gun on the table there and step away from it. If you turn around holding the gun, he will shoot you. Only load the number of bullets that you want to fire in each round. Don't put any in your pockets. I'm explaining this to you because you're a first-timer. These are my rules. To protect me. Don't take them as a threat. They're just the rules.'

I nodded, holding his gaze. I hadn't done a lot of shooting at all, but these seemed to be basic gun club rules. Just with a stronger penalty if you ignored them.

'You done any shooting before?'

'Some, not much.'

'Not a member of any shooting clubs, then?' The words 'shooting clubs' were emphasised, sneered at almost. The professional judgement on the amateurs.

'No.'

'Good. Maybe you won't think you're John Wayne then. What have you used before?'

'I've fired semi-automatic pistols before, just target range shooting.'

'So you know how to load a magazine and strip the gun down?'

'More or less. I know how to load and eject. Stripping it down I might need a refresher on.' I felt like a total beginner. It was embarrassing.

'Okay. Mick said you ought to have a double action revolver. You know what that is?'

'Yeah. You can just pull the trigger, you don't have to
pull back the hammer each time, pulling the trigger cocks it
automatically.'

'Yes, but you've never used one before?'

'No.'

Castle looked at me dubiously. He was probably wondering why Mick had sent him this total novice. I could see him
deliberating. Probably about whether to throw me out or not.

'Okay. If you want I can give you a semi-automatic pistol
instead of the revolver, if you're happier with something you
know. But the revolver is mechanically much easier. You
might be better off with it.'

'Look,' I said, 'you're the expert. I don't want to waste
your time. You tell me what you think and I'll go along with
it. I'm a beginner. Unfortunately, I'm going to have to learn
quickly.'

'Okay,' he said and gave me a sort of resigned smile.
'Mick said you might need help. He also said I wouldn't have
to explain things twice.'

'I hope not,' I said.

'First thing then, what do you want the gun to do?' He
carried on as I started to answer. 'I mean what kind of situation is it for? Are you going to need rapid fire, or single shot
accuracy? Are you going to be up against one person, or several? What sort of distance are you going to be from your
target? Are you going to be in a crowd? Are you worried
about hitting passers-by?' he looked at me and smiled, 'or
don't you give a damn? All these things are important, so
don't give me the details, just the situation.'

'One man,' I said, 'as close as I can get. I'd like to do it
with one shot.'

He smiled again. 'We'd all like to do it with one shot, man, all of us.'

I'd worked out what was wrong with his smile. It had no humour in it. He carried on.

'So it's at close range, say within fifteen feet.'

'I hope so.'

'Is it in a crowd?'

'No. Does that make a difference?'

'Oh yes. In a crowd you might have to conceal the weapon. Self loader pistols are flatter and smaller, easier to hide.' I started to say something, but he was in full flow now, a professional on his subject, maybe showing off a bit to the beginner.

'Also you might want to use a silencer in a crowd, causes less panic and confusion, although they don't silence the gun, just suppress the explosive noise. You still hear the mechanical sound of the gun.' He glanced across to the big man and half laughed. 'Unless we get him an old Welrod.' It must have been an in joke and I didn't get it. Castle turned back to me again. 'Old World War Two pistol,' he said. 'The nearest thing yet to a real silent gun.' If there was a joke, I still hadn't got it.

'But silencers are difficult to hide, they're usually bulky things, stand out a mile.' He smiled again. 'Not like in the movies. And then there is the problem of the bullet passing through your target if you've got a powerful gun and injuring somebody else as well.' He looked at me to see if I was getting queasy at the thought. I wasn't. He dropped the lecture bit and got back to business.

'Not in a crowd,' he said.

'No.'

'And you don't need a silencer? I'd advise you against it unless it's absolutely necessary.'

'I don't think I need one.'

'And since you want to take him with one shot, you won't need rapid fire.'

'If you say so.'

'Okay. I'd stick with the revolver then. If you only want two or three shots, then that should do. It'll be safer for you than a semi-auto. Less to go wrong mechanically. If a semi-auto pistol jams on you,' he turned to the locker and got one out to show me, 'you have to rack the side to clear the stoppage.' He demonstrated. It seemed pretty quick to me. He saw my expression. 'Yeah,' he said, 'but you'll be slower.' He put the automatic back and picked out a large revolver to show the difference.

'On a revolver, pull the trigger and a new cartridge comes into the firing line.' He looked at the gun in his hand. 'You know, if you want to stop the man in one shot, this will do it.' He handed the gun, unloaded, to me. The last time I'd seen a gun close up was when Smith had pulled one on me and it had scared me to pieces. Now I was holding what would make us equal. I hoped. It was cold and dull and heavy. It felt like a dead weight in my hand.

'What is it?' I asked.

'Smith and Wesson Hunter .44 Magnum. Bullet will go right through him.'

'Sounds good.' I surprised myself by how cold I sounded. Castle took the gun back.

'Yeah, but if you miss with the first one, which you might well do, then it's difficult to get an accurate second shot in quickly. The recoil is too heavy. Especially for a novice.' He turned back to the locker, put the .44 away.

'If you do want a semi-auto, I've got some Russian pistols with less recoil. Lot of Russian weapons on the market in the last few years, since the country split.' He took two guns out of the locker and handed me the larger of the two.

'Tula Tokarev .33. Very powerful gun. Takes 7.62 mm bottleneck cartridges and has no safety. That's an old gun, but clean. This one is the Makarov 9mm. It's replacing the .33 in Russia as the official state weapon. More police oriented. Less powerful and has a safety catch. This is a new gun, might need time to bed in.'

'These are all semi-autos though, right? And you think I should take a revolver.'

'Yeah, probably.' He sounded slightly disappointed. He handed the Russian guns to the heavy and picked up the revolver he'd first taken out.

'I was going to give you this one, a .38 special snub-nosed with an enclosed hammer, but I'm not so sure now. It's easy to use and safe to carry, but it's not so accurate if you let him get away from close range and it's not got real stopping power.'

'You mean if I shoot someone with this he might not fall down?'

Castle made a see-saw motion with the flat of his hand.

'He might and he might not. He might fall over just from the shock of being shot, or he might not notice it at all. 'Specially if he's really hyped up, or on crack or something.'

'I don't think that's likely.' I couldn't see Smith as a druggie. At the same time, I couldn't see him falling over from shock either. 'So what do I do?'

'What you do, Jones,' Castle said, 'is you make sure you hit something vital, preferably more than once and with something heavier than this snub-nose.' He put the gun back. 'What you need is expanding ammunition. Something that will do damage.' He was half talking to me and half to himself. 'That's it.' He pulled out a bigger gun and handed it to me.

'Smith and Wesson 686, taking .357 magnum expanding bullets. A stopper of a gun.'

I weighed it in my hand. 'It's a bit bigger than the last one, isn't it?'

'Got to be, Jones, got to be. I could give you a smaller gun that takes the same bullets, but there'd be no point. If you fire an expanding bullet from a short barrelled gun, it won't expand when it hits your target and you've lost the whole point of using it. The 686 here, has a six inch barrel which is long enough to use the bullets effectively. It's also safe to carry around and it's easy to use. No safety to worry about, unlike the autos, it hits very hard and I'll even throw in a speedloader for you.'

'What's a speedloader?' I asked and immediately wished I hadn't. It was obviously something that everybody ought to know.

'A speedloader,' Castle said slowly, 'is a simple device that allows you to load all the cartridges into the revolver's cylinder at once instead of one at a time, hence saving time, hence "speedloader". You said you haven't used a revolver before so I'll show you how to do it in a minute, but I think this is the gun for you.'

I looked at the weapon in my hand. Somehow it didn't look as vicious as the .44 Magnum had. I held it out in front of me as Al had showed me. It felt good and bad at the same time. There was a difference between holding a gun on a practice range and holding one prior to buying and using it.

'What do you think?' Castle asked me.

I glanced at the big man who looked bored and at Castle who obviously thought that this was the right gun.

'I'll go with what you say,' I told him.

'Good.' He spoke to the heavy. 'Get me the ammunition for this,' and then to me again. 'Do you need a holster of some kind?'

I thought for a couple of seconds. 'No, I don't think so.'

'Okay, that saves us a fair amount of hassle fitting you for it and sorting out the best draw for you.'

Castle showed me how to load the bullets singly and with the speedloader. Then he set up a target on the range at about twenty feet, which was a little longer than I thought I'd need. He also gave me sponge ear plugs which looked clean enough, so I put them in.

'Don't fire single shots,' he told me, 'fire in groups.'

'Groups of how many?' I asked.

'Depends on who you're shooting at and how many of them there are.'

I remembered Mick saying not to fire too many, since we'd be paying for them later. Castle retreated behind the clear screen with his minder and I stood with my back to them facing up the range. I glanced over my shoulder at them and saw that the big man had his own gun in his hand. I wondered if anyone had ever died standing where I was standing now.

I loaded three bullets into the cylinder and took Al's right handed firing position. Gun in the right hand, right arm extended, but not fully. Left hand supporting the right hand and the butt of the gun, taking the weight of the weapon. Left thumb over the right thumb and left arm bent slightly more than the right. Both legs bent slightly, a little more than shoulder width apart, the left foot a half step further forward than the right.

Relaxed.

Breathed in and as I breathed out, slowly squeezed the trigger.

The explosion seemed louder than when I'd last fired a gun. The recoil much stronger. I steadied the gun as fast as I could and fired again. I was aware now of the strength of the recoil, tried to adjust to allow for it and fired the third shot.

I put the gun down on the table and stepped back from it before Castle stepped past the screen towards me. My heart was pounding and my mouth was dry. Not so much from the gun, but because I'd seen Smith in front of me as I fired.

'Go down and bring back the target.'

He wouldn't walk in front of me.

I brought back the human upper body silhouette target without enthusiasm. I might as well have left it there. I'd missed completely twice and hit the white paper surrounding the silhouette once. Not too impressive. Castle wasn't worried though. Of course, he wouldn't be there when I had to shoot someone.

'Don't worry, Jones, it takes time to get used to a weapon. But remember, if you cock the weapon – pull back the hammer, then you're on what is, relatively, a hair trigger. You should be able to do that for the first shot if you're not going for speed. After that, it's faster to just pull the trigger, but then you can get a drag effect as you pull it all the way through. That's what happened to you just now. I saw you trying to relax, but you have to relax more, while keeping those hands steady. Put the target back up and try it again.'

I walked the twenty feet to the hooks and put the same target back up again. It was hardly marked so there was certainly no point in changing it. I walked back, aware of the two men's eyes on me. The big man's indifferent, Castle's with slightly more interest. He knew Mick and he was probably wondering what my connection to him was.

This time I loaded six bullets for two bursts of three each. Settled into position. I wasn't interested in practising drawing the gun and firing, I was going to be holding the gun when I met Smith, not trying to beat him to the draw.

Breathed in and out again. This time I didn't just see Smith in front of me, I looked for him. Cocked the gun and the first shot went true. I felt the second kick and pulled the gun back for the third. Paused, cocked it again for the first shot of the second set. Fired them off, learning from the first three.

I checked my position after the final shot. It seemed to be good, but I'd tensed right up again. I laid the gun on the table and went to collect the target. Castle checked it with me.

'That's better, you're settling to it.'

There were three shots in a ragged group at the top of the chest and two slightly lower. One bullet was missing completely. Probably the second shot that I'd felt kick away. Before he moved back behind the screen, Castle said:

'What you've got to do, Jones, is stop fighting the gun. You've got to become comfortable with it, as well as becoming used to it. When you shoot at something the gun must be a part of you, not something separate. The bullet is coming from you, not from the gun.'

'Deep,' I thought, 'very deep,' but I didn't say it. I needed all the help I could get.

I loaded three more bullets and this time tried to relax, not just myself, but with the gun. In a strange way what Castle had said seemed to help. I controlled the recoil better and realised what Castle meant by 'dragging' the gun while pulling the trigger all the way through. Two shots in the chest and one on the surrounding white paper higher up. I'd been aiming for the head on the third shot. Two to stop the man and the third a kill shot to the head.

I fired off another eighteen shots after that. I know that Mick had said to go easy on the range, but this was important. I needed it. By the time I'd finished, the power of the weapon wasn't scaring me anymore. It was reassuring me.

When I'd finished, Castle took the gun and asked me how much ammunition I wanted to take away with me. I didn't need too much. I asked him for enough cartridges to fully load the gun and the speedloader. If I needed more than that I'd be in real trouble. I'd wanted to ask Castle how I'd done for a beginner, but I thought it would make me sound desperate. As it was, he offered his opinion anyway.

'You don't have a bad eye, Jones, with a bit of practise you could be good.'

He looked at me and smiled that humourless smile. 'For the moment though, if you are going to shoot at somebody, I would say get as close as you can, make sure you land with the first shot and then follow it quickly with another two or three.' He stopped smiling. 'And pray that whoever it is, isn't shooting back.'

The heavy was wiping over the gun and speedloader. No prints.

'One more thing,' Castle said. 'The gun is clean now. There's nothing to tie it in to anything else. You can drop it at the scene if necessary and it won't come back to me or you, unless you leave your calling card on it. If you want to hold on to it, that's up to you, but nothing comes back to me.'

It wasn't a threat, just a statement.

And that was it. The practice session was over. The big man held on to my gun and bullets and Castle led the way out of the room and up the stairs. The big man followed me. At the top of the steps I was given the glasses and put them back on again. The heavy took my arm again, but without the same grip this time. I heard the front door open and smelled fresh air. Well, fresh compared to a basement shooting range. We went out and the big man helped me into the cab. Same seating arrangements as before. Again there was silence throughout the drive. At a guess and because Castle was thorough, I thought the return journey would take exactly the same amount of time as the first trip. I let my mind wander. It made its own way all the way back to the first time I'd ever been on a shooting range.

I was eighteen and Al took me to a club range. I was shooting next to another teenager who reckoned himself a bit. We were using .22 Browning semi-automatic pistols and he seemed to know what he was doing. We both let off ten shots. My target came back first with one shot on target and one shot that just clipped the edge of the circle. Eight complete misses. Right off the paper. My shooting partner laughed his head off at that. Until his target came back with sixteen shots all over it and no-one could tell who'd shot what or where. It shut him up, but I decided then, on my first visit, that guns were not for me. I'd been shooting only two or three times since then and certainly not in the last four years. I never got any kick out of it and from a practical point of view it seemed to me that you'd be more likely to get hurt if you carried a gun than if you didn't, never mind the fact that sooner or later you were bound to get pulled for it. Al thought the same. 'Only if necessary,' he would say, 'and most times it isn't. Not in this country anyway.'

I pulled myself back to the present. The gun, my gun, was now necessary. I wondered what became of the know-all teenager from the gun club. He was probably playing paintball somewhere in the Kent countryside.

After about twenty minutes driving, Castle said, 'We won't drop you exactly where we picked you up, we'll leave you nearby.'

Standard security. I might have told someone where the meet was and asked them to wait there for me to return. It suited me though. I didn't want to be dropped back in that particular place anyway.

'The main road, Commercial Road, will do me fine.'

There was no answer. A couple of minutes later he said, 'Okay, you can lose the glasses now.'

I took them off and squinted against the sunlight. It wasn't that it was sunny, just that the glasses had blacked everything out. We were on Commercial Road approaching the top of Cannon Street. I resisted the temptation to look at my watch. I'd wait until I was out of the cab to do that.

'This is you, Jones.'

As I got out of the cab, the big man pushed an opaque carrier bag into my hands. The gun and bullets. The cab was moving off before I had both feet on the ground. I thought he could have said 'good luck' or something, but I suppose it's not the sort of thing you say in his business. For all he knew I was going to try and kill one of his best customers or even a friend of his. I wondered if you had friends if you were in that sort of business.

*

I was squinting after the taxi when I realised that I was holding the carrier bag tightly and it was gun shaped. I tucked it inside my jacket and crossed Commercial Road towards my van. There were two policemen walking away from me further up the street. I felt a nervous jump as the realisation that I was walking through London Town with a gun in my hand hit me. I thought perhaps this was part of what Castle had meant. Become comfortable with your gun, but it felt like everyone who looked at me would know, must know straight away, that I was carrying a gun. But they didn't. I understood now why psychos get a kick out of this. The idea of fooling everyone else on the street, of feeling more powerful than everyone else, superior to them.

I reached the van, opened it, sat inside and tucked the gun, still in its carrier bag, under the driver's seat. I sat still for a minute and got a grip of my mind. What did I have to do next? I had to phone Tony about the van and I had to get over to Paddington. That was okay, I had plenty of time but I wanted to know about Julot, so – Broussier!

I'd forgotten about Broussier!

Christ! He was sitting in my old bedsit waiting for me to turn up and tell him how to get to Trafalgar Square. Could I phone him instead of going all the way back there? No, Broussier wouldn't answer the phone and if Mex answered it he would have to go and get Broussier. Even Mex might recognise someone whose face had been all over the newspapers for two days. No, I had to go back there, which meant I was pushed for time. I wanted to get to the factory early, in fact, very early. Smith might get there ahead of time and I wanted to be there before him. It was no use sitting here kicking myself for forgetting Broussier, I just had to get a move on and sort it out.

I checked my watch. It was ten to six. Great. I'd hit the rush hour as well. I started the van and swung back northwards. I felt a bit sorry for Broussier. He'd been sitting still, waiting for me to come back and help him for a while now. I'd spent some time house-sitting with Al and it was boring even when you thought something might happen. Broussier would probably be climbing up the walls by now.

I thought back to the first time I had helped Al on a static job. Most people employ house-sitters when they're away for a while, so that the house looks occupied and they won't be burgled. Al house-sat for people who knew someone was going to break in and wanted to catch them doing it. And not so that they could be handed over to the police.

We were in the Hertfordshire countryside. A detached

house set in small grounds and we sat in the dark, barely whispering, since the place was supposed to be empty. I didn't know who the house belonged to, nor why anybody would want to break into it, but Al had said come along so I did, trusting in him the way I didn't trust in anyone anymore. How old was I? Seventeen? Something like that and jumping at every sound. To a young city boy, the countryside was full of unfamiliar sounds that could have been anything from a rabbit going through a hedge to an intruder cutting pieces of glass out of a window. I ended up sitting in a darkened room, straining to hear a noise that I didn't really want to hear. When it came, a definite shuffling sound from the rear of the house, I hadn't got the faintest idea what to do. Luckily, Al hadn't chosen that moment to have a pee – we had plastic bottles for that; no noise and definitely no flushing of toilets in a house that was supposed to be unoccupied – and he pulled me gently back into the darkness of the room and told me not to move. When the man entered the room we were waiting in, Al stepped forward unseen and hit him hard in the throat with an open palm, moved into him and leaving his hand there in a grip on the man's throat, stepped through and took him to the ground. Just in case the guy was still a threat, Al followed him down and put his right knee through the guy's floating ribs into the floor. It was conclusive, frighteningly quick and it left me completely out of breath.

Al tied the man's hands and feet together with plastic packaging strips – the kind that can't be untied, they have to be cut off – and signalling me to be quiet and to follow him, we checked out the rest of the house. Well, he checked and I maintained the rearguard a little way, okay, a fair way behind.

The house was empty. We locked it behind us and searched the grounds, which was really scary because Al thought it would be better if we split up. We could cover more ground like that. After ten or fifteen minutes we found a car parked which we opened with the keys that Al had taken from the man. Finally, when Al was satisfied that the intruder had been on his own, we returned to the house. I asked Al why he hadn't gagged the man as well as tying him up.

'Who is he going to shout to?' he said. 'Anyway, it isn't easy to shout with a bruised throat like that and busted ribs. He won't even want to breathe in case he cuts his own lungs.'

That seemed a fairly good answer, so I shut up. Back at the house, Al made a phone call and we sat around waiting for someone to arrive. I didn't know who and I didn't want to know. I did want to know one thing though.

'Why did you bring me along tonight? I mean, you didn't need me here, did you?'

He smiled at me. 'I like your company. Anyway, it's good education for you. And I might have needed your help; there might have been two of them.'

'Right,' I said, not knowing quite what I would have done if there had been two of them. Probably held my breath for twice as long as Al dealt with both of them.

I asked Mick about this soon afterwards. We were sitting in his flat listening to some rare recording of Big Joe Turner just before he died.

'What is it with Al? Why does he want me along on these jobs?'

'That is a good question, son, a very good question.'

Mick was hunched over his guitar, trying to play along with the tape. Not succeeding really.

'You going to answer the question, or just carry on murdering that song?'

He didn't put down the guitar, but he did stop playing.

'I can't answer it, because I don't know the answer. Al works his own agenda, always has done and it's no use anyone else trying to figure out what he does or why. Maybe he thinks he can use you, once he's taught you a few things. Maybe he thinks that you're worth training up. I don't know. Believe me, I don't want to know everything that he's involved with and neither do you. When he's ready to tell you, he will. Until then, keep your mouth shut and learn everything you can. Al isn't right about a lot of things, but he's the best at what he does that you'll ever meet.'

At the time, I think that was the most I'd ever heard Mick say in one go and I was impressed enough to shut up and listen to him. Later, I asked Al directly why he was taking me on like this. It was the one question he never gave me a straight answer to. He said things like, 'Well, we're mates aren't we,' or, 'You're on your own just like I've been and you'll never survive unless someone teaches you a few bits and pieces.' Perhaps as Mick said, he'd seen something in me that he could use, but I never felt used by him, although I worked for him, or with him quite a lot. I preferred to think of him as a friend and I still do. If there was a hidden agenda, I never worked out what it was, although there were plenty of things he did that I wasn't asked to be a part of and times when he just wasn't around for a while.

At his funeral there were several people that I didn't know and I thought I'd met most of Al's circle. A couple of women, which didn't surprise me, but also several older men and two younger, all of them hard-eyed and close-mouthed. I asked my old boxing trainer who they were, but he didn't know them at all. I asked Mick about them, but all he said was, 'Don't ask me questions that I don't want to know the answers to.'

Which reminded me that all this time after Al had died,

Mick still hadn't told me all the details of his death. I'd have to ask him again and this time stay until I got an answer out of him. It was something I needed to know and something that I had a right to know. But it would have to wait. There were other more pressing matters, like overtaking this idiot in front of me who was driving down the middle of the road at fifteen miles an hour holding everyone up, while the traffic in front of him steadily pulled away. You don't get too many chances to make up time during the rush hour and when you get them you've got to take them. If he'd have pulled in slightly, all the traffic behind him could probably have got by fairly easily. As it was, we all had to nip out and in again when we could. I saw my chance and took it. He hooted me as I went past, so I stuck a finger up at him and he hooted me again. Typical Sunday driver. Either that, or someone who didn't live in London and didn't know the London driver's rulebook. Page five clearly states, 'If there's a gap, use it. If there's an inch, take it.'

I accelerated to catch up the line of traffic ahead and focused my mind again. I thought hard. If I'd forgotten Broussier, had I forgotten anything else? I went over everything in my mind, driving on automatic as everybody else does in London traffic jams. It all seemed to hang together. I couldn't think of anything that I'd missed. True, as Mick said, I didn't know exactly how I'd react and as Linda had said, I didn't know exactly what I was going to do afterwards, but I was sure I could sort those things out. All I had to do was to keep to schedule, get to the factory ahead of Smith and shoot him. Shoot him dead. I felt the cold heat again. What had started as a crazy idea was actually going to happen.

Maybe I'd thought that somewhere along the line something would stop it. A problem with the gun, or Mick talking me out of it, but no, the whole thing had come together and was going to happen. I had the gun, I had set the rendezvous and I felt strong. I'm ashamed to say it, but driving across London I felt good and I felt powerful. Ashamed, because I was driving on a schedule to kill someone. Maybe not one of the good guys, but it was still a life. And I'd convinced myself that it was all right to take away that life. I'd convinced myself that this was what I had to do. Morality was gone now, I was running on a track. I'd set myself a schedule and I was keeping to it. I didn't have to think about anything, just keep to the timetable. It didn't occur to me at the time, but it was almost like being a soldier, except I was receiving orders from myself.

I made it to my old bedsit by seven. I watched my speed, the last thing that I wanted was to be stopped for speeding, but it wasn't necessary to keep too close an eye on it. It's almost impossible to speed through the London traffic at peak time. On the way I had a good idea. It was about time. On my ratio of one every three years, I must have been due. I stopped at a discount store and bought a baseball cap, a scarf and a dark jacket. For Broussier, not for me. He had to get to Trafalgar Square without being arrested and the clothes might help to cover him up a bit. All the caps in the shop had American football team names on them. I didn't think Broussier would know the difference between a Chicago Bear and a Miami Dolphin, so I got him one that said New York Jets. It might help keep away the London sharks.

When I reached the flat, I drove past it along the High Road and back again, checking once more the parked cars and anyone hanging around. Pat's granddaughter was still on his stall. Everything else seemed clear of strangers. I drove up the side road by the flat, parked the van a hundred yards or so up the street and walked back. Given that I'd forgotten about Broussier, it was lucky that I had the keys to the place with me. I'd attached the van key to their key ring.

I opened the door to the foyer and quietly went up to the first floor flat. I still needed to check that it was clear. It would be stupid to start getting careless at this stage. I stood outside the flat door for a minute, listening hard. I could hear Mex singing out loud. That almost certainly meant it was clear. If there was anyone in there with him they would have made him shut up by now. He was singing *Yellow Submarine*. It sounded like one of the Clangers on acid. I opened the front door, quietly stepped through and closed it gently behind me. Not because I thought anyone dangerous was inside, but so as not to let Mex know I was there. His voice was coming from the kitchen. Maybe I could sneak past to my room without him seeing me. I couldn't.

'Hey there, Inglis, how you doin'?'

'I'm fine, Mex, but I might be away for a couple of days.'

'Yeah, I seen the note you lef' me. It's okay, me an' Linda survive widdout you for a while.'

He didn't know Linda was gone yet. Her door was shut and he wouldn't dare open it. I walked down to my old room. Mex's voice carried after me.

'I ain' seen your fren' at all. You sure he's here?'

'Yeah, Mex,' I called back after him, 'probably just knocked out with jet lag or something.'

Inside the room, Broussier was definitely not knocked out. He was pacing up and down, which isn't easy in such a small space and when the door opened he almost jumped on me.

'Where have you been? I have been going mad waiting here, listening to that idiot singing to himself. I thought you were not coming back.'

Anyone would think he was pleased to see me. He sat, no, he sank down onto the bed and rested his face in his hands. He was a relieved man.

'I was going crazy. I thought maybe you were leaving me here.'

I didn't think that it was a good time to tell him that I'd almost forgotten him.

'No, Jean,' I said calling him by the name Julot had used and noting that Broussier accepted it, 'I said I'll be back and I am. You've got plenty of time, so stop worrying. I'm going to give you enough money to get you to Trafalgar Square, plus a little extra, just in case. I'll also write down all the directions exactly, for how to get there. But first you have to tell me about Julot.'

There was a silence, He was wondering whether to lie to me or not. He chose the wrong option.

'I don't know any Julot.'

I reached down and grabbed a handful of his thick hair, pulled his head back and hit him open handed across the face as hard as I could. It left a mark you could see through his tan. Still holding his head back, I said, 'You lie to me, I'm going to break you up.'

'No,' he said, 'I'm not lying, I – '

I hit him again, same place, just as hard.

'I'm trying to help you, Broussier, so tell me who Julot is, or I'll dump you back in the shit where you belong.'

'Okay,' he said, 'okay.' He was breathing hard.

I let go of him and waited.

'Julot is the man I used to work for. It will be his people that I meet tonight.'

'What's his part in this?'

His head was in his hands again. 'He wants something that I have.'

'What do you have?'

He hesitated for a second and then brought out a small,

flat cardboard envelope from his trouser pocket.

'This,' he said and put it back again. 'It's a computer disc. A new one, a prototype.'

I thought for a moment things were falling into place.

'Who does it belong to?' I asked.

'No-one,' he said and then went on. 'I took it from Julot, but he stole it from someone else, the company that developed it.'

'Worth a lot of money?'

He nodded.

I held out my hand and reluctantly he gave me the disc. It didn't look like much to me. I handed it back, which surprised him.

'I don't want it,' I said, 'I don't want Julot on my case.'

'Thank you,' he said. He realised that I could take it from him and there would be little he could do. 'I need this for tonight. I give them the disc back, they let me live.'

He didn't seem too happy about it, but that was his problem. If he'd been stupid enough to try and cross a man like Julot, he should count himself lucky to get away with his life intact. There was still something I needed to know.

'Who is Smith?'

'A buyer, who wanted to take it by force. If you hadn't stopped him, I wouldn't have anything to trade tonight.'

It figured. It all worked and it was a relief that Smith and Julot weren't connected. I couldn't believe that Broussier would be lying to me now. He looked broken. I didn't tell him that Julot himself was in London. It might have finished him off and I wanted him out of here and away from me. But he had to understand some things first.

'Listen, there are two things you have to do for me, okay?'

'Sure.'

'If anything does go wrong, then you have to leave me out of it. Both me and this place. Tell the police you slept rough or something, but nothing about this place and nothing about me.'

'Of course, you don't exist at all.'

'And the second thing is that if something goes wrong with the man that's meeting you, you can't come back here. I won't be here and Mex won't let you in. I don't know how you're going to get out of London, but if it goes wrong, you're on your own.'

'It is okay. They will have a passport for me. It is part of the deal.' He looked at the carrier bag of clothes. 'Those are for me?' he asked.

The other carrier, the one with the gun in it, was inside my jacket. I hadn't wanted to leave it in the van. I didn't plan on being in the flat for too long, but it was long enough for someone to nick the van. I didn't want to have to call Mick and tell him I'd lost the gun within an hour and a half of getting it.

'Yeah, they're for you and if you're caught, you stole them, right? Or you found them in the park, if you don't want to get done for theft.'

'Okay, are we going now?'

He was eager to be moving and I couldn't blame him. He'd been cooped up here for almost two days and on the run for another two. The nightmare could be almost over for him and the nearer we get to the end of trouble, the faster we want to move. I felt bad about slowing him down, but I had no choice.

'*We* are not going anywhere. You are, but not yet. You've got to be at Nelson's Column by 10.30, so if you leave by nine that will be fine. Any earlier and you'll be hanging around for too long, which is not a good idea. And you're going on your own. I don't exist, remember. In fact, now I come to think of it, I'm not even going to write anything down for you. I'll give you directions and you can write them yourself. And you can tear the label out of that jacket as well, I'm not leaving you with anything that can tie in with me.'

'You are right, yes. We must not be careless, even now.'

'Especially now,' I said.

I gave him precise directions for getting to the nearest tube station and told him which train to get and where and how to change. I even drew him a map of Charing Cross tube station, as best I could from memory, showing him which exit to leave by if the Trafalgar Square exit was closed. I left him studying the directions and went down the hall to the payphone to call Tony. I tried the car lot first, hoping he was still there. I didn't want to call him at home in case I had to speak to Marie. I was lucky. I hoped it was the beginning of a trend.

'M and T Autos.' Tony, using his telephone voice.

'It's me, Tony, Garron.'

'No, don't tell me, you smashed it.'

'No, I haven't smashed it.'

'You scratched it.'

'I haven't scratched it either.'

'Well what is it then? Don't tell me it's a social call, I was about to go home.' He paused. 'Did you see Linda last night?'

'Yes, I did.'

'And?'

'And what?'

'And what happened?' He sounded impatient.

'Nothing happened.'

'What do you mean "nothing happened"? Did you get her phone number at least?'

'No.'

There was a pause, then, 'Christ, this is like pulling teeth. Are you going to tell me or not?'

'She walked out on me.'

'Oh,' he said. Then, 'Why?'

'I said the wrong things.'

'You're a fool, you know that? I think you had a chance of something there.'

'Yeah, well...' I wanted to change the subject. Tony did it for me.

'You wouldn't phone me up to tell me that, so what is it?'

I took a deep breath. 'I've got a bit of a situation,' I said, 'with the van.'

There was silence. Then he said, 'What sort of situation?' His voice was threateningly wary.

'Er, well, it's insured isn't it, I mean for theft and everything?'

'No, it's not! It's insured as part of my stock, but if you're driving it, it's got to be under your insurance. What's happened? Someone's nicked it, haven't they?'

'No, no-one's nicked it, just calm down a minute and listen.'

'I don't want to hear anything that does me out of eighteen hundred pounds.'

I felt bad about this. Really, I'd taken advantage of Tony and now I wasn't going to give him any option but to go along with me. But I'd needed a car for tonight and I hadn't wanted to go into all the details with him. At the same time, I didn't want him on a charge of aiding a murderer if I got pulled tonight. This was all I could do.

'No-one's going to do you out of anything, all right? But I have got a problem and I need to use the van.'

He started to interrupt, but I carried on. 'I'm not using it for anything criminal, but I suddenly need to get somewhere tonight. I will have it back outside your yard by – ' I did a quick calculation. 10.30 at the factory and I didn't intend being there long after that. I added some time on plus travelling, ' – by 12.30 tonight. One o'clock latest.'

The payphone was running down its units. I put some more coins in.

'What I'll do, is I'll phone you at home from that call-box outside the car lot to tell you that it's back. If I haven't called by one, then you phone the police and report it as stolen. They'll find it pretty quickly, or you'll get the insurance back. I'm sorry about this – '

'No, you're bloody not!' He sounded angry, to say the least. 'You bloody knew about this before you took the van, didn't you?'

I didn't say anything.

'Didn't you?'

'I wasn't sure, Tony, I didn't know if – '

'And you couldn't just ask me for a car for the night, you had to do it like this. What is it, you don't trust me now?'

'No, mate, I just didn't want to get you involved.'

'Involved!' he shouted. 'Whatever it is you're doing, you're using my sodding van!'

He calmed himself down. I could hear him breathing at the other end of the line. When he'd got control of himself again he said, 'What's going on?'

I didn't reply.

'Look,' he said, 'I pulled you out of East London, looking like a piece of trampled rubbish and I didn't ask you anything. I move your neighbour to a new home and she asks me not to tell you where she is and I don't ask why. You want my van to move a few bits and pieces and I don't say a word. Now I'm asking you straight out, what's going on?'

What could I tell him? Nothing. I couldn't say anything to him. Even if I could have lied to Tony, which he would have spotted, he knew me too well, I couldn't think of anything plausible. I said the only thing I could say, which was also the worst thing I could say.

'I can't tell you, Tony. I'm sorry, but I can't tell you.'

There was quiet on the line. When he spoke, he spoke quietly.

'You stupid bastard. What are you trying to prove?'

I didn't know what he meant.

'You've always been the same. Whatever you're doing, you've got to be doing it on your own. You can't let anyone in.'

I still wasn't sure what he was getting at. I just wished he could see it from my angle. I couldn't get him involved. I'd promised Marie. I couldn't ask him for anything straight out. Then, as he was talking to me, I realised something else. I didn't want Tony involved. I didn't want his help. I didn't want anybody's help. I just wanted everyone to leave me alone to get on with it. My way. Maybe there was a bit of the 'I got myself into this, so I'll get myself out of it' attitude, or maybe I thought that if I let anyone else in, they would persuade me, convince me, that I was in the wrong. Maybe I didn't want to be persuaded. Maybe I was just a stupid bastard.

' – you got now, Garron?'

'Sorry, Tony, I didn't catch that.'

'I said, how many friends have you got now?'

'What? I don't know. I haven't counted recently. I know a lot of people.' I wasn't sure how we'd got on to this.

'Yes, you know a lot of people and most of them you haven't seen in ages and half of them were hangers-on from your boxing days anyway. How many real friends have you got? Now. Here. People that you see and talk to properly. Not just people that you know or that know you.'

I hesitated. 'I don't know. Not that many I suppose.'

Tony wasn't in the mood for being kind.

'I think you're over-estimating.'

He didn't give me time to think about that.

'In the past twenty-four hours, you've lost Linda and you've lied to me. And you expect me to say "okay, don't worry about it, 'cos after all we're mates". Well, being mates works both ways, Garron and I think you've forgotten that. So remember it fast, or you're going to turn around one day to an empty world!'

He slammed the phone down.

I looked at the receiver in my hand. I looked at the wall. I looked around me. I think I was looking for something to hit, but Mex was back in his room. Maybe I shouldn't have told Tony anything about the van, but I hadn't wanted to leave any loose ends. And his van left uncollected near the West End would be a definite loose end. I'd thought I was doing the right thing. All I'd done, though, was piss him off. And use up all my loose change.

I sat in the kitchen for a while. Maybe I should just walk away. Pack Broussier off, take Tony's van back, lose the gun and let Linda go her own way. She didn't want me now anyway. But even as I thought this, I knew I couldn't walk away. And not for all the reasons I'd already thought of. There was a new reason. I'd gone too far. I felt that I was committed now. Al used to say that when you'd decided to do something, you had to do it. I knew what he meant by that. It's like going into the ring having decided that you're going to knock the guy out. But you win on points. A good performance and you've still won and as far as everyone else is concerned that's fine, but you know that for yourself, you haven't quite won. Because you went in to do something and you didn't do it. You did enough, but sometimes enough is not what you need. You need to do what you set out to do. What you set yourself to do. Jake La Motta against Sugar Ray Robinson. The last time Robinson won, but the Bull never went down and that meant that in some way, he'd won and Robinson knew that in some way, he hadn't beaten the man.

I'd set this kill up. I'd taken the decision, for what I'd thought were good reasons. Maybe it was wrong. But I felt committed. I had to do this now. I couldn't back out. I couldn't stop short of what I'd told myself I was going to do. Or Smith would have won. Even though I would have got Broussier and Linda and myself away from him, he would have won. And I didn't want him to win. Anything. Ever again.

I stood up, left the kitchen and walked back to my room, cold fire playing in my stomach.

*

Broussier was in good spirits now, but still restless, anxious to get going. That was tough. He had about an hour and a half to wait and that was all there was to it. I didn't have that long though. I wanted to get moving.

I gave Broussier ten pounds, much more than he needed to get to the meet and also gave him some last minute instructions. Things like using the ticket machine and not the ticket office, not browsing in shops if he was too early, not asking people the time and so on. What he really needed was a babysitter, firstly to take care of him and secondly because two people are often less conspicuous than one. But that couldn't be arranged, so he would have to manage on his own. If he was half as good at looking after himself as he was at thanking me, then he'd be all right. It was getting embarrassing. Now he wanted to write down a number or an address to send me money when he got home. The guy was incapable of thinking straight.

I told him he couldn't have a contact point for me, but if he gave me a number in Brussels I might, but only might, get in touch. He started reeling off numbers, but I stopped him and pointed out that I didn't need the international and area codes. I could get them from the operator. He gave me the Brussels number and seemed surprised when I didn't write it down. I told him I'd remember it. I didn't know whether I'd ever call the number, but I took a few seconds to plug it into the memory bank. No mnemonics or anything, just the straight number. I thought that it would stick, but I didn't really care either way.

Then we shook hands and I told him to try and avoid Mex when he was leaving. I took a last look round my former home. I wasn't sentimental about it. I hadn't been there that long and the only good thing about the whole place had been Linda and she was gone now as well. I left Broussier standing by the bed. I hoped he would be all right, but it was no longer my problem. Unless he was pulled by the police. If that happened I couldn't be sure that he wouldn't tell them about me and this place. If they started to pressure him, he'd probably crack and if they investigated this flat, it wouldn't take them long to come up with my name, but since I wasn't about to shoot Broussier as well as Smith, there was little I could do about that. As I walked down the corridor, Mex poked his head out of his room behind me.

'Hey, Inglis, you goin' out now?'

'Yeah, Mex, see you later.'

'Hey, can you take out the rubbish bag wid you? The one in the kitchen?'

I thought about it. I would probably, hopefully, never see Mex again. Linda was gone as well. He might even think that we'd gone off together, which was a nice thought. So why not do something for him as my last act in this flat.

'Yeah, sure, Mex, I'll take it.'

'Thanks, man, I see you later.'

I pulled the bin liner out of the swing bin in the kitchen and knotted it. Holding the gun inside my jacket against me with my right hand, I hefted the bag up with my left. I don't know what we'd thrown away in the last two or three days, but it was heavy. I made my way to the front door. This was ridiculous. Going off to kill someone, but having to put out the rubbish on the way. Exit first murderer stage left, with gun and large black bin liner.

*

I threw the rubbish in one of the large council wheelie bins outside and walked to the van. It was crazy, but I was feeling for the gun every thirty seconds even though I knew it was there and it couldn't move without me noticing. Inside the van, I tucked it under the driver's seat again and checked my watch. Twenty to eight. Plenty of time. I thought Smith would get there early, perhaps an hour earlier, by 9.30, so I was aiming for an hour earlier than him. As I drove down to Paddington, I wondered why I could think my way into killing Smith, but not Broussier. It wasn't a 'good versus evil' thing. For all I knew, Broussier might be responsible for far worse things than Smith, yet I was discounting that. Perhaps it was their personalities. Broussier seemed like a nice guy – Smith wasn't. But I hoped I was more objective than that. So what it came down to was one of two things. Either it was purely utilitarian; Smith was the threat therefore I had to get rid of him, whereas Broussier was no threat unless he talked to the police, or I was taking Smith's treatment of me personally. I preferred the first option. The second meant that Linda was right and I wanted her to be wrong.

I tried to blank my mind. I wanted a clear head, not one full of arguments and counter-arguments flying around inside it. I felt really keyed up. Maybe this was what any criminal felt like. The secret knowledge that he, amongst all the other people and all the other cars on the streets, had a purpose. But I wasn't a criminal. I was one of the good guys, right?

I drove past shops, houses, people, cars, catching glimpses of them as I passed by, unusually aware of their presence. It was impossible not to think of anything at all. My mind was bouncing from thought to thought, idea to idea, image to image, like a pinball machine triggered by I don't know what. I suddenly realised that my breathing was getting faster and shallower. I was beginning to sweat. I'd never been a pill popper, but I wondered if this was what it was like to be on speed. But I wasn't on drugs. This was my head doing this. I could control it. I must be able to control it.

I pulled over to the side of the road, switched off the engine and got out of the car. Took some deep breaths and listened to my heart pounding. What the hell was wrong with me? I was just driving down the road and suddenly I was gasping. I stood there for two or three minutes, letting the cool air chill the sweat on my forehead, before getting back into the van and sitting there for a moment. I needed to relax. I needed something to occupy my mind. I needed something to focus my thoughts in a different direction. I needed something! But I didn't have anything, just the radio. I switched it on, moved the dial around and got lucky. I don't know which station it was, but Ricki Lee Jones was easing and toying her way through *Easy Money*. I switched on the engine and checked the mirror, indicated and pulled out, stabilising myself, back in a routine again, the routine of driving. I'd tensed up. It was as though I had a grip on my mind and

I didn't want it running too far ahead of me, in case I didn't like where it went. The thing was, though, I wasn't sure what it was I didn't want to think about. Inch by half inch I relaxed the grip on my thoughts and allowed them limited freedom.

Easy money. Well, that was what a lot of things came down to in the end. Money. The rest was probably covered by sex and power. All right, stick in a PS for love and 'charitable good deeds', if you chose to ignore the odd ulterior motive here and there.

The people I knew when I was growing up wanted power of a kind. The power to control their own lives. But they couldn't get it. Not by fair means and usually not by foul either, not for long anyway. For their power they needed money and the hard reality was that whilst most of them weren't starving, they were struggling. And struggling is only worthwhile if you have the possibility of getting somewhere. Take away that possibility and all you have is a lot of tired people using all their energy to tread water and stay afloat. That was the grim reality. They had no money, but somehow they got by. They had no choice. We lived in council flats, on estates that some people wouldn't or couldn't live on, but it was liveable. There was poor health, kids who didn't bother going to the schools, the threat of violence, people who drank too much. Lisa said nobody lived here, just existed. Everyone knew somebody who was a drug addict. Everyone trying to keep their kids on the straight, but some of them giving up. Everyone wanted something else, but could see no way of reaching for it.

Except me. I knew the reality, I lived in it. But I was getting out. I had my dream. I was going to be a champion and it didn't matter how long the odds were. There were one or two others that I knew who wanted out and didn't use crime as their way of grabbing a moment or two of power. Pete tried to become a pro musician and is now eking out a living up north. Tony sweated for his own business and got it. Ailsha got her 'A' levels and went off to college, though what happened to her I don't know. A couple of guys went into the army. And me – I nearly made it. I so nearly made it. But even though the dream died, I was still out. I had a better job, a little more money, a little more control over my life. Until I realised that moving up a financial division isn't far enough. You still struggle. You still tread water, it's just the pool is slightly cleaner. And the way it turned out, I ended up sitting in my bedsit waiting for something to happen, wanting something to happen. And it had. And now the waters were turning murky again.

*

I stopped off on the Harrow Road for chocolate and a drink. It had suddenly occurred to me that I'd be sitting in the factory for maybe two hours and I should have at least something in my stomach. The grocery store that I stopped at had a special offer on some 'Acme' type washing powder. The shopkeeper practically tried to give me two boxes. I didn't take them, though. It said on the box that it was great stuff for getting gravy off T-shirts, but it didn't mention how it was for getting blood off hands.

I drove past Paddington station and parked up on Craven Road on a single yellow. It was way past 6.30, so the parking restrictions would be finished. I wouldn't have to nip back to feed a meter. That idea had its funny side though. Getting a parking ticket while you left your van to go and commit murder. I walked up Praed Street, past St. Mary's Hospital, my mind still moving from thought to thought, but slowly now, not racing out of control. I knew a nurse once who worked at St. Mary's. Or was it a nurse called Mary who was at some other hospital? Or maybe it was someone called Mary who was a patient at a hospital. I gave up. Whoever and wherever she was, she certainly wasn't thinking about me right now, so why should I rack my brain about her. Still, I hoped she was doing all right. Maybe I crossed her mind every now and again. But I didn't think so. If I did, it was no doubt in the same half-nameless, blurred way that she'd just arrived in mine. Hell of an epitaph. Here lies a half-nameless, blur-faced man who crosses someone's mind once every few years. I pulled myself together. I had enough to think about with the present without wallowing in day-dreams about the past.

I reached the Metropole and cut around the back of the hotel. I was almost at the factory now. It had been closed for quite a while. Sooner or later someone would develop it in some way. Until then it was surprising that it was still empty. If there's a vacant building in the West End, someone usually takes a temporary lease on it. This place by rights should have been a storage centre or a car park by now.

It was a medium sized detached building on the end of a side road. There's a school or day centre or something opposite, which would be closed now and the offices next to it should be empty as well. I'd first come here about three and a half years ago, just before Al was killed. The place had only just been closed down, but Al made it his business to know when useful buildings became available. He met me there one evening, pulled his car up by the side wall and unloaded four large boxes. He showed me where to break in at the back, the front was bricked up and we stashed the boxes in the darkness of the factory. I stayed with them whilst Al went off somewhere else, returning a couple of hours later. We spent the rest of the night and the following day watching over these boxes as though our lives depended on them.

Once it was dark again, we took them back out the way we'd come in, loaded them back into Al's car (not his, hired for the occasion) and he drove off. I never knew what they contained and I never asked. It crossed my mind that they might not have contained anything worthwhile. It might just have been a test for me. Al did that a couple of times, tested me out for nerve or character. I never knew if that was for his benefit or mine and as I said, he died before I found out if there was some further purpose to the testing.

The building was on two levels. The ground floor was the factory itself, a high-ceilinged, stone floored area, which had once resounded to the sound of heavy machinery churning out a living for its workers. Now it lay empty, a silent monument to the 'sound business practices' that had closed it down. There were two staircases, one wooden and one stone, at either end of the factory that led to the offices above.

I knew all this from memory and as I approached the building I hoped my memory was right. I also hoped no-one had replaced the boards over my little broken window at the back. If they had done I'd have to break them off again. It was my only way in.

They hadn't.

I climbed through and dropped the six feet or so to the floor. It was nearly dark outside, the street lights were just coming on and there was enough light from through the broken boards half covering my entry point to see about three feet into the factory. After that it was pitch black. Not just dark, but a heavy blackness that you could feel. One of the few places you come across where it really makes no difference if you close your eyes or not. I stood for a few minutes to see if my eyes grew accustomed to it. They didn't. Your eyes can only become used to a change in light. They can't deal with total blackness.

I gave up and pulled out my Mini – Maglite. I wanted to find the stairs. I wasn't worried about tripping over anything, the place had been cleared out, but I didn't want to walk into any walls. I also didn't want to tread on any rats or other creatures. Put your average human in a totally dark place and not only do they become totally disoriented, they also start wanting to know that there's nothing 'out there'. Now I'm not afraid of the dark, but I'm as afraid as the next man. It's a control thing. If I can't see anything then I can't control what happens to me. Besides which, I didn't think that anyone would see the torchlight. There were no windows at the front and only one at the back that wasn't completely boarded up, so I switched on the torch. Stone floors and stone walls. Some scurrying sounds as things moved out of the light. I was facing the front of the building. I could see the door to my right that led to the stone staircase. I moved the other way, towards the wooden steps. I wanted to be upstairs when Smith arrived.

Treading quietly, although I don't know why since there was no-one there to hear me, I walked the length of the factory to the wooden stairs. I used these instead of the stone ones because I had to check them out. I needed to know if they were still usable or had rotted away. The answer was they were usable, but noisy. Almost every step sent an echoing creak through the building. That would be useful though. An early warning system to tell me when Smith was on his way.

At the top of the steps I turned and walked down a narrow corridor, again the length of the building, but this time back the other way. I could see the door, leading to the top of the stone stairs at the far end. To my right there were offices, some without doors, but all of them dark. For some reason there were no windows at the back of the building upstairs. Al had said it was a very old factory, which made sense. They would never build wooden staircases and windowless offices now.

To my left there were also offices, but these and the corridor were lit dimly by the street lights from the road in front. The windows here were not boarded. Probably, somebody thought they were too high to be broken. That person was wrong; most of them were smashed. After all, to a young vandal, the higher the window, the greater the challenge.

But it was as I had remembered. Pitch black downstairs, but dimly lit upstairs in the streetside offices with a hazy, dull orange glow from the lights outside. My idea was to wait up here for Smith. He'd arrive downstairs and realise Broussier wasn't there. Then he'd make his way upstairs and along the corridor and I'd step out from one of the offices and shoot him. If he shouted to me from downstairs, I'd answer him and tell him to come up where it was lighter. It seemed straightforward enough.

I looked at my watch, tilting it towards the street windows to see the time. It was a quarter to nine. I sat myself down in the middle office, hedging my bets against which side Smith would come from. I guessed the wooden stairs, since they were immediately visible from the factory floor. The stone staircase was hidden by doors both upstairs and down. You had to know it was there, or have a good look around to find it. Still, I couldn't be sure, so I stayed in the middle. I sat on the floor of the office just inside the doorway, leaving the door open. Rested my head back against the wall and pulled my knees up. I put the gun down by my side on the floor. I realised suddenly just how tired I was, but there was a feeling that I'd done it. I'd pulled all the threads together and got them to meet at this point.

I took a couple of deep breaths and felt my neck and

shoulders relax. It was nice to be sitting down. It had been a long, long day. I sat up with a start. I'd known I'd have a long wait, but it never occurred to me that I might fall asleep, that I'd have to fight to keep myself awake. I stood up. I doubted that I could fall asleep properly, at least not if I could help it, but I might doze a bit and the last thing I wanted was to wake up with Smith standing over me. I thought about this for a minute. If Smith came up via the wooden stairs then I'd hear him. I'd have to, they creaked like they were about to break and the echo magnified the sound. If he came up the stone staircase though, I wouldn't know he was coming. I intended to be looking, but I needed a noise just in case I wasn't one hundred per cent alert.

I walked down the corridor to the door at the top of the stone stairs and tested the handle, checking the angle that it went to before the latch was released and the door would open. It was quite a big angle. I took out all my keys and put them together on one keyring. Slipped the ring onto the door handle. Now if someone opened the door from the other side, the keys would slide off the door handle and fall the three feet to the floor I tried it for sound. Loud, but not necessarily loud enough to jerk me awake if I was in the middle office. I'd have to stay here in the end one nearest the stone staircase.

I settled down in that office but then got the jitters that I was feeling too tired and the keys might not be loud enough, so I found a piece of broken glass from one of the windows and balanced that on the door handle as well. Better, as they say, safe than sorry. Then I checked that the gun was loaded and that the speedloader was full and in easy reach in my trouser pocket. Then I realised that I was an idiot because I'd put the speedloader in my right pocket and it had to be in the left one, since my right hand would be holding the gun and

I'd be going for the speedloader, if I had to, with my left. So I swapped it over and settled down again, concentrating on not falling asleep. It should have been easy. After all, this wasn't what you would call a relaxing situation. But the act of sitting still was lulling me and although I could have stood up and moved around, I didn't want to. I was fairly sure that Smith would be here early, but I didn't know when and if he did come early I wanted him to think he was here on his own. He'd have to check that of course, which is why he'd come up here, but I didn't want to be moving around making noise, or showing myself at the windows.

I felt myself relaxing, so I concentrated on the one thing that I hadn't really thought about in detail, killing Smith. Oh yes, I'd thought about it, thought about how to do it. About stepping out into the corridor and shooting him, but now I started to visualise it. Al always said that visualisation was one of the most important things to practice.

'If you've got to do something that you've not done before,' he said, 'see yourself doing it. Visualise yourself doing that action time and time again, in every last detail. Then, when you find yourself in that position, you will react. Because you've been there before. Your mind has already done that action, it's not new to you.'

He told me this soon after he started to teach me bits of street-fighting, but I used it in the ring as well. My boxing trainer liked the idea, but then he was also a mate of Al. I remember the first time I went to his gym, sent on from the boy's club. I was expecting someone like Burgess Meredith out of *Rocky,* but this guy was big and loud and not as old. His voice boomed out.

'You call me, "Boss". That is because this is my gym and I run it. Therefore I am the boss here. No name, just "Boss". Got it?'

Me, a nervous sixteen year old, just nodded

'Al tells me you can fight. But this is a boxing ring, not a fighting ring. So most of his stuff goes out of the window. Most, not all. I'm not interested in whether you can fight, I'm interested in whether you can be a boxer.'

And so it started. What had gone before was kids' stuff; this was the real thing. And I've got to say, it's not pretty. It's primitive. Legitimised savagery. When I knocked out my first fighter in a real match, I felt something so strong. You might say primeval. Some might say shameful, or disgusting. But it was a sense of being alive, of being vital. A sense of your own power. Yes, at the expense of someone else, but that's one of the basic schemes of this world. Maybe that's what I wanted to feel again. Maybe that's why I was going to kill Smith. I couldn't admit it, even to myself, but perhaps what I wanted was that feeling again, magnified a thousand times. That power-crack again.

So I sat and saw the scene in my head, once, twice, ten times, fifty times, heard Smith on the stairs, heard his tread, stepped out, raised the gun and just blew him away. I ran the film at normal speed and in slow motion, seeing the bullet hitting him, seeing his face distort, the falling body, the flailing limbs. End of story. I also ran the aftermath. Wiping the gun clean, removing the unused shells, placing it on the floor by the body. Collecting my keys, wiping down the door handle and the piece of glass, making sure not to tread in Smith's blood when I left. I felt good. I felt strong. Everything was set. Even if I wanted to, it was too late to change anything now.

– *It's not too late.*

That little voice again. It had been silent for days. Probably I'd been too busy to hear it.

– Oh yes it is.

– No it's not. You can get out.

– Chicken out, you mean.

– It's not chickening out, it makes sense.

– They'll come after me.

– Maybe, maybe not. At least you won't be boarded up in some hole in Camden, waiting for the police to come and knock on the door.

– If the police come, they won't knock on the door, they'll kick it in. Besides which, they won't care too much if someone like Smith gets shot.

– Perhaps not, but they'll still want to know who did it.

There was a pause. I don't know how you can have a pause in a conversation that you're having with yourself, but there was. I think I was waiting for the little voice to say something else and I wasn't quite prepared for what it said next.

– You can't let it go can you?

I thought about that.

– No.

– And you can't even work out why you can't let it go.

– No, not really.

– 'Cos it's so mixed up inside that stupid head of yours, that you can't straighten it out. You gave Linda all those reasons and you told Mick that you had to do it, but the truth is that you set your course at the beginning and now you won't change it.

– No... I don't know.

– You do know. You know that even if your reasons were right when this started, they're not the only reasons now, are they?

– That's not true.

– Isn't it? When did pride and anger come into it? Or were they there from the beginning?

– It's not pride. It's... it's a need to control, to control what I do, what happens to me.

– And for that you're going to kill?

— People have killed for less.

— *Yes, but not you.*

I couldn't answer myself on that one. I had to listen.

— *Everyone is controlled by others. We give control of our lives to other people, to institutions.*

— Yes, but not me.

— *You know, Tony was right, you really are stupid. And stubborn.*

— Yeah, but I've got here, haven't I?

— *Where's here?*

I wasn't sure. I looked around at the traffic flowing past. I started to get up, but I couldn't manage to stand. What was stopping me? I looked down. I was chained round my waist to the iron post behind me. The traffic flew past, getting closer with each passing car. I had to get out of here, but I couldn't move. I looked around me wildly. There was a key on the ground to one side. It had to be the key to the chain holding me. I reached out for it, but it was too far away. I twisted and stretched, but it was no use. The cars were getting closer. There was an articulated, bearing down on me. It was a couple of hundred feet away, but getting nearer, rushing towards me. I threw my hands up in front of my face and the dim office came into focus. I jerked myself up, half expecting a chain to restrict me and stood there for a minute, readjusting to the silence of the building after the noise of the dream. Instinctively, I checked my jacket pocket for the gun. It wasn't there. I had a moment of pure panic before I remembered that I'd put it on the floor next to me. It was still there. Well of course it was. I picked it up, the weight of it a reassurance to me.

I paced about a bit calming myself down, trying to recreate that sense of power that I'd had before, but it wasn't easy. I wasn't going to doze off again!

I went to the door where I'd left the keys and the piece

of glass and removed both of them. I wouldn't need them now, I was going to stay wide awake. The glass I wiped clean and put back by the window where I'd found it. The keys went back in my pocket and I wiped down the door handle.

I moved back to the middle office and paced around in there for a minute or two, staying clear of the windows. Did a couple of leg stretches to loosen up. I'd been hunched over for a while. Then I settled down again to wait. I looked at my watch, tilting it as before, to the light. 9.25. Smith could be here at any time now. I felt a pulse beating at the base of my throat. I tried to breathe deeply, but quietly, to slow the pulse rate. It didn't want to know. It was suddenly very cold in this big, empty, dark building.

*

Fragments – flashbacks – what do you think about while you're waiting to kill someone? What dances through your head? Faces, people, words, ideas, things that sweep down from somewhere, from nowhere, flash through your brain and then fly on again, leaving you grasping at a thought, a colour, a residue, confusion.

I tried to clear my head. I tried to think like I assumed a professional hit man would think – a contract killer. He'd be detached, cool, a workman just doing his job. He wouldn't worry about how long he had to wait. He'd just sit here calm and easy, another job, another payday.

But I couldn't be like that. Not now, maybe not ever. I kept looking at my watch every two minutes, certain that Smith would be here by 9.30, worrying when he wasn't. Did he know somehow? Had he been watching me? Did he know where Broussier was going to be?

I got a grip on myself and threw out these thoughts. Things were still going according to plan.

– *Maybe he's not coming.*

– He's coming. He wants to kill Broussier. I mean he really wants to do it and not just for business now. He's missed him twice, so now his reputation is on this as well.

Smith had believed me when I'd told him I'd bring Broussier to him. He thought he'd scared me bad enough and he wanted to believe that he was going to get another crack at the Belgian, so he believed me about setting him up for this killing ground. Smith would be here. He wouldn't think that –

A noise.

From the factory below.

I stood up and strained to hear something. Anything. But there was nothing. The sound didn't repeat itself. Maybe it had been from outside and not downstairs. Maybe I was jumping at shadows. I didn't sit down again though, I'd only be up again the next time someone blew their nose three streets away.

Christ, what was I doing here? I should have run, taken the chance Smith was bluffing. I could have gone up north and visited Pete, maybe taken Linda with me. We'd be sitting now in some pub up in North Lancashire talking about music and old friends and drinking beers at half the price we'd be paying for them in London.

Would Linda have gone with me? I mean, we weren't exactly lovers, we hadn't even kissed yet. But we'd connected somehow at some point and not just since this business had started. We hadn't 'gone out' together, but we'd had a few drinks, watched a few films, even gone shopping together and managed not to get on each other's nerves. Maybe this was how it was supposed to work, gradually, bit by bit, working into a relationship almost without trying, rather than deciding to try and bash one into shape. But something had happened between us and the more I thought about it, the more I realised that it was what I wanted. What I needed. But now I was going to throw it away. I knew that if I killed Smith, Linda would never think of having any kind of relationship with me. There are certain lines that some people won't cross over. For anybody. There are some things, that if you do them, people can't see you the same way again.

I went out once with a girl when I was still quite young. I hadn't learned, though Al had told me, not to react to things that people said to me.

'They're only words,' he said. 'You're the one that gives meaning to them. If someone calls me a bastard, so what? It's just a word. If someone calls my mother a name, it doesn't matter. My mum wouldn't want me to get into a fight 'cos someone called her a name. They're just words, not to be taken personally.'

The next night, someone called Al a 'dirty Jewboy kike' and he broke the guy's jaw and nearly ripped his head off. I took my life in my hands afterwards and reminded him of what he'd told me the day before.

'That's different,' he said. 'Some Nazi calls me that and he's not insulting me personally, he's having a go at what I am and I'm not having that. If I let that go, then next time he'll say "dirty Jewboy" and maybe push someone over and then the time after that, maybe beat the crap out of someone else and it'll be my fault for not stopping it right at the beginning. If it's personal, forget it. If it's racist, do something about it.'

I could have pointed out that I wasn't likely to get the racist comments, but it didn't seem like a good time to argue.

Anyway, I was sitting in this sort of pub/club with this girl, trying to make a good impression. I'd only just turned pro as a boxer and she was impressed by that, but I wasn't well known yet and I was off my own patch by a long way.

One of the guys in the place said something to my date as I was buying the drinks and then when I'd come back and sat down again, he came over and said something else to me as well. To be honest, I don't really remember what it was, but it triggered me off.

I took the table into him and then with him into the wall. Then I dropped the table and just started pounding him. It's lucky I didn't kill him. I thought I'd hit him a couple of times. Apparently I hit him about a dozen times. Then, before anyone else joined in or called the police, I grabbed the girl and pulled her out of there. Yeah, I know, real Captain Caveman stuff, but I was still young enough to be influenced by *The Sweeney* and she was too young to know about women's lib. Still, I got my come-uppance. She walked off and left me that night. She couldn't handle what she'd seen. Boxing was all right – that was legitimate, glamorous even in her eyes, but in that club I'd crossed a line that she couldn't deal with. She'd never be able to look at me without seeing the animal that could so easily have killed someone that night and she couldn't handle that. And I couldn't blame her.

And now I was about to do it again. Cross a line that would change someone's perception of me irrevocably. Perhaps that was my real problem. If someone put a line in front of me, I had to cross it. I had to see what the view was like from the other side. Smith had not only put a line in front of me, he'd described it to me, dared me to cross it. The problem for me, as he saw it, was that it was too big a step. The problem as Mick saw it, was that once I'd stepped over, there was no going back. They were probably both right. But I was going to do it. Or at least try. Neither Mick nor Smith could stop me now, only I could stop myself. And the only reason that I could think of for stopping was Linda.

To kill, or not to kill? I grinned to myself. It's not often that I quote Shakespeare, let alone misquote him deliberately. Most of my quotes come from the movies. If Smith walked in now I could say to him, 'of all the offices in all the factories in all the world, you had to walk into mine' and shoot him dead. It wasn't funny, but allowing for the fact that I was under stress, it could have been worse.

I was rambling mentally. My brain was racing again. I did some deep breathing and checked my watch for the umpteenth time. Ten to ten. Where was he? Why didn't he come?

– *Relax, he'll be here.*

– You've changed your tune.

– *Well, you're committed now. He'll be here soon. Even if you left now, you might not get away before he arrived.*

– So you're on my side again?

– *I've always been on your side, you idiot. But now we've got to focus properly. Forget about everything else except killing Smith.*

– I have.

– *No you haven't. You're still thinking about Linda.*

– You're right.

– *Well, you'd better admit something to yourself.*

– Yeah, what's that?

– *You'd better admit that you want this more than you want her.*

– That's not true.

– *She's not enough to stop you going through with this.*

– There are other things to consider. They all add up to having to do this.

– *Yeah, sure. Like you really care about what happened to Harwood and Nelson and what could happen to Broussier.*

– I do.

– *No, you don't. They're just the excuse that you're using. You want this for your own reasons and Linda isn't enough to hold you back.*

At this point I trod on the little voice and squashed it flat, which was probably what I should have done long before. I'd had enough of arguments, reasons and decisions. I was here, Smith was on his way and that was that. I wasn't interested in all that stuff that kept going around and around in my head. The same points, the same questions. It had been driving me mad constantly for two days. Now it was going to stop. I didn't care just then about right or wrong, or about consequences. My mind was set. As Al said, 'You weigh things up, you make the best decision you can and you stick with it.'

I checked the gun again. I checked the speedloader. I checked my watch. Just before ten o'clock. He was cutting it fine if he wanted to get here before me and Broussier at 10.30. I had been so sure that he would. It was the professional thing to do. The realisation suddenly hit me. But of course, he wasn't dealing with professionals. He thought of me as an amateur. He didn't need to get here too far ahead of schedule, since I, as an amateur, would be arriving on time and no earlier. Half an hour would do him fine. No need to sit around getting bored for any longer.

I checked my watch again. Ten o'clock. He'd be here now. Any minute. Right now he'd be approaching the building. He'd park just around the corner and walk up to the factory. He'd be looking at the bricked up entrances. I could walk over to the windows now and look down on him. I could shoot him from here, but I'd probably miss a clean kill and he might get away and even as I'm thinking this, the moment passes and is gone. He'll know that there has to be another way in at the back of the building and walk around the side. He sees the broken boards on the window, shines his torch inside and sees the empty factory. In through the window. Would I hear him drop to the floor downstairs? I strained hard, but I couldn't hear a thing. It might be just that bit too far away.

Right now he'd be taking his bearings. The torch would be moving in an arc around the factory downstairs. I was tempted to sneak along to the top of the wooden staircase to find out if I could see a light moving around. I didn't though. All things come to those who wait. I had to stick to the game plan. If I waited, Smith would come to me. If I moved, I could mess everything up. He might hear me, or I could find myself in the wrong position when he arrived up here.

Downstairs it would be deathly quiet, but that wouldn't worry Smith. After all, he was the only person in the place. It was supposed to be quiet. And deathly quiet would suit him fine.

He'd be having a good look around the place. Not moving about, just letting his eyes follow the torch. He'd be looking for cover, somewhere to stand and wait for myself and Broussier. Somewhere that he could stay unseen, until he was ready to step out and confront us. The pillars; they were big enough.

Having looked all the way around, he'd notice the door on the right and the wooden stairs on the left. Which way would he go? Left, I pleaded with him, left, I urged him. I stood upstairs in the doorway of the middle office, looking at the door to the stone steps, but straining to hear a sound from the wooden ones. I willed him to go left, to take the wooden stairs. It was a better position for me. He'd be moving now, slowly, still panning the torch from side to side in front of him, sending the rats rushing out of the beam. I could see him smile to himself, wondering how long it would take for the rats to pick Broussier's bones clean.

Now he's at the bottom of the wooden staircase. He looks at it the same way that I did, not sure if it's safe or not. Shines the light upwards. Does he have to go upstairs? Maybe he looks at his watch. Five past ten. Enough time to check out the upstairs if he wants to. Well, he should do this properly, just in case there's some old tramp who has made his home here.

Making the decision. Testing the banister. Come on man, it's just a set of steps. Nothing to be worried about. It's not going to –

A noise.

A creaking sound that echoed through the building. My stomach turned and I felt the pulse in my throat again. He was on the stairs. I turned to face the direction he'd be coming from. The sound didn't repeat itself. He'd stopped, wondering whether to carry on up and risk the noise again. But there is no-one else here, so it's all right. The creaking again. Another step. Come on man, you can climb stairs faster than that. Come on!

Another step and another. How many were there? I hadn't counted. A mistake. A careless mistake, but it wouldn't matter. I would see his head the moment he got three or four steps from the top. I moved into the office and stood behind the door, looking out through the crack by the hinge. Almost the same position that I'd been in when I'd watched Nelson die. But this time I'd chosen it. A perfect view and cover until I wanted to show myself. I would wait for him to make his way fully into the corridor. The steps continued. I held the gun loosely in my right hand by my side. Breathed deeply. My heart was beating so hard, I thought it would give me away.

Another creak and another. His head appeared and then his shoulders, rising into view as if through the floor. My mouth went dry. There was something wrong. It wasn't Smith!

I felt like I'd been hit with a heavy body blow. It wasn't him! And then I realised how stupid I was. What a naive fool

I'd been. Of course Smith wouldn't come here alone. It wasn't just Broussier that Smith wanted dead. It was me as well. There was no way he was going to let me go, after I'd seen him kill Broussier. He wanted me to bring the Belgian here so that we'd both be killed at the same time. Smith might not even be here at all. This was just a killing job. He could leave it to his pet gorilla to do. And his pet gorilla, complete with plastered up nose where I'd broken it, was at the end of the corridor and advancing towards me, checking each office as he went.

I didn't know what to do. All that planning, setting everything up and I'd got it wrong, completely wrong. I'd missed something so obvious that I deserved to get shot for it. And now I would be.

The sweat broke out on me. I tried to think. I had maybe three quarters of a minute before he reached me. Was he here on his own? If I stepped out and shot him, would that bring someone else running? I couldn't think straight, I'd been knocked totally out of my stride. I was going to die.

Shoot him. I had to shoot him. If anyone was downstairs to hear the shot, they'd think that he'd shot me or Broussier. That was it! Shoot him and fire two shots. Now. Now!

I tried to lift the gun. But I couldn't. I'd frozen. My hand, my arm, wouldn't work. The gun was too heavy for me. It was just a dead weight. I looked down at it, the sweat pouring off me, panic flashing in my head. He was in the next office, he was coming to kill me and I couldn't move. I couldn't move!

He was clear of the next office.

Shoot him.

Approaching this one.

Lift the gun. Shoot him.

Pushing the door open.

Shoot him!

His eyes met mine. Registered surprise. I wasn't supposed to be here. Glanced down and saw the gun and the surprise changed to resolve. His gun came up fast and my left hand smashed down on his wrist, knocking the gun from his grip. It did that on its own, I swear I never moved it. At the same time, I dropped my gun and brought my right hand up in a strike to his throat. It didn't get there. His left forearm was in the way. His momentum was forward and I had none. I hadn't moved my feet yet, I had no kind of balance. He launched into me, his left hand reaching for my face and I fell backwards, my instincts snapping into gear, back now to what they knew how to deal with and away from the shock of the unexpected, from the shock of having control of what was happening snatched away from me.

But I'd lost the initiative. As I fell, I tried to hook one of his legs with mine, to bring him down with me, to give me something to work on when we hit the floor. I tried, but I missed it and he was falling deliberately on top of me, not making the most of his position, but landing a split second after I did, knocking the wind out of me and sending a wave of pain through my ribs and back as they suffered their second beating in four days.

I'd somehow pinned his right arm against my body, but his left hand was grabbing at my eyes, too low, but I couldn't do any more than twist my head from side to side and keep hold of his arm at the elbow to stop him bringing his fingers higher to within striking range. I tried a hit to his groin with my knee, but he smothered it with his legs and I was in trouble. We lay there for a few moments, each straining for an opening, for the single strike that would give one of us the advantage and the chance to finish it. Because this was going to the death and both of us knew it.

But I also knew that with every passing half-second the odds were growing in his favour. He might not be well trained, but he was bigger than me, heavier than me and stronger than me and the longer this went on, the better it would be for him. I thought about nutting him as I'd done before, the plastered nose was a good target, but his head was lower than mine, so that was no good, but I had to do something. I could feel my strength going and my ribs on the left were on fire and if I stayed here like this for another few seconds I would just be overpowered and this man would claw at my eyes and then lift my head up and smash it backwards against the floor until it pulped.

My right hand was still holding his left arm at the elbow and I took a chance and managed to slide it in between the arm and his body and began to push outwards, forcing his arm away and his fingers further from my eyes. He was stronger than me, but I had the better position to do this and besides which, I was scared and desperate and believe me that helps.

There would be a critical moment when he would realise that he couldn't force his hand back to my face and he would give up and let it go back and bring it up again on the inside and I would be finished because I didn't think that I could get my own hand back to cover myself in time. I knew all this because although the move only took maybe two seconds, my brain was racing, not working things out with conscious thought, but running on instinct, which is much faster.

So I had to do something before he made his move and I'd known that before I'd started forcing his arm out wide, so when I had enough space, maybe sixteen inches, between my hand and the side of his head, I stopped pushing outwards and slammed the heel of my palm the other way into his temple, twisting myself as best I could to get more power behind the blow and rolling my head in case his arm came flying in again.

It did, but it missed. Partly because I'd turned away and partly because his head had dropped to one side, dazed from the palm strike. I brought my left hand up behind his head and grabbed his hair as near to the front as I could, pulling his head up. I'd let his right arm go free, but I wasn't going to give him the chance to use it. Holding his head up with my left hand, I smashed the base of my right forearm near the elbow into the plaster on the bridge of his nose. There was a low grunt of pain, but he was strong and still there and I couldn't get enough power into the blow to finish him, so I pulled his head backwards by the hair and twisted my body hard and managed to roll him off me. But he was recovering from the palm strike and I didn't think I'd have enough strength to push him away far enough to give me time to reach for the gun, so I carried on rolling with him, leaving him face down on the floor with me behind him. He was trying to push himself up with his right hand and I couldn't let him do that, so I moved my left hand from his hair to the right side of his head and slipped my right hand under his jaw from behind and twisted hard and felt his neck break.

I sat there, half on the man's back, holding his head at that grotesque angle, listening to the echo of the crack fade away. I just stayed there, my breath coming in tidal waves, looking down at him, looking down at this man who had wanted to kill me. Who would have killed me. Then I gently rested his head down on the floor and pushed myself off him.

I didn't stand up. I wasn't sure that I could. I moved on all fours away from him and put my hand on his gun. I looked around for mine but I couldn't see it. Then I spotted it near one of the walls. Too far away for now. I slumped down with my back against the side wall of the office, my head still hammering, my breathing still uncontrollable.

I couldn't stay here. I had to get out, but I was so tired. I sat there waiting for the shakes to come but they didn't. Maybe I was too tired to shake. I waited to feel something. I wanted to feel something. I'd just killed a man. I needed to feel some kind of emotion, but there was nothing. Just a heavy tiredness and an aching hurt in my body.

I had to move, I had to work out what to do next, but not yet. No shots were fired. There hadn't been much noise. I could sit here for a while and get myself together again. No-one would have heard anything and be coming to investigate, not unless they were already inside the building. I had to check that out, but I didn't have the energy. And I came up with some good reasoning for sitting still. If someone else was in the place and they'd heard the fight, then they'd be coming up here to see what had happened. If they hadn't heard anything, they would still come up eventually, to find out where their colleague was. Either way, all I had to do was sit here and wait for them. That was good. My brain was working again. Now I just had to concentrate on breathing normally and stopping the noise inside my head.

God, I was tired. I was hit by a sudden moment of panic. Was I bleeding? Had he drawn blood? I didn't want to leave traces of my blood behind. I looked at my hands. Nothing. I put my hands to my face, moved them around, took them away again. Still no blood. Maybe I'd got away with it. I checked my jacket where I'd hit him with the elbow strike. That seemed clean as well. I relaxed a bit and sat back again. I wanted to close my eyes, but I couldn't. I had to wait in case anyone else was here. And in case there was, I had to do something else. I just couldn't work out what it was. I made an effort, concentrated. The gun, I had to get the gun. The dead man's weapon was nearer than mine, so I reached for that, the movement making me dizzy. I had to sit back again.

It can't have been long that I stayed like that, only a few minutes, but it felt like an age. Sitting with my back against the wall, a dead man's gun in my hand and his body stretched out nearby. And that hammering inside my head.

*

The door was opening. The door at the top of the stone staircase. It was obvious what the sound was the moment I heard it. It was a heavy door and it hadn't been used for years, it was bound to make a noise. I should have checked for that when I first got here.

Sit tight.

Let him come to you.

Footsteps. He wasn't trying to be quiet. There had been no shots. There had been no trouble. There was no reason to be silent. And since there was no need to be silent, he called out the dead man's name.

'Jerry?'

That was strange. Funny almost. I'd always thought of Jerry as a mouse and here he was, a full grown gorilla. I wished I hadn't heard his name. It made it more personal. I preferred to think of him as a gorilla.

'Jerry, you there?'

Smith's voice. It was Smith's voice.

He was here. He had taken it personally. He wanted to see me and Broussier dead himself. He was looking in the offices at the end of the corridor. I could get up. I could sight down the corridor.

Sit still.

Sit quiet.

Wait.

I checked the gun that I'd picked up. A semi-automatic.

The safety was off. I slowly pulled the slide back to cock the gun. There was a double click. It was as quiet as I could make it, but it was there. Had he heard it? He might have heard it.

Footsteps in the corridor.

And then I noticed something. My breathing was normal. I was calm. There was still a buzzing in my head, but only I could hear that and it wasn't a problem. I was calm, in control again, back on track.

Smith turned into the office and saw the dead man first. He was good. He didn't rush over to him or call his name again. He just stood still and looked around the room. As he turned his head, he saw me sitting, back to the wall, aiming the gun at his chest. He'd been crouching slightly, now he straightened up. His gun was in his hand, but held loosely by his side and pointing to the ground. If he moved to bend his arm and bring the gun up, he'd be dead before he got into a position to fire.

'Let it drop,' I said.

'Yes.' The gun hit the floor.

'Kick it away from you.' My voice sounded strange, dull and flat. He pushed it to one side with his foot. Not quite far enough, I thought.

I held the gun steady and looked at him. He had nerve. He didn't even look like he was sweating. He probably thought he still had time. I hadn't shot him as he'd entered the office and so why shoot him now? Why wait, unless there was something else that I wanted, some deal to be done.

He was wrong. I hadn't pulled the trigger when he'd come in because I wanted him facing me when I shot him. I wanted him to know that it was me killing him. I wanted to see his face as I did it.

There would be no more talk. I had nothing to say to him. I sighted the gun.

'How did you kill him?'

I almost answered before I realised it was a trick. Ask a question, get a response, get the man talking.

Shoot him.

I didn't need to answer him.

Shoot him.

I would have done, I should have done, but Smith was still composed. He still didn't know, still didn't realise that I was going to kill him. I wanted him to know. He had to know. Maybe he did.

'Broke his neck,' I said.

Smith let out a low grunt and shook his head slowly. Shuffled his foot slightly. I didn't like that.

'Don't get used to moving,' I told him.

He raised his hands slightly in resignation, another movement in itself.

I didn't like what was happening. A few seconds ago I had him stone-still, silent and surprised. Now he was recovering, moving and talking.

'That's twice I've underestimated you, Garron,' he smiled at me. Smiled at me. I couldn't believe it. He had real nerve. He carried on. 'Am I getting old, or are you an exceptional character?'

He was so good. Putting himself down a bit, building me up a bit. The only thing was, I knew what he was doing. My face hadn't changed expression. I don't think I'd even blinked. The gun stayed steady, sighted on his chest.

I could let him talk himself out, wait until he realised it was useless, see if he cracked, but that was dangerous. I was too tired, the gun was getting heavier, my left arm ached too much and Smith was still on his feet and capable of moving quickly. Better bring him down to my level.

'Knees, down on your knees.' Restrict his movement.

He got down slowly, one leg at a time. Gave a short laugh.

'Not good for the trousers, these hard floors.'

The only problem with him kneeling and I hadn't seen it, was that his gun was now too near him. I knew he hadn't kicked it far enough away. He'd also moved himself nearer to me as he'd knelt down. He was now only eight, maybe ten feet away and only three or four feet from the gun. Being on his knees, though, it was a more difficult movement to reach either me or the gun.

'Don't worry,' he said, 'I'm not going to go for the gun. I think I've got a better chance without it.'

When I didn't answer that, he went on.

'You see, if I went for the gun, you'd shoot me. You'd have to. Self preservation. A case of me or you. Bit like Jerry there.' He gestured behind him, arm movement again, getting me to accept the idea of him moving, giving himself that extra split-second when he went for me.

'He tried to kill you and you had to kill him or die. Self-preservation. But I'm not going to try and kill you. There'll be no reason for you to shoot me.'

I didn't say anything, just kept the gun steady and I think it upset him.

'Think about it,' he said. Was there a shade more urgency in his tone? 'You have no reason to fire that gun.' He looked around him. Too much movement, too much bloody movement.

'Broussier's not here, right? Did you see him again, or not?'

I said nothing.

'It doesn't matter. If he came to you, then you would have helped him. If he didn't, it's because he didn't need you. Either way he's out, probably back in Europe by now. And that's it. My interest in him, in you, is finished. I've got no personal vendetta against you, I can just walk away.'

His voice echoed for a moment, then there was quiet again. He was sweating now. I could see a slight shine on his forehead, picked up by the dull glow from the lights outside. My silence was unnerving him.

'Just walk away,' he'd said. Yeah, right. I wanted to say something now.

'That's it, is it? You just walk away?'

I could see him relax a little. He'd got a response. I was talking.

'Yes, that's it. It's over. I made a mistake about you and it's cost me. Cost me time, money, status, even one of my own people, but now it's over. I tried to use you and you didn't let me. That's where it finishes.' He stopped for a second and drew breath. 'I'm parked across the road. You let me walk out and you can watch me through the window, walk to the car and drive away. And that's the end.'

I shifted my weight slightly. Bent my arms more to bring the gun nearer to me. It was getting heavy.

'What about Linda and the paper seller?'

'They're out of it as well. I'm not interested in them.'

I don't know if my look changed, but he realised he'd made a mistake.

'All right, the newspaper man was unfortunate, but he'll be out of hospital soon, if he's not out already.'

'And Harwood?' I said, 'and Nelson?'

His face registered surprise for a moment, no-one was supposed to know about Nelson. He recovered himself quickly, but he didn't answer straight away, trying to gauge the right way to go, the right answer to give. What he didn't realise was that it didn't matter what he said.

'Come on, Garron, you don't really care about Harwood.

You're right, he shouldn't have died, but it happened. You killed Jerry, he killed Harwood. And Nelson – it was his way of life that killed him, not me. Don't try to tell me that you'd shoot me down in revenge for him, I wouldn't believe you.'

I made him wait for a couple of seconds.

'No, you're right,' I said.

It was a critical moment. He visibly relaxed, dropped his eyes, sank lower on his knees. I saw him swallow. I said;

'There is something you're missing.'

He looked up at me again.

'You said it was business and you were just using me as part of that business. But I'm not a businessman. I might have taken it personally. Maybe I don't need a reason to kill you. Maybe I just want to.'

He knew now. He finally understood. He looked at me and I knew what he saw. A blank face and dead eyes. And I recognised what I felt. Cold fire. Calm rage. I sighted the gun for his head.

'You can't,' he said. It was a weak protest. 'You can't –'

I pulled the trigger and blew him away.

*

He was dead. The body had been jolted backwards, but the momentum hadn't been enough because he'd been on his knees and he'd rocked forwards again and then slumped to one side. His hand lay a few inches from his gun.

I stood up. Shakily. My legs were weak. I didn't know if that was a reaction to killing a man, or from sitting down with all that tension running through me. I stood over Smith, careful not to tread in the blood that had fallen, or the growing pool of it that was seeping from his head wound. His face was turned away from me into the floor. I stood back a bit, sighted the gun and fired once more into the side of his head. I don't know why I did that. He just seemed to need it.

My head was clear now, but I wasn't thinking. I didn't need to. I was working on automatic, running through the list of things that I'd thought out before. I wiped the gun down carefully and gave it back to Jerry. I tried to remember which hand he'd been holding the gun in. I was pretty sure it was the right one. I put the gun into his hand and put his left hand in place as though he'd been supporting it in the classic grip. Made sure he left his prints all over the gun, not just the handle and trigger, but the slide and safety-catch as well. Then I dropped it a few feet away from him. The police would know that there had been at least one other person here, whoever had killed Jerry, but it wouldn't be obvious that Jerry hadn't killed Smith.

I wiped over the door and door handle in case I'd touched them, but that was about all I could do. I don't know much about forensics and I wasn't sure what the police could find and identify. I'd probably left clothing fibres and even hairs on the floor during the fight with the gorilla, but it couldn't be helped. I'd just have to make sure the police didn't find me to match anything up.

I started to leave when I remembered my gun. It was near the side wall. I didn't need to leave it here now, I hadn't used it. The gun was clean, I could hang on to it. As I picked it up, my wrist hurt. I hoped I hadn't messed it up again on the gorilla's head. I checked the speedloader was still in my pocket and walked out. I didn't look back as I left the office. There was nothing to look back at.

I went down the wooden steps and stood at the bottom in the darkness, wondering if they might have brought a third person with them. I doubted it, but I held the mini-torch in my left hand supporting the gun as a precaution. Panned the gun and the torch around the factory. Nothing. No-one there. Just the same scurrying sounds as the rats moved. I wondered if they ever made it upstairs. I hoped so.

At the broken window I stopped for a moment to gather my strength. It was about six feet above the floor and there was nothing to stand on, so I'd have to jump and pull myself up. It would be difficult given that I had a left arm that didn't want to work, a right wrist that probably wouldn't take the pressure and I was drained. I put the gun and torch on the sill and jumped up. Managed to lock out my arms and stayed there for a second, hurting and wondering if I could pull myself through, or if I'd be found here by the police, trapped in the factory because I'd been too tired to escape.

A hand grabbed my arm and another the collar of my jacket. I was pulled forward and landed on the wet ground outside. It wasn't too bad a landing, but I wasn't in any condition to land anywhere, soft or hard and it hurt. I started to move, expecting to see armed police and dog handlers. Someone had heard the shots; someone had dialled 999. Instead I saw Julot standing a few feet away from me in the rain, a gun in his hand. From where I was on the floor, he looked even bigger than before. I think at that moment I would have preferred the police.

'Don't do anything stupid,' he said. His voice was quiet, steady.

I wasn't going to do anything stupid. I wasn't capable of it. I stayed where I was, half sprawled on the ground. After a few seconds I said;

'You're supposed to be meeting Broussier.'

'Someone else will meet Jean. I was more interested in you and Smith. They are both dead?'

I nodded.

'Again I am impressed,' he said. 'I am pleased that you were the one who came out. Otherwise I would have had to kill them myself.'

'But they were the buyers for the disc.'

Idiot. Shouldn't have mentioned the disc, but I was too tired and I wasn't thinking straight. It could cost me my life. It might already have done.

Julot smiled and shook his head.

'They were working for me, and they made mistakes. Because of you they made mistakes. And then they began to chase around trying to correct those mistakes. I don't like people who chase around, they cause disturbances. A loose end that is necessary is okay, if it is an efficient, well organised loose end. If it is not...' He shrugged.

'Am I a loose end?' I'd said it almost without realising I was speaking.

It seemed like there was a long pause.

'No,' he said, 'I don't think so. You do not have access to people who could hurt me and besides,' he flicked a glance at the factory, 'I know where the bodies are. You are not a loose end.'

'Even though I know about the disc?' I asked because he already knew and I wanted to be sure.

'No, Garron, you do not know about the disc, you only think you know.' The gun disappeared and for the first time since I'd seen him pointing it at me, I thought that I might get out alive.

'The disc is a fake. I stole it because it does not work. I did not even steal it properly, the company that made it almost gave it to me, to save their reputation and I suppose their shareholders.' He shrugged. 'They promised something that they could not deliver.'

'You mean all this was for nothing, for a hoax?'

'No, Garron.' Julot's voice was suddenly hard. 'This was to save my reputation, which is very important to me. I promised to keep the disc off the market for them, that it would just disappear. Vincent, the man you protected, he is working on a similar product. I contacted his boss and also promised him that I would keep the disc off the market, for a price. He of course thinks that the disc works perfectly. I win both ways, for very little work.'

'Until Broussier nicks it and tries to sell it on. Smith was supposed to get it back, but I messed it up for him.' I was sitting up now, though I thought it was safer not to stand. 'You've been very tolerant of me.'

'I respect you, Garron, in one or two ways you are a bit...' He didn't finish, but then said; 'Maybe one day I might put some business your way. On my terms of course.'

He backed away a few paces and disappeared around the end of the building. I stayed where I was. I stayed there until I was sure he was well away and until I felt strong enough to move. The gun and torch were lying on the ground beneath the broken window. I picked them up and dried them as best I could. It was still raining and cold, but I hardly noticed that I was soaked.

I walked back to the van a different way, coming around the back of Paddington station, concentrating on putting one foot in front of the other. In the back of my mind was the thought that I should feel something, but I didn't. Not relief, not remorse, not shame, not elation, not even that power-crack. Nothing. That was wrong. I knew that I should have some physical reaction; the nerves had to come down, the muscles had to relax, but there was nothing. No shaking, no sweating, no loss of control, just an emptiness. Julot would have killed Smith and Jerry. I'd killed two men for nothing.

But I pushed these thoughts to the back of my mind. I still had to finish the night's work. It wasn't until I was back at my flat that I could relax. Then I could collapse if I had to and no-one would know. Until I got there, I had to stay in control of everything, which meant not doing anything that could disturb the balance of what was going on in my head. Just keep putting one foot in front of the other.

Reached the van. Everything happening by remote control. Keep the mind occupied with a routine, don't let it dwell on what you've done. I wondered if Broussier had made it to Trafalgar Square on time. It didn't matter. I couldn't do anything else for him now.

I started to drive slowly back towards Tony's car lot, the rain hammering on the roof of the van. I found myself gripping the wheel too tightly and sitting forward on the edge of the driver's seat. After a couple of minutes driving somebody flashed their lights at me. It jolted me. Then someone else did the same. And a third car. I suddenly realised that I hadn't switched on the van's lights. The moment of panic subsided and I tried not to think of what could have happened if a police car had stopped me for that. Nothing would have happened, I told myself. They wouldn't have known.

It took me a while to reach the car lot because I was driving so slowly. I had no energy to drive any faster. There was a light on in the office behind the parked cars. I left the van on the road in front, stepped over the low wall that hemmed the cars in and walked to the office. One foot in front of the other, still on automatic. The door opened and Tony came out. I should make an effort, talk normally to him. I couldn't. I held the keys out to him and he took them.

'Thanks,' he said. 'I thought I'd wait here for you, I didn't want you calling me at home too late, waking Marie and the kids up.'

I didn't say anything. I didn't even know if it was late or not.

'You don't look too good, mate, are you all right?'

'I'm okay,' I said. I didn't sound it, even to me.

Tony looked at me doubtfully, then went on, 'Look, earlier on, what I said...I might have been a bit hard on you, not wrong, just a bit over the top. I – '

'No,' I broke in, 'you were right and you weren't too hard. It needed saying.'

'Yeah, well...'

I turned to go.

'Hold on a minute, there's a message for you. Linda called. Must have been before I came back here tonight, 'cos it's on the answering machine. I left it on there, since I knew you were coming here later.'

I followed him into the office.

'Over there,' he said, pointing to the machine as he picked up his coat and keys.

I pressed 'play'. Her voice, a little distorted by the machine.

'Hi, Tony, this is Linda. Sorry to use you like this, but can you get a message to Garron for me?'

I felt Tony watching me. He'd heard this already.

'Tell him he's an idiot, but I forgive him. I know he's not going to go through with what he was planning... okay, I'm fairly certain he won't go through with it and as long as he doesn't, tell him he can get in touch with me on – '

Click.

I switched it off.

It was all I could do. I couldn't lie to her. When I didn't call, she'd know. And maybe she'd try to understand. If she wanted to.

I didn't look at Tony. He'd work it out. Or not. I turned away from the machine. The next call would clear her message.

I left the office, walked between the cars in the rain. Tony caught up with me at the pavement.

'How're you getting home?'

'Don't know. Buses I suppose.' I hadn't thought about it.

'Take the old Escort on the corner there, I don't need it for a few days.' He gave me a set of keys. 'Can't have you getting on buses at this time of night. You might get mugged or something.' He tried for a smile, but I didn't.

'Thanks,' I said, 'I'll get it back to you.'

'No rush, mate, no rush.' He hesitated. 'You sure you're all right?'

'Yes.'

'Okay. Call me, we'll get together at the weekend.'

'Sure.'

He turned away and walked to the van. Going to put his eighteen hundred pounds inside the lot for the night. I opened the door of the Escort and got in. Put the key in the ignition, but didn't switch it on. Sat there for a minute, the rain running down the windscreen and blurring the world.

There was a tap on the passenger window and I didn't even jump at the noise. Tony's face. I reached over and wound the window down.

'You left something in the van.' This time I did jump. My right hand shot involuntarily to my jacket pocket. The gun was still there. Tony handed me the cassette tape through the window, said 'call me' and turned away again. I put the tape into the player, but didn't switch it on. Wound the window up, started the car and drove home.

It was crazy. Tony going back to his family and I'd just killed two men. The car that just passed me at the lights, on its way somewhere and I'd just killed two men. I had this feeling of unreality, no, not just a feeling; it was unreal. Cars going by, people moving around and two dead men in a factory in Paddington.

Did I do it right, Al? Did I do it right?

Maybe it hadn't happened. That's what it felt like, but I knew it had happened. The words flew around in my head. "I've just killed two men."

I felt the sweat starting and the pulse beating and I tried not to think about anything. Keep driving. Get yourself home. Be safe. *I've just killed two men.*

I got to Camden at just before midnight. The streets were empty. No people and few cars. I parked up and as I switched the engine off, the silence hit me. Even the rain had stopped. I didn't want silence. I wanted to hear something. The sound of the engine, even the sound of the rain on the roof of the car, had kept me sane. Now there was no sound. Just rising panic and the words in my head. *I've just killed two men!*

I switched on the radio/cassette, wanting the radio, getting the tape.

The blues again. The same song as before. How long ago was it? A day? A lifetime? Drawing me into its truth. Talking to me. Speaking to me.

I don't know, but I've been told,
It ain't your age that makes you old,
It's what you've done and what you've seen,
And all the things you might have been.

What you've done and what you've seen,
And all the things you might have been.

I sat there and let the tape run out, waiting for the shaking to stop and wondering how old I was.

*

But if you survive, you carry on. You have no choice.

The car door is there; you open it and get out. The steps

are there; you climb them. The front door is there; you unlock it and go in. Close it behind you.

Home.

Safe.

And not even alone. Cat's eyes in the dark from across the room, staring me out. I didn't move into the room. I sat down where I was and leaned back against the wall. I didn't want to scare him away. I wanted him to stay. I wanted the company. After all, we weren't that different. Both of us were hunted and hunter. Both of us ran sometimes strong, and sometimes scared. Both of us were killers.

I closed my eyes, concentrated on nothing, tried to focus on nothing. Al's voice came at last.

'The bad guys died and the good survived. What's wrong with that?'

I don't know, Al, I don't know.

I could see him standing in front of me, looking down at me, a half smile on his face.

'Better than the other way around though, isn't it?'

Yeah, I thought and almost smiled back at him. Better than the other way around.

*

Epilogue

The man half raised his hand in recognition, then thought better of it and let it drop back to his side. He stayed where he was, the lion's statue standing guard over him and waited for the contact to reach him. It was good of them to send someone he knew, someone he would recognise, not just a nameless London contact.

It was raining and cold, but there were still a handful of people scattered around the Square. The contact was a slim man, dressed for the weather. A longish overcoat and a hat which was now pulled down over his forehead and eyes. He stopped in front of the tall man and smiled warmly at him. Put out his right hand. The other man almost took it, before he realised what he was supposed to do, but he recovered himself in time and placed a small flat cardboard envelope into the outstretched hand. It was over. Relief and gratitude showed in his eyes. He didn't think anything of his colleague leaning in towards him, didn't see him take the silenced gun from an inside holster, almost didn't feel the two shots enter his heart at an upwards angle. The expression in his eyes hardly changed. He was dead without even realising he'd been killed.

The killer replaced the gun and leaned the taller man back against the base of the statue, careful that no blood leaked on to him. He was three or four strides away before the body began to fall sideways. He was out of the Square before anyone took any notice. That was what he'd been most concerned about, an observant or interfering passer-by. The security cameras didn't worry him. The only feature they might pick up was his moustache and that would be gone before he checked into his hotel. The gun would disappear piece by piece.

He felt himself relax, felt the tension ease away. It was never easy, using a silencer at point blank range, he would have preferred a knife, but those were the instructions and it had been a good kill. He looked around him at the bustling city. He liked London. He would enjoy the next day or two, before returning home.

*

Look out for

Another Man's World

Joe Stein's second thriller,
which is to be published by
bluechrome in September 2007

For an exclusive preview of *Another Man's World*, visit

www.joestein.co.uk